MURDER IN THE CARDS

A Tom Logan Mystery

Tony Piazza

OTHER BOOKS

By Tony Piazza

Fiction

Anything Short of Murder
The Curse of the Crimson Dragon
A Murder Amongst Angels
Murder is Such Sweet Revenge

Nonfiction

Bullitt Points: Memories of Steve McQueen & Bullitt

Short Story

My Most Precious Gift
Published in the anthology
The Best of SLO NightWriters in Tolosa Press
2009-2013
Edited by Judythe A. Guarnera

Death Hides Behind a Mask
Published in the anthology
Deadlines: Murder and Mayhem on the California
Coast Vol. 2
Editors: Susan Tuttle, Barbara M. Hodges, Marie
Marcy

ACCLAIM FOR TONY PIAZZA

"Earnest and dutiful, the narrative (of *A Murder Amongst Angels*) aims for the minimalist prose of Raymond Chandler but often channels the overly procedural narrator of noir B-movies. And more concerned with nostalgia than invention, the plot hits the right notes as it crescendos toward a well-orchestrated coda. A sentimental caper that mostly follows the genre formula, with a few refreshingly original flourishes."

– Kirkus Reviews

"Mr. Piazza has quite a knack to transport readers to old-time Los Angeles. He draws them in to assist in solving his cases. The period and scenes of the three stories within *Murder Will Out* are all deftly written with well-drawn characters and highly suspenseful drama. The situations are suitable to the time and keep readers turning pages at a high rate."

– Viola Robins
Reviewer, InDTale Magazine

"*Murder Will Out* is a 'can't put it down' page turner. This is a great addition to any Chandler Fan's collection. Overall five stars and winner of the International Review of Books badge of achievement."

– Kathy Denver
Review Editor, The International Review of Books

"One-time San Francisco actor turned novelist Tony Piazza has resurrected the concept of the ludicrous but exciting adventure yarn with *The Curse of the Crimson Dragon*. Enjoy living in the literature of yesteryear? Then you'll savor leaping headfirst into these pulpish pages. The flowing action and excitement never let up, even during the expository or exotic love scenes, as Ryan faces down every kind of life-threatening situation. The sweat never stops pouring out of Piazza's prose. If only more writers reminded us of how much fun reading was in the days of *Planet Stories, Argosy, Fantastic Adventures*, and *Blue Book*!"

– John Stanley
*Author of **The Creature Features Movie Guide***

"Old-fashioned adventure and thrills with clearly defined good guys and bad guys, a throwback to another era. I've read both of Piazza's novels and each takes me back to a time and place that I enjoyed spending time." (*The Curse of the Crimson Dragon*)."

– Dave Congalton
Radio talk-show host, screenwriter, and author

"It's almost impossible to set *Anything Short of Murder* down once I start reading. I have a special love for Tony Piazza's breathtaking characters. I feel their personalities jump right out from the pages and into my mind's eye where they dazzle and spellbind me from beginning to end."

– Cookie Curci
Freelance journalist

"A fast-paced ride in the tradition of the wonderful 1930s era mystery writers who wrote such great classics with a light sophisticated touch. I've read all of Mr. Piazza's Tom Logan's mysteries and *Murder is Such Sweet Revenge* is definitely one of his very best efforts writing in the genre. High marks for the characters, situations, fun and witty dialogue, and the whodunit factor that truly is a surprise. Just when I thought I had it figured out...well, you know how that goes. Terrific surprise ending and fluid writing from scene to scene and chapter to chapter."

– Paul A. Fahey
*Author of **The Short and Long of It***

"I thoroughly enjoyed this mystery (*Murder is Such Sweet Revenge*) with its unusual murder weapon, all the wonderful suspects, the ambience of the hotel and its resident ghost, Tom's adorable dog, the many twists and turns, the surprising ending, and at the end, the hint of more adventure and mystery solving ahead for Tom and Rita."

— Marilyn Meredith
*Author of **A Cold Death***

"What more can a mystery addict desire? ***Murder is Such Sweet Revenge*** has it all! A colorful cast of characters is brought together in an ideal setting on Coronado Island in what becomes one of the best page-turning mystery novels I've read in years. If you've never set foot into the Hotel Del Coronado, here's your chance to do it with style, finesse, and all the suspense that exudes from this historic place."

— Frank Scozzari
*Author of **From Afar***

"In this delightful romp in the classic noir genre (***Murder is Such Sweet Revenge***), Tony Piazza has captured the glamour and allure of the 'hard-boiled detective with a heart of gold.' There are twists and turns galore in this imaginative tale that in places will leave you breathless."

–Susan Tuttle
*Author **Write It Right** series and **Tough Blood***

"I grew up reading hard-boiled detectives and PI's in the mode of Shell Scott and Matt Helm, both flawed but with a work ethic that always rose to the occasion. With Tony Piazza's hero, I can still enjoy my favorite style in Tom Logan and even the same era. I could have said protagonist, but with Tom Logan, hero fits better. (***Murder is Such Sweet Revenge***)."

– Barbara Hodges
*Author of **Hounded by Death***

"Seekers of fast, satisfying mystery reads are sure to love ***Murder Will Out***, by Tony Piazza. The dedicated film historian, writer and, sometime actor is inspired by the golden years of tight, bright pulp-fiction writing of Dashiell Hammett, Raymond Chandler, et. al., and he transports you there via dead-on detail, dialog and detective action. What's more, he invites you to care about his characters. Good stuff!"

– Carole T. Beers
*Author of **Ghost Ranch***

For my late parents who taught me that anything was possible with hard work and persistence, and my dear Lord, who not only supplied me with the resources and gifts but instructed me in how to use them wisely.

ACKNOWLEDGMENTS

"Murder in the Cards" is a work of fiction, and even though I know my readers may be tempted to blur the lines between fact and fiction, I ask that you do not. A number of the characters, as well as a few of the locations in this book, were modeled after real-life persons and places of the past, but in no way are meant to suggest that they are these characters themselves. Please keep this in mind as you are reading.

There were other characters in this story that were created with the help of friends and family. For the sake of privacy, I will not mention their real names, but I want to especially thank them for letting me borrow portions of their names, and in a couple of instances their real backgrounds to bring certain characters alive in this story.

However, I will make a mention of the dog, Buddy, who is in this book, and was in my previous Tom Logan mysteries. He was based on our dog, a gentle, loving

Cocker Spaniel who was the best friend a person could ever ask for. Some of the antics you will, and have, read about in this series was based on actual incidents we experienced during the 16 years he graced our home. He will be missed, but lives on in this series.

As I've written in my previous books, composing a story is only a part of the process. It requires an excellent editor to make a good book even better. Once again I have the services of one of the best – Sue McGinty. Having worked as an editor for a major publishing house, as well as an expert in the mystery genre (an author herself of the exceptional Bella Kowalski mysteries), she was the perfect choice to mentor me in writing this series. I should add, however, that any errors that remain in this work are mine and mine alone.

People do take notice of your covers, and my novels have been fortunate to have a very talented young man as their designer. A very special thanks to Liam Heckman, my graphic artist extraordinaire.

Writing is a lonely affair, especially for a spouse who has to spend hours alone while you pound out your story on the keyboard. Many thanks to my wife, Susan, who puts up with those lonely times, as well as attending the many book signings, talks, and meetings in support of my career as a mystery author. She has assisted me from time to time with information on 1930s fashions and details on old Los Angeles in general. Her family ancestry goes as far back as Pueblo Los Angeles, and fashion design was her former profession.

Finally, I also want to thank my family and friends, whose continued support has been a real blessing.

1

HONEYMOONS AND MURDERS

"Falling is a common death in the Grand Canyon. How many were pushed is anybody's guess."

— *Anon*

rand Canyon, October 1933
Here I was dangling over a chasm where angels fear to tread, and simultaneously asking myself, "why?" One misstep and I could be playing the harp, along with these same angels. Just before stepping over the edge, a rope tied securely around my waist, I took a final glance at Rita whose concerns were evident. She had been a bride for less than a month, and we weren't relishing the idea that she soon could become a widow.

This wasn't my idea of a second honeymoon. In truth, we never had a first. The murder of a bestselling author cut that one short, and this was our second attempt within a couple of weeks. As luck would have it, no sooner had we arrived at the Grand Canyon, even before checking into the *El Tovar*, a man was seen being pushed by another over the rim. Heavy snowfall had blocked all access roads, so no law enforcement in the form of sheriff or park ranger was immediately available to investigate, and as fate would have it, I became "Johnny on the Spot." The desk clerk had seen my Private Investigation Card and had no reservations about eliciting my help – even though he knew it was our honeymoon. So, here I was, risking life and limb, out in the freezing, wind-swept cold, instead of cuddling up with my new bride in front of a blazing fire.

The body lodged on a narrow ledge that jutted out approximately forty feet down the canyon wall. A half dozen heavily clothed men and women gathered on the rim trail above me, four of them tightly support-ing the rope from which I hung. That previous spring the Civilian Conservation Corps began building stone walls along the rim between the *El Tovar* and *Bright Angel Lodge*. This portion of the rim was beyond the construction, several yards up the trail, past the Hopi House, and opposite *Verkamp's Curios*.

"Can I start feeding the line?"

The question was shouted from above by an ath-letic-looking fellow who had located the rope to which

I was attached. There seemed to be enough length to reach the body. At least I'd hoped so. I wasn't planning to make this trip twice.

"Go ahead," I called. "But start letting it out slowly."

I felt the tenseness ease, giving me some slack to start the descent. There was snow and loose earth, so I had to consider each placement of my feet. This kept my attention focused on the wall ahead, instead of the ground, which ended some 2,000 feet below. Occasionally I did have to look down toward the ledge where the body had landed, to align my position and gauge the distance. I kept those examinations brief to keep my knees from buckling.

"You doing OK?" It was my friend from above.

Before I could answer, I momentarily lost my footing, and for a short, heart-stopping moment was suspended in the air by the rope before regaining a foothold.

"You OK?" he repeated, this time more frantic.

"Yeah," I shouted back. "I'm OK, but I can't say the same for my shorts."

A brief chuckle filtered down from the crowd on the rim. Most likely due to relief, and not my sorry attempt at humor. "Give me a moment," I continued. "I need to catch my breath."

"Sure thing," came the response.

I inhaled and then let the air out of my lungs slowly. A vapor formed in front of me. It was cold, just above freezing, but still, I was sweating. I chanced another glance at the body below. Another 20 feet I reasoned.

"I'm ready," I announced.

They started feeding me more length, and slowly I covered the distance without further incident until I reached the rocky shelf where the body had lodged. The ledge was just a small outcropping of limestone about five feet wide and ten feet in length. The body was near its edge but wedged at an angle between two jagged rocks. The way it was unnaturally arched told me the spine was likely broken, a fact confirmed by the sporadic jerking of the body. There was still some life in it, although quickly ebbing away like the ever-growing pool of dark blood gathered around the skull and foaming from the lips.

"Can you understand me?" I asked, leaning close to one ear.

A fedora still covered his head, inexplicably attached despite the fall. It had slid forward, the brim touching the bridge of the wearer's nose. To examine his eyes I gingerly removed the hat. A pile of shoulder-length platinum blond hair fell out. The 'he' was a 'she.' I looked closer. She seemed familiar, although at that moment I couldn't figure out why. She was attractive, even near death, and battered as she was. For a second her eyelids fluttered and then opened with a start. I felt her hand grip hard on my right wrist. Her actions told me she had something urgent to say. I leaned closer.

"What?" I whispered.

Despite the convulsions of her body and the pain, she drew upon whatever strength she had to utter two words. "The Gypsies."

"What about them?" I asked, but there was no response. Her brown eyes clouded over in death.

2

THE INVESTIGATION BEGINS

*"The true mystery of the world is the visible,
not the invisible."*

—*Oscar Wilde*

I froze my backside on the ledge as a couple of guys above searched for a line to haul up the body. The view of the plateau below was spectacular. The Bright Angel trail could be seen snaking its way through the snow to the Indian Garden and beyond to Plateau Point. I would have appreciated the sights more if I wasn't perched like a Bighorn Sheep on the canyon wall. And talk about cold. I was dressed for winter weather, but sitting on that ledge, I soon realized that a Southern Californian's definition of cold and an Arizonian's were vastly different. However, in my defense, this weather was an anomaly for October. Snowfall usually begins the following month.

"You still doing OK?" my athletic looking friend yelled down in his deep, commanding voice. It seemed he had now taken leadership of this hastily formed group of rescuers. "We're still trying to scare up another rope. Do you need anything in the meantime?"

"Yeah," I called back. "A Saint Bernard with a keg of brandy."

He laughed.

"Sorry, we don't have one handy. I'll see what I can get you later. Deal?"

"Deal."

Since it would still be a few minutes before we could remove the body, I decided to move around and keep the blood flowing to fight off the chill. Rising from a sitting position into a haunch, I carefully searched through the corpse's clothing hoping to locate something that might identify her. I still couldn't shake this feeling that I knew her from somewhere. The man's suit she wore was clearly not her own. It was a size or two too big for her, and at places, you could see where she had tied it up so it would fit. I went through the pockets, but they yielded nothing. Not a hanky, nor even a pack of cigarettes. If I were to discover her identity, it would have to be topside, where hopefully someone would recognize her.

It took thirty minutes before another rope was lowered, and an additional fifteen to slowly pull her up. The trick was to keep her from catching onto something projecting from the face of the cliff. I wasn't worried about her slipping through the rope. The way I secured her under the arms guaranteed that she could make the journey. My concern was that she might get hung up on something, and that's why the slow ascent with me verbally guiding those pulling the rope – warning them of possible obstacles. Once the body safely made it to the top, the rescuers turned their attention to me. The trip up was, fortunately, less eventful than the one down, and it was with profound relief when my feet finally stood again upon the path along the rim.

"Tom, I was so afraid!" Rita was the first to greet me with a hug and a sigh of relief. "I thought I was going to lose you."

"I wouldn't let that happen, doll," I replied, grinning down at her. "Besides, I'm not about to give Aunt Katherine the satisfaction."

The second person to greet me was my athletic friend who walked over to introduce himself.

"Good job," he began, thrusting out his hand. His grip was strong and dry. "My name is Jim... Jim Rollins."

"Mine's Logan... Tom Logan and this is my wife, Rita."

"Pleased to meet you, Mr. Rollins," said Rita.

"Jim... please," he responded, taking her offered hand. "You must meet my wife, Liz." He turned to me. "I have an idea. How about joining us for dinner tonight? I promised you a drink. I have some genuine

Kentucky Bourbon back at the cabin… been saving it since the start of Prohibition for a special occasion. Good a reason as any to crack it open now. How about you two join us at the cottage, and we can go to dinner from there?"

"Well," I hesitated, looking toward Rita for guidance. She nodded enthusiastically. "OK, sounds great. What time?"

He looked at his watch.

"It's four-thirty now… say five o'clock? That give you enough time?"

"Could we make it six?" I suggested. "I'll need to see about securing the body, and I was hoping that I might find someone who could ID her."

"You mean you don't know who she is, Tom?" Rita interrupted. She sounded incredulous, which piqued my interest.

"Well, no, not exactly."

"*That is Norma Daniels*, the moving picture actress."

That explained why she seemed so familiar. I wasn't much for dramatic films, but she had starred in a score of them for Warner's. Mostly historical dramas – period pictures, which I may have seen. Rita was the person keen on them. Daniels' image also graced the covers of numerous fan magazines – *Photoplay, Silver Screen, Movie Mirror,* and so on. Especially lately, since her high profile separation from a San Francisco newspaper exec.

"Why would anyone want to kill her?" Rita asked, a frown creasing her brow.

"Jealousy, anger, envy... you name it," I responded. "Perhaps even mistaken identity. She was wearing a man's suit."

"You know *that is strange.*"

"Tell me about it," I replied dryly.

"No," she said, "I mean, the plot of her last film... it was about a young peasant girl who tried passing herself off as a man to get into the court of King Louie the Fourteenth and be close to her love." Rita looked earnestly at me. "You remember, Tom. We saw it at the Warner's Downtown Theater. *Royal Ransom,* was the name of the picture, and John Barrymore was the male lead." I shrugged my shoulders, and she continued, "It was paired with that funny Laurel and Hardy film, where they are Doughboys in World War One, and after the war they get a lunch wagon, and then hide a friend's little girl from people who want to place her in an orphanage."

"That I remember," I answered. "But, I must've dozed through the rest."

"You know nothing about culture," she concluded in a huff.

"Sure I do, sweetheart," I responded, pinching her on the cheek. "I married you, didn't I?"

Rollins cleared his throat, "About dinner tonight?"

"We'll join you at six, Jim?" He nodded. "Where should we meet?"

"We have a cottage at Bright Angel Camp. There are only two. We're the first just down from the office.

We can have a quick drink there and then go to the cafe. Sound OK?"

"Perfect."

A crowd had gathered around the body, which was now lying covered in the center of the trail. I moved away from Rollins to address them.

"Anybody witnessed what happened here?"

They all silently shook their heads, except one gentleman who spoke up, "I didn't, but I know who did." Before I could respond, he continued, "A waitress over at the El Tovar. I don't know her name, but she had a uniform. She's one of the Harvey Girls."

I made a mental note to place her at the top of my 'to do' list. Next, I asked if anyone knew a place where we could store the body. Someone suggested the ice-house down by the depot. Any shed would've worked considering the temperature, which was close to freezing. However, the small, square building adjacent to the Santa Fe Railway station was convenient, and its owner cooperative. The structure was solid, constructed of native stone and framed in thick wooden beams. Using a brass key, the owner unlocked the barn-like door and slid it open. Rollins and I carried the body inside. There was an empty wooden pallet at the far corner, several feet from the stored blocks of ice. We settled on that spot to lay the body.

"What's the matter?" Rollins sensed something was bothering me. Perhaps it was my hesitation upon leaving.

"There's something I need to check, but I'm not sure…" An idea entered my head. Rita had followed us to the icehouse but decided to wait outside. I left Rollins a minute to speak with her. Reluctantly she agreed to what I'd suggested, and then Rollins and I traded places with her as she privately went about my request. Ten minutes later she returned.

"You were right, Tom," she confirmed, and then frowning. "Although I'll have to ask you later how you'd guessed it."

I made sure that icehouse was locked tight before leaving, and gave orders to the owner about safeguarding the body until the authorities arrived. I could tell Rollins wanted to ask me something. He waited until we started toward the lodge before discretely pulling me aside. Rita in the meantime had continued climbing the stairs that ran up the hill.

"Just now… your wife said that you were right about something?"

"Oh, that," I answered with a smile. "I had her check the body. The victim wasn't wearing undergarments."

"How *did you* guess that?"

"Intuition," I replied. "But knowing Rita, it might take some convincing."

At the entrance to the El Tovar, we parted ways – Rollins to the Bright Angel, and Rita and I into the inviting warmth of the hotel's 'Rendezvous Room,' a large space constructed of dark, richly-stained logs and broad rafters. Window seats, easy chairs, and small tables in the arts and crafts style were creatively placed about the immense space and gazed down upon by numerous game trophies, which hung from a plate rail that circled the room. Rita and I dashed for the stone fireplace in the corner, where logs were burning brightly, emitting the occasional snap and crackle of freshly cut wood.

"I could stay here all night," Rita sighed, as she held her hands toward the warmth of the fire.

I looked at my watch, and replied, "Unfortunately we have just over thirty minutes before we have to meet the Rollins."

"Gosh," Rita exclaimed. "We better get moving. I want to freshen up a bit."

"You go ahead. I want to visit the front desk." I looked at my watch again. "Meet me here no later than five forty-five. That should give us plenty of time to get to the cottage."

Rita bounded up the stairs as I leisurely strode over to the reception desk. There a clerk sorted through the mail. He turned after I tapped the bell.

"Can I help you, sir?"

"I'd like to know if a Miss Norma Daniels is staying here."

He hesitated a moment, then pulling the register book toward him, ran his index finger deftly down its margin. After repeating the action on four other pages, he firmly announced that she wasn't.

"She must be," I insisted. "Platinum blonde, about five foot one."

"I'm sorry, sir, but there is no 'Daniels' registered here."

"She might have checked in under another name," I offered. "Or come in with someone else. She's a motion picture actress. I'm sure you'd recognize her."

"I'm sorry."

"Perhaps someone else was at the desk when she had signed in."

"That could be," he said. "And who exactly *are you, sir?*"

Before I could answer, Tennyson, the Assistant Manager who had originally asked me to look into this crime, interrupted, "It's OK, Gary. I'll take care of it. Continue attending to the desk."

Tennyson motioned with a subtle wave that we move off to the side. Once there, he continued in a hushed voice, "What did you discover?"

"Plenty. For one thing, it was a 'she,' and not a 'he' who was pushed."

"A woman." He seemed surprised. "That's remarkable, but she was dressed in a man's suit."

"Just wait. It gets better." I had his attention now. "Ever hear of the moving picture star, Norma Daniels?"

"Who hasn't?"

"Well, it was she who was pushed into the canyon." This revelation stunned him to silence, so I continued, "Which, brings me to the question I asked your guy at the desk; is she staying here?"

"What did he find?"

"That she wasn't registered."

Tennyson retrieved the book and checked for himself. "He's right. There's no 'Daniels' listed here."

"Could she have registered under an assumed name, or maybe with a man and they registered as a couple?"

"Unless they'd signed under something obvious like Mr. and Mrs. Jones or Smith, I couldn't say. I don't see anything like that here, nor do I suspect I will. They'd be cleverer than that. However," he concluded, "there's no real way of telling."

"She's here. She has to be," I reasoned. "I can't imagine her in a tent-cabin, nor at the automobile campgrounds. Perhaps," I conceded, "at one of the cottages, but there are only two, and I know the occupants of one."

"The tent-cabins are not available during the winter," Tennyson informed me. "And the campgrounds are pretty basic. I know the family who rents one of the cottages – regulars named Reynolds. They have done so from October to December for the last three years. Is this the same party you know of?"

"No, mine's called Rollins."

"So, unless, Miss Daniels likes roughing it..."

"Which somehow I doubt."

"Then she has to be here," he concluded.

"I agree. Any way we could narrow down the list?"

Tennyson examined the register again.

"We have 103 rooms accommodating approximately 250 guests, and they're all occupied at the moment. You're talking a pretty big task."

"How many suites with private baths?"

"Twenty-five. Why?"

"She's a movie actress. She'll want her privacy."

"OK, but twenty-five is still a big number."

"How many of these suites were occupied recently?"

"Ten. But why just recently?"

"Because I doubt Miss Daniels would be able to hide for long without being discovered. Even disguised, her chances of being recognized by someone – a housekeeper, or waitress, for instance, would increase considerably. Since we haven't heard of her before now, it's safe to assume she must've registered recently."

He looked again, and his eyes brightened.

"Four registered in the last couple of days. Two today, which included you and your wife, and a couple from Maine, and two yesterday – one of which is a single woman."

"What's the name?"

He rechecked the register.

"One person in a suite with bath, American plan, $12.00 per day, rented to a Roberts, Miss Lydia Roberts. She gives an address in San Diego."

"Who checked her in?"

"Oddly enough, I did."

"Do you remember what she looked like? I assume you've seen Miss Daniels in the movies. Could it have been her?"

"Sure, I've seen her in films many times," he admitted. "And now that you make the association, yes it's possible. She has the same build; however, I couldn't see much of her face. She wore a large hat and dark glasses, but I did see some strands of her hair. It was red. Miss Daniels is a blonde."

"No problem there," I said. "She probably wore a wig."

"Well, there you have it," he concluded. "Looks like your best bet."

"Definitely worth a check. Where's this suite located?"

"Second floor – Miwok Suite."

I spotted Rita coming down the staircase, so added quickly, "Could you find out if a Miss Roberts is still occupying this suite? And if not, could you arrange that I get a look at it – say, tomorrow morning? That is unless the law gets here first." I started to turn away, but another thought hit me. "I believe there was a witness to the murder."

"Yes," he replied. "Unfortunately she's not available at the moment."

"Tomorrow?"

"Of course. Not a problem. And I'll be putting a call through to see what the status on the sheriff and the rangers is."

"Good. Tomorrow, then."

3

DINNER WITH THE ROLLINS

*"Hell Hath No Fury like a Woman
Scorned."*

—*William Congreve*

The Rollins were lodging in a cozy cottage nestled among some Douglas Firs, down the hill from the Bright Angel Camp Office. The structure was constructed of wood, painted rust with an apple green trim around its windows. Native stones formed its foundation and were the primary material of a fireplace whose chimney rose above its shingled, slanted roof. A path of swept earth bordered by more stones led up to the entrance – a single door painted the same color as the trim. Inside there were two double beds, a small kitchen, and sitting room complete with table and chairs. There was also steam heating, electric light, and a bath. Here were all the comforts of home in a rustic setting at a price of $4.00 per day. Quite a bargain considering our room at the El Tovar was $20.00.

Jim introduced us to his wife Liz, an attractive, pure-blooded, blue-eyed Italian from Philadelphia. James was a mixture. His mother was Scotch-Irish, his dad, Russian. Roginsky was his original name, but it was legally changed to Rollins when he decided to become a stage actor, as was Liz. She left the stage to become a full-time wife. They had no children, but four Cairn Terriers were now waiting at home with Liz's mother. We had that in common. Our Cocker Spaniel, 'Buddy,' was back in Los Angeles being watched by the Clancy's. We learned all this within ten minutes of our "hellos." After that, Jim and I sat down for some serious drinking while the ladies drifted off into the kitchen chattering about the canyon and its sights.

"What do you think, Tom?" Jim asked, smacking his lips. "Isn't that the smoothest Kentucky bourbon you've ever tasted?"

"Definitely worth the wait." I agreed.

"Another?"

"I wouldn't say no."

He refilled the shot glasses and slid mine over to me.

"I have a confession to make," he began.

"What's that?" I asked. My glass paused midway to my lips.

"Well, perhaps," he corrected with a sparkle to his fair eyes, "a proposition."

"What kind of a proposition?" I asked, trying to keep the wariness out of my question.

"I'm a stage actor – Broadway, summer stock, repertory; you name it. I love my profession and work very hard at it. When I take on a role, it ceases just being a character in a play – I become that person. That takes work, and plenty of research, which brings me to my proposition. In two months I'm playing a detective in an off-Broadway production called 'Footsteps in the Dark.' Having never really known a real detective, or followed what he did," he concluded, "I thought, hey, here's my chance to do some real research."

I fumbled around for a moment, searching for a response. This petition was unexpected, and I wasn't prepared to answer. Fortunately, our wives returned at that moment announcing that they were famished, and we hastened on to the restaurant in the Bright Angel Lodge. I did mumble to him as we left the cottage that I would give it some thought but cautioned that if it happened at all, it might only be for one day. I was planning to hand the investigation over to the proper authorities as soon as they arrived.

The Bright Angel Coffee Shop was a no-frills café furnishing a la carte meals daily. The décor was not as elegant as the El Tovar – simple wooden tables and chairs, a few booths, and a cashier stand complete with a glass case displaying sundries – cigars, cigarettes, gum, candy, and a handful of souvenirs. Not to say that the place wasn't without charm. It was warm and airy and had that same rustic feel found in its cottages. Plenty of rough-cut wood panels, lodge poles, plaster and native stone went into its design, and it was amply lit by electric lanterns at night and through several windows by day.

After hanging our heavy coats on a peg near the entrance, we located an empty booth beside a window on the canyon side and eagerly claimed our seats. We were all starving and couldn't wait to place our orders. There's something about cold air that gets an appetite going, and the frigid drop of temperature that evening was a factor. A waitress must have sensed our hunger because she was over in an instant with water, menus, and a pot of strong, scalding hot black coffee.

"What's good?" I asked the Rollins after the waitress left us a moment to decide on our selections.

"Their 'Old Timer's Stew' was excellent," Jim Rollin offered. "I had some last night."

"Sounds like a winner," I agreed.

"I had the Chicken Fried Steak," his wife volunteered. "It was good as well."

"It all looks good to me," Rita exclaimed.

In the end, I stuck with Jim's suggestion, and Rita went with Liz's. The Rollins decided to try something different and selected the boneless trout. There was a noted silence after the waitress disappeared with our orders. Liz was the first to break it, with an offhanded remark directed toward me.

"Jim was telling me you're a detective."

"Yes," I said.

"With a police force?"

"No. Private Investigator."

"Like Spade and Marlowe," she responded, more animated. "Or like William Powell in that new movie, 'The Kennel Murder Case!'"

I laughed.

"Not exactly. Authors like to glamorize this business. Aside from today, I'm not usually in the habit of stumbling onto murder cases..."

"That's not true, Tom," Rita interrupted. "What about our honeymoon?

"Well," I began, but Liz cut in.

"You two newly married?"

"Yes," Rita replied. "About two months. This trip was supposed to be our second honeymoon. A murder ruined the first at the hotel where we stayed – a resort on Del Coronado Island. Tom was asked to investigate – and in the course of this investigation, we got to meet William Powell. He was staying there – and so was Carole Lombard. We even went to the horse races with them."

Liz Rollins leaned forward. "Really." Rita now had her full attention. "Do tell. First about the murder."

"Perhaps this isn't the place..." I broke in.

"There was this bestselling mystery author," Rita continued to my chagrin. "A real self-centered jerk discovered in his room with his brains..."

"Rita!" I warned under my breath, polite, but firm enough that she listened.

"Sorry. I got carried away."

"No. It's all right," Liz insisted. "This is interesting. Please continue."

That was all Rita needed – a little encouragement from a co-conspirer of her gender.

"Tom eventually flushed out the murderer," she persisted. "But not without some close calls along the way. He's very clever – not the murderer – Tom."

"Rita," I interrupted again, blushing in modesty.

She chose to ignore me, rambling on instead.

"There was another case last year. I'm sure you've heard of the actress/ comedienne Gertrude Hurd…"

"Oh!" Liz exclaimed with delight. "I read about that. Was your husband involved?"

I gave Rita a nudge under the table.

"Involved," she continued after giving me a nudge back. "Tom practically solved the case all on his own."

I looked at Jim. From the look in his eyes, I could tell he sensed my discomfort. I shook my head and shrugged helplessly in his direction.

"Tom," he said. "I was wondering. *Why were you asked in on this murder?* Couldn't they get the sheriff or park rangers to investigate?"

"I questioned that myself," I replied, grateful for the clever way he delivered me from my dilemma. "I was told that the snowfall had closed the roads and that's why they needed my help, but I wondered why there weren't any rangers on site."

"I can answer that," Liz interjected. "I heard a child had gone missing at the North Rim, and all available rangers were called over to help with the search."

"Just the 'Logan Luck,'" I concluded solemnly, right in time for the arrival of our meals.

The stew looked and smelled good. It was served in a bowl and accompanied by a sourdough roll and side salad. Rita's Chicken fried steak looked equally delicious. A generous portion of meat, breaded and covered with thick country gravy, sided with fluffy mashed potatoes and green beans. The Boneless Trout Fillet selected by the Rollins was covered lightly in seasoned flour, sautéed, and served with Citrus Butter. Sides included brown rice, mixed seasonal vegetables, and a side salad.

We ate our entrees silently, except when we felt out of politeness, that small talk was necessary. Mostly it revolved around the canyon, stories of other travels, and a little about our backgrounds. Thankfully nothing more was said about the murder. I'd had enough violence for one day.

"Liz and I go in for these real challenging vacations," Jim Rollins commented at one point. "You know, mountain climbing, white-water rafting, and such. We were planning to take a mule ride into the canyon, but this unexpected weather messed it up."

"I would think you'd have plenty of challenges living in New York," I responded with a smile. "Like trying to catch a cab."

"That kind of a challenge we can live without. It's why Liz and I choose National Parks for our vacations. When you live in the big city, places that offer room to breathe are an attraction."

"Amen to that," I agreed. "Los Angeles is still growing, and we are spreading out some, but I can see in a few years we may become just as overcrowded."

There was silence after that, but then Liz, unfortunately, decided to bring up our former conversation.

"Speaking of challenging. It must've been scary hanging over that cliff today."

"Yes... yes, it was," I responded, shortly, hoping it would end there. It didn't.

"Jim said the actress Norma Daniels was pushed off the cliff. That's kind of ironic. I mean, I was just reading an interview she gave to *Movie Mirror* where she revealed that she was scared of heights."

"Not anymore," I commented dryly. She didn't catch it.

"What do you plan to do next?"

"All depends, if the law shows up, hand this mess to them. Short of that, follow up on some leads."

"Like what?"

"To begin with, speak with the witness..."

"Was there a witness?" Liz seemed surprised.

"Yes, a waitress from the Harvey restaurant. I didn't have time tonight, but I plan to catch her first thing tomorrow morning."

"Then what?"

"Probably snoop around her room and see if I can discover anything of interest."

"Oh, this is so interesting," she cried. "Will you be interrogating the staff?"

"'Interrogation' is a bit extreme. However, I will be questioning some of them."

At this point Jim broke into the conversation, addressing me.

"Which brings up what I'd asked you earlier. If the law doesn't show, do you mind if I tag along tomorrow?"

"Well... Jim," I began slowly. "As much as I would like you to..."

Rita must have sensed my discomfort because she jumped in.

"If possible, Tom prefers to work alone. And when he doesn't, I usually..."

Jim interrupted again, only this time directing his comment to Rita.

"I was hoping you might keep Liz, company. If I'm following your husband around..."

"But...but..." Rita sputtered.

"Oh, yes," Liz chimed in. "I would love your company. Maybe we can check out the *Hopi House*. I hear they have some lovely Navaho baskets and rugs for sale..."

"Yes, but..." Having trouble finding the words, Rita turned to me with pleading eyes. I just smiled back. Knowing Rita like the back of my hand, I figured she was already planning to play Watson to my Sherlock. Now faced with a choice, I saw an opportunity. A way to keep Rita out of my hair, while I conducted the investigation. For one thing, I thought Jim would be less obtrusive than Rita. And second – and more importantly, I wanted to wean Rita from her involvement in my cases. Twice now a dangerous situation arose during an investigation, and both times Rita was right in the middle of it. On one occasion she was even taken hostage, and I feared murdered by the suspect. I never want to re-live that experience.

"You know, Jim," I said after a moment. "Perhaps you should join me." I turned to Rita.

"I think it would be a nice change of pace, doll, you having some female company. Maybe you can find a rug for the apartment."

"I was thinking more along the line of a tomahawk," she murmured between her teeth, and then smiling sweetly for the Rollins' sake, "Yes, Liz, I'd enjoy shopping with you tomorrow."

Dessert came. Hot apple pie minus the ala mode. Vanilla ice cream wasn't appealing because of the cold weather. However, re-fills of hot coffee sounded good. Both Jim and Liz chattered happily over their cups, pleased with the arrangements for tomorrow. Rita, on the other hand, had suddenly become morose. I knew there would be hell to pay once we were alone. She didn't disappoint.

"Tom," she snapped, as we sloshed our way up the path which wound its way back to the lodge. "I thought you enjoyed spending time with me."

"I do, doll. Why do you say that?"

"Then explain what happened back there. I mean, Liz is nice and all, but you know I'd rather spend tomorrow with you."

"And if it were just a regular day I'd also enjoy that too. But it's not – its work."

"I've accompanied you on your cases before," she persisted. "I've even helped."

"Yeah, almost helped me into an early grave with worry."

"That's not fair, Tom. You know I can take care of myself."

We walked into the lobby of the El Tovar. Tennyson was still on duty at the desk, and as he spied us, he gave a frantic wave and rushed over.

"Mr. Logan... thank God," he said, breathlessly. "I've been trying to reach you."

"What's the matter?"

He looked around, and then struck by the proximity of the other guests, quickly lowered his voice. "There's been an unfortunate incident... with the body."

"Has someone tampered with it?"

"Yes," he answered sharply.

"In what way," I prompted. "Mutilated it. Stole it? What?"

"You'll have to see."

I sensed that was the end of the conversation, so I turned to Rita.

"Sweetheart, head up to bed. I'll join you after I finish checking this out."

"Couldn't I…"

"No!" I responded, firmly. "You stay here and keep warm. I'll fill you in when I get back. I promise."

"But…"

"When I get back," I repeated.

For an instant, she searched my face. Then sensing my resolution, huffed, turned sharply on her heel, and with a slight toss of her head started up the staircase.

"Oh, and honey…" I called. She paused midway without turning. I continued, "Don't forget to set the alarm. I'm supposed to meet Jim at seven, and you're to join Liz around nine. I'm sure you'll have fun shopping."

"Forget the tomahawk," I heard her mumble under her breath. "I'm starting to think bow and arrows!"

4

ICEHOUSE INTRUDER

*"A thief is not the one who steals, but the
one that is caught."*

—*George Bernard Shaw*

The outside temperature had dropped several degrees lower than during our earlier walk back to the El Tovar. Away from the lights of the lodge, it was pitch dark. I couldn't see but a few feet in front of me. If it weren't for Tennyson's flashlight, the trip down the steep, icy steps would have been difficult.

As we neared the icehouse, I noticed a figure bundled up in multiple layers of clothing warming his hands over a coal fire. At our approach, he came forward to greet us.

"This is Collins," Tennyson said by way of introduction. I shook the man's offered hand. He had a firm grip. "Collins works in maintenance. He volunteered for this watch."

"I commend your sacrifice." I indicated the metal drum with its glowing coals sheltered beneath a pine. "That can't provide much relief in this weather."

"I do OK, sir. I don't mind the snow much. Different story if it was raining."

"Collins was the man on duty during the break-in," Tennyson explained. Then turning toward the man. "You'd better tell Mr. Logan about it."

"Sure. So sorry about the break-in. I'd only left my post ten, maybe fifteen minutes at the most…"

"About what time?" I interrupted.

He rubbed his chin.

"Maybe seven, seven-thirty."

"Where did you go?"

"Restroom over at the depot."

"Did you see anyone hanging around?"

"No. Just the Station Master. He was at the depot building."

"But nobody outside? Strangers?"

"Not that I noticed."

"What happened next?"

"On the way back to my post, as I passed the ice-house door I noticed the lock broken. I didn't go in, but slid the door open just enough so I could look in…"

"Were the lights on or off?" I interjected.

"Off."

"Then you couldn't have seen much."

"Yes, that's correct."

"Hear anything?"

"No, it was quiet." I could tell that he wanted to say more, so I waited. "I did right, didn't I," he continued with some hesitation. "I mean – *should I have gone in?*"

"No, you did fine," I replied, setting him at ease. "Who knows what you could've encountered? Perhaps the person inside was armed."

"My thoughts exactly," he said more confidently. "Next I ran up to the lodge and alerted Mr. Tennyson. He got a couple of men, and we returned to the icehouse..."

"About how long did that take?"

"Ten minutes at the most."

Here Tennyson took up the narrative.

"I brought the flashlight with me and through the gap in the door shined the beam around the inside. The intruder was gone."

"You sure, Tennyson?"

"I could see from wall to wall. It was empty – except for the corpse, of course."

"Was the door as you left it?" I addressed this to Collins.

"I believe so."

"Therefore," I reasoned, "this person had to be in and out of the icehouse within the time you went over to the depot. Which tells me, this person must've been watching you at your post to act so quickly. The big question is 'why'?"

"I don't mean to be cryptic, Mr. Logan," Tennyson began. "But you'll have to see this for yourself."

Tennyson directed me toward the icehouse entrance. The beam of his flashlight landed on the lock. I saw that a crowbar had jimmied it. There was an impression on the frame where its heel had dug in. Using my handkerchief to preserve fingerprints, I slid open the door just wide enough so we could pass; then used it again to switch on the lights. The temperature inside was barely tolerable. Much colder than I remembered. We could see our breath. Immediately I searched out the body. It was laid out as we had left it, but with an obvious difference. The man's clothing the dead woman had been wearing earlier was now gone, and her naked body draped from neck to mid-thigh with a gunny sack.

"Is this what you saw from the doorway?" I snapped.

"Yes," Tennyson replied.

"And the gunny sack? Could it have come from here?"

He motioned to the corner. "On that shelf. We use them to carry ice."

I found this gesture on the intruder's part very telling – preserving of the girl's modesty. I filed it away for later reference.

I nodded, and then indicating the body, suggested: "We better take a closer look."

Gingerly I lifted the sack away. Just as a doctor who examines his patient with detachment, I ran my eyes over her petite form, looking for evidence. A professional doing his job. After assuring myself that there were no apparent signs of disturbance – at least visible, the coroner might say otherwise – I tucked the gunny sack back into place around the body.

"Aside from the missing clothes," I said, turning toward the two men, "I can't see anything unusual on the torso. Now, let's take a look at her hands. Whoa, what's this?"

There was a piece of paper wedged between the thumb and forefinger of her right hand. This was something new. I distinctly remember examining her hands earlier and could swear it wasn't there then.

Again with the aid of my handkerchief, I easily manipulated it free from her fingers. The slip was approximately 5 ¼ inches by 3 ½ when opened along its fold, and crème colored, with the words 'El Tovar' embossed in gold lettering across its top. It had been taken from one of the notepads available in all the guest rooms. Written on it were three words: *R zbunare Este Sigur,* in a careful hand using black ink.

"Looks foreign," Collins suggested. Both he and Tennyson were looking over my shoulder.

"I wonder what it means," Tennyson added.

"I don't know," I replied. "But it's a clue." I tucked it into my notebook. "And sooner or later we'll need a person to translate it." I looked at Tennyson. "That reminds me, what's the word on getting someone over here?"

"We shouldn't expect anyone sooner than tomorrow night. The Rangers are still digging themselves out on the North Rim. The road is packed with snow. And the sheriff has been notified. His office is in Flagstaff, about 74 miles from here, but all roads are closed down."

"Then it looks like I'll be continuing tomorrow as planned." I headed for the door. "In the meantime, we'll need to get this lock fixed, and Collins, I hate to ask, but could you return to your post?"

On cat-like feet, I crept into our suite. The lights were out, but no sooner had I taken a few careful steps into the room, when a bedside lamp clicked to life.

"Sorry, honey," I whispered. "Did I disturb you?"

Of course, I knew better. Rita hadn't been disturbed at all. In fact, she had been sitting up in bed, pillows propped behind her, waiting anxiously for my return.

"You thought you'd get away with it," she stated.

"Away with what?" I was all innocence.

"What's the story?"

"You want to hear a story?" She nodded, so I sat close to her on the edge of the bed. "OK. Once upon a time, there were three bears..."

"Not a bedtime story," she admonished. "I want the real scoop."

"Then, there was only one 'bare.'"

"Tom! Stop stalling."

"Honestly there was only one 'bare' – the corpse itself. Someone stole her clothes."

She stared at me for a long moment and then said with disbelief, "No."

"Cross my heart, doll."

She still wasn't convinced.

"I can't – No. You're putting me on."

"Nope."

"But, who would be that bold? I mean, taking a chance like that with the place being watched just to remove a dead woman's clothes."

"That's the million-dollar question, doll – and the other is, 'why?'"

She bit her lip in contemplation.

"It had to be her killer," she surmised.

"Possibly," I admitted.

"Perhaps there was something on or in the clothing that might identify the killer."

"Again, possible. However, there was something left with the body that wasn't there before. A note, folded in half and left between her fingers."

"Really." She pulled herself up even further in bed. "What did it say?"

"Here, read it for yourself." Using my handkerchief, I removed the paper from my notebook and held it up so she could read it – cautioning her, of course, not to touch it.

She read it over a couple of times. I could see her lips moving as she silently mouthed the words. After a pause, she asked, "Do you know what it means?"

"It's all Greek to me, doll."

Her eyes brightened.

"Perhaps that's it."

"What's it?"

"You said she said something about 'A Gypsy'…"

"Gypsies," I corrected. "Plural."

"Alright – 'Gypsies,' plural. Maybe the note is written in Gypsy."

"Gypsy isn't a language. But, perhaps you might have something. It could be Romany. It's the Gypsy language. To be sure, we'll need someone who can read Romany." I quickly corrected myself. "Or suggest that to the sheriff, or rangers, or whoever it is that takes over this crazy case!"

I started to replace the paper in my notebook, but Rita held up her hand.

"Wait." She reached for the pen and notepad sitting on the bedside table and copied the words down. "When we get back to Los Angeles I'll contact a translator at the university. If for no other reason, I'm curious myself."

"That's what I love about you," I commented after kissing the nape of her neck. "You are efficient." She giggled, and I delivered another behind her right ear. "Still mad?"

She nodded, so I kissed her chin, and asked, "Still want to chop me up with a tomahawk?"

"No," she cooed.

"Shoot me full of arrows?"

"I don't think so?"

"Then how do you plan to kill me?"

She moistened her bottom lip seductively, and responded in a husky voice, "*Like this.*"

Reaching up, she pulled my face close to hers. Instantly our lips parted. At first, our kisses were gentle, almost caressing, but soon became more passionate.

Breathless, we both separated and I started to undress swiftly.

"Tom," she began after drawing the covers back and scooting over to make room. "*Is that all you love about me* – being efficient?"

Slipping in beside her, I answered into her dreamy eyes, "Oh, there's a lot more. I'll tell you about it in the morning."

5

QUESTIONING THE HARVEY GIRL

"Those waitresses (Harvey girls) were the first respectable women the cowboys had ever seen – that is, outside of their own wives and mothers."

—*Erna Fergusson*

I was ten minutes late meeting Tennyson and Rollins the following morning. I didn't offer an excuse. After all, I was technically on my honeymoon, so let them think what they liked. However, they must've guessed. I could tell by the stupid grins on their faces. I mumbled a hasty apology and addressed Tennyson.

"So, what did you find out about Roberts?"

"I contacted the maid on duty this morning," he responded. "Miss Roberts didn't answer her knock. I instructed her to go back and check the suite.

Apparently, Miss Robert's bed hadn't been slept in. I consulted the registration, and she's still booked for three nights. I then spoke with the night clerk – she didn't check out. And a moment ago I looked in her suite's mail slot and there's no key. It seems nobody has seen Miss Roberts since early yesterday morning."

"Exit Roberts, enter Daniels' corpse," I concluded. "She could be our girl. However before we take a look at the suite – Regarding this witness to the murder…" I referred to my notebook. "I wasn't given a name, but someone identified her by uniform – as a Harvey Girl. I take it you know who she is?"

"Yes," Tennyson confirmed. "Sally – Sally Ann Iverson. She was hysterical after it happened. The restaurant manager gave her the rest of the day off – sent her back to her dorm."

"Is she OK now?"

"Yes – came back to work this morning."

"Is she available?"

"She can be. She's in the dining room – serving breakfast with the other girls."

"Good. Could you fetch her? I want to hear her story."

"No problem, Mr. Logan. You can use this private area for her interview if you like." He indicated the door on our left, just before the main dining hall. Rumor has it that it was expressly added for Teddy

Roosevelt who liked to eat dinner in his muddy boots and riding gear. I'm not sure if that was true, but the moose head hanging on a nearby wall was shot and donated by him.

"Thanks, Tennyson," I acknowledged. "Now, could you get the girl?"

As the Assistant Manager crossed toward the main dining room, I indicated to Rollins that he accompany me. We entered the private area, christened, 'The Roosevelt Room,' and located chairs at a small table. Here we waited among panels of dark wood with elaborate scrollwork and a wall decoration consisting of a plate rail exhibiting antique china dishes. Beneath the ceiling ran a border of deer hieroglyphics, Native American in design, and reproduced from a pictographic site at the top of the Bright Angel Trail. A good fifteen minutes passed before Tennyson appeared with the girl.

Miss Iverson was tall, perhaps close to six feet. She was young, fresh-faced, scrubbed and polished. Decidedly cute, but in a juvenile sort of way despite her height. She wore no make-up. This was prohibited by the company – especially when on duty. For Iverson, however, this was not a problem, being blessed with a flawless complexion, underscored naturally by rosy cheeks and full, pink lips. These attributes, combined with her innocent, china-blue eyes, created an impression of a cherub; although a farm girl from Middle America was probably more faithful to the facts.

She was dressed in the official company uniform of starched white apron over a black blouse. It wasn't an attractive outfit. In truth, it wasn't designed to be, with its long black skirt, clerical-looking "Elsie" collar, opaque black stockings, and clunky black shoes. The outfit was intended to de-emphasize the female physique, making it less attractive to the male. The regulations also dictated that hair should be restrained in a net and tied with an approved white ribbon. Miss Iverson's honey-blond hair was done up in that fashion; and by the manner that it was layered, you could tell it was long. The only adornment allowed on the uniform by the company was the Harvey pin, which was worn above the breast near the left shoulder.

Both Rollins and I rose as she entered. I offered her a chair.

"Don't keep Miss Iverson too long," demanded an unfamiliar voice – thin, and nasally. I looked in its direction. A third person, an older woman was standing behind Tennyson. "She's serving breakfast in an hour, and we're expecting the usual rush. You understand me, young man?"

"Miss Lonsdale," said Tennyson quickly. He looked embarrassed. Here evidently was a woman who was used to being obeyed. Tennyson explained further, "She's the 'House Mother.'"

"House Mother?" I queried.

"Yes, our senior Harvey Girl. She watches over the others – keeps the young ones in line."

I looked Lonsdale over. She appeared fortyish, with a slim build, and severe features. Like Iverson, she was wearing the Harvey issued uniform.

"You heard my request, young man," she repeated. The gold-framed pince-nez, bounced on her beak-like nose as she said it. The lenses magnified two dark, beady eyes that looked sternly in my direction. "We can't have her tied up all day."

"We'll keep it brief, Madam," I promised.

"You better," she snapped. And after a pause: "Do I need to stay?" She lifted her chin proudly, and a strand of her silver-streaked hair worked its way out of the net.

I smiled genially. A warm, full-toothed grin.

"I assure you, Madam, her virtue's safe with us."

Apparently, Miss Lonsdale lacked a sense of humor. She scowled in my direction and stormed away. Tennyson exited soon after, but not so dramatically, which left Rollins and me alone with the girl. I shut the door discretely and sat so Miss Iverson was facing me.

"Miss Iverson," I began after clearing my throat and smiling encouragingly. "I was told you witnessed the crime that occurred yesterday?"

"Yes," she replied after a fashion. "It was terrible. I'm embarrassed to say that I went to pieces afterward."

"Understandable," I consoled. "Do you feel strong enough to tell us now?"

"Yes. I believe so."

"Please do." I noticed the delicate lace handkerchief in her hands. She was twisting it. "Take your time," I added. "There's no rush. Whenever you're ready."

"Yesterday," she eventually began, "during my break, I left the hotel to visit a friend who works at the curio shop."

"Vankamp's?"

"Yes, that's correct."

"What time?"

"Ten thirty."

"Exactly?"

"Yes."

"How can you be so sure?"

She furrowed her brow and replied, "The serving staff gets a break after the morning crowd has cleared. The dining room stops serving breakfast at ten, and we had pretty much cleaned up everything within a half hour. I rushed out, not even stopping to put on a coat. I remember that because once outside I regretted it. However, since my break was short – we only get a half hour, after which we set up for lunch – I decided to brave the cold and visit my friend. And, oh," she added. "Something else. I heard the train whistle announcing its approach to the station. According to the schedule, it was due in at ten thirty."

"My wife and I were on that train, and yes," I confirmed, "we pulled in exactly at ten thirty. I remember looking at my watch and marveling that we were on schedule. So, how much after that time did you witness the murder?"

"No more than a couple of minutes. It's only a few yards walk along the path to the store. I'd just reached the entrance when I heard …"

"Let's return to that in a minute," I quickly interrupted. "But first – regarding the time – you're saying that the murder occurred sometime around, or shortly after ten thirty-two a.m. Is that correct?" She nodded. I recorded it in my notebook. "Good." I jotted a couple of more things and then looked up expectantly. "Continue."

"I had just reached the entrance to the store when I heard a shout, and turned to see two men arguing near the rim."

"How far away were they?"

"Oh, gosh. I'm not very good at judging these things." I waited as she mulled it over. Finally, she concluded: "Maybe fifty yards."

"Could you make out any of their words?"

"No… no… wait. Just before the one man pushed the other over the edge, I heard him say; 'How could you do this to me,' or 'why are you doing this to me' – something like that."

"The murderer said this, not the victim?" I asked, seeking clarification, and noted her response in my book.

"That's correct. He raised his voice, furious-like, and then soon after gave him a shove."

I hadn't at this point corrected her in regards to the gender of the victim. The fewer people who knew a woman was the victim, and that it was the movie actress, Norma Daniels, the better. It would come out soon enough, and then the place would become a circus. Hopefully by that time it would be out of my lap and into the ranger's, or sheriff's, or whoever inherited this mess.

"Could you describe them?" I continued, pencil poised.

"There again, I'm afraid I'm not a very good witness."

"Please try."

"OK." Once more she paused to reflect, and then began slowly, "The man who shoved the other – I remember thinking he looked like a sailor – heavy, dark blue coat and Watch Cap."

"What about his face?"

"No, not at that distance – and besides he was wearing a muffler. A dark color as well."

"What about size? Height for example?"

"He could've been taller than the victim."

"And build? Thin, medium, heavy?"

"Hard to say the way he was bundled up."

"If you were to guess?"

"He wasn't fat. Maybe medium. Although he could've been thin."

"Anything else?"

"Yes. The other person – the man who was killed – he seemed out of place."

"How do you mean?"

"He wasn't dressed for the cold – thin, brown suit and fedora hat. Not exactly what one would expect to be wearing in this weather."

"And that's all you can remember regarding the two men?"

"Yes," she answered, and then her eyes suddenly glazed over, as if her thoughts had turned inward. "Wait a moment. I do recollect something else. The murderer – he had something in his hand – I believe it was a red cloth. He was waving it around when they were arguing, and after pushing the other fellow off the cliff, I saw him toss it away."

I sat up when she said this, and turned quickly toward Rollins.

"Jim, could I ask you to run out and search the area where we pulled up the body?"

"For this red cloth?" he asked. I nodded. "I'm on my way."

"And if you locate it," I called after him, "pick it up carefully. Don't use your bare fingers. We wouldn't want the local officials accusing us of contaminating the evidence."

"I've been observing how you do it," he said, smiling. And then tapping his breast pocket, "I have a handkerchief all ready to do the job."

Rollins left the room, and I picked up the questioning again.

"When all of this was occurring: the argument – the killer pushing the victim off the cliff. Did you notice anyone else around? Anyone who could also have witnessed it?"

She thought carefully again and then answered, "As I mentioned already, it was freezing. Normally there would've been more people about, but I didn't see a soul." She hesitated, then said, "Well, perhaps that's not entirely true. I did think there was someone else in the area when this was occurring – much closer than me – just off the path and farther up the trail. But when I looked again, this person was gone. I can't see how anyone could've disappeared so fast, so perhaps it could've been my imagination."

"This person? Any description?"

She shook her head.

"I'm sorry, no. I'm a lousy witness."

"No. You're doing fine. Did you see this other person before, during, or after the killing?"

"I can't say. It was just an impression. All I can say was that he was gone afterward."

"So, you think it could've been a male?"

Again she shook her head.

"No. Not really. I just said, 'he,' but it could've been a 'she.'"

"OK. We'll leave it at that. What did you do after witnessing the murder?"

"I was pretty shaken up. I ran into the store shouting to everyone what had just occurred."

"Where there a lot of customers?"

"Not many. Maybe four or five. They ran outside – I don't know why, maybe to help."

"And you?"

"My friend sat me down and made me drink some tea. I was trembling badly. When I had calmed down a bit – although still trembling – she walked me back to the dining room at the El Tovar. Miss Lonsdale took one look at me and summoned the hotel doctor. He advised rest and gave me a sleeping draught. Then my friend took me to the dorm, I took the draught and slept through the night."

I started to ask the name of her friend when a knock on the door interrupted me. It was Rollins returning.

"That was quick," I said, as he retook his seat at the table. "Any luck?"

"Yup." He unfolded his white handkerchief revealing the red cloth folded inside. "Located it in the bushes. It wasn't hard to find once you knew to look for it."

I used the end of my pencil to spread it out on the table. It was a red bandana, imprinted in black with a paisley design.

"Is this what you saw the killer waving around?"

"Yes. It could've been."

"I know this next question may seem unusual, Miss Iverson, but bear with me…" I carefully observed her. "Does 'Gypsies' suggest anything to you?"

"Gypsies?"

"Yes."

"I don't understand."

"It's what the victim said before dying – 'The Gypsies.'"

"No, I'm afraid not."

"You're sure?"

"Positive."

I consulted my notes.

"Could you give me the name of your friend in the curio store?"

"Yes, of course. It's Rebecca Stewart."

I made a note of it, and then looking up: "Is there anything else you might want to add to our discussion?"

"No. I don't believe so."

"Then thank you, Miss Iverson. You can return to your job now." I rose at the same time she did and presented my card. "If you think of anything else, please don't hesitate to contact me. You've been very helpful."

I escorted her to the door. I could tell by her modest response to my last statement that she still felt her contributions were minimal. But, in fact, I had learned some valuable information, not the least of which was the discovery of the bandana.

"Rollins," I said, once I shut the door behind her. "Let me ask you the same question I posed to Miss Iverson – but framed somewhat differently."

"OK, fire away."

"What does this red bandana suggest to you?"

"I don't know. Billy the Kid – cowboys – bank robbers." He laughed at his response.

"How about something less wild west, or even American."

He shrugged, so I answered: "How about Gypsies? An article of their apparel, perhaps?"

6

SEARCHING FOR CLUES

"In solving a problem of this sort, the grand thing is to be able to reason backwards."

—Sherlock Holmes, *A Study in Scarlet*

The Miwok suite was located on the second floor down the east corridor from the ladies lounge. As we neared its door, a maid appeared from an adjacent suite. The girl was small in stature, perhaps in her late teens. She had dark skin with high cheekbones, a pug nose, and shiny, blue-black hair parted in the middle and braided, so it hung mid-length down her back. She was carrying a pile of dirty towels, which she dumped into a laundry cart.

I addressed her.

"Excuse me."

She seemed startled by our appearance.

"Sir?" Her almond-shaped, brown eyes darted from my face to Rollins.

I read the name tag on her uniform.

"Debbie?"

"Dibe," she corrected. "It's Navajo for lamb."

"Hi, Dibe. I'm Tom Logan, and this is James Rollins. Were you the person who reported that the occupant of this suite had not slept in her bed last night?"

"Yes, sir," she answered. "Mr. Tennyson asked that I check."

"Did Mr. Tennyson also tell you that we would like to take a look inside?"

"Yes, sir. He said that I should allow you in."

"Could you do that for us now?"

In answer to my request, she removed her passkey and inserted it into the lock. Then pushing the door open, she stood aside so we could enter. As she started to follow, I asked, "Could you wait outside, Dibe? Continue working if you like. After we're finished, I may have some questions for you. So, please stay close."

She nodded and returned to sorting the linen on her cart.

This suite was much smaller than the bridal suite that Rita and I were occupying. It also lacked a canyon view. Rollins stood aside as I made a careful circuit of the bedroom. I could feel his eyes observing me as, with a handkerchief in hand I pulled one drawer open after another searching its contents. A woman's personal items were still here, neatly tucked away in bureaus, cabinets, and closets. These indicated to me that she had either left in a hurry or was expecting to return. If the latter, then the occupant was most likely Miss Daniels.

Rollins'curiosity got the better of him.

"Find anything of interest, Tom?"

"This stuff is expensive. Something you might expect a movie actress would own. Classy clothes – unfortunately, no personal labels – and a jewelry box loaded with the real McCoy. I can't imagine a lady voluntarily leaving these items behind."

"Purse?"

"I found a couple of handbags. One 'everyday,' and the other 'evening.'"

"Wallet, or ID inside?"

"No. Those were missing. On the other hand, there wasn't any identification found on Miss Daniels' body either."

"Then perhaps this woman isn't Daniels. Just a tourist who wandered off."

"To where?" I queried. "Overnight – and in this weather?"

He shrugged.

"Furthermore," I continued, "Tennyson said that the suite's key is missing. Normally a guest would drop it at the front desk when leaving."

"I don't recall you finding a key on the body?"

"I didn't," I sighed. "That would've made things too easy."

Dropping to my knees, I looked under the bed. There I discovered a hat box, which I fished out and opened. Sadly it was empty, except for a papier-mâché head form and several hat pins.

"Anything?" Rollins asked, trying to peer inside.

"Maybe. It could've been brought along to transport a wig, but then it could have been for a hat." I thought for a moment, and then an idea struck me. Immediately I left the bedroom, crossed the sitting area, and switched on the light in the bath. Opening the medicine cabinet over the sink, I removed a hairbrush and examined it.

"Bingo," I uttered under my breath, but loud enough for Rollins to hear. He had followed me and was now standing near the entrance.

"Something encouraging?"

"Yes, strands of platinum blond hair. By all accounts, Miss Roberts was a redhead. The owner of this brush was a blonde like Daniels."

I tapped my fingers pensively on the edge of the sink for a couple of seconds, and then slipping past Rollins, re-entered the sitting room and crossed to the suite's exit. Next, leaning out into the hall I got the maid's attention.

"Dibe, if you don't mind, we're ready for you."

Her cart had moved up the hall, and she was dumping trash. Immediately she set down the wastepaper basket and joined us. I offered her a chair in the sitting room, but she declined. I sat on the arm of the settee and Rollins leaned against the door jamb of the bath.

I started with a few simple questions regarding her employment. Like, for example, 'Did she enjoy her job?' and then commented on 'what a beautiful place to be employed.' I wanted to set her at ease. I could tell that she was nervous. Once she had relaxed, I began my questioning.

"Did you see the woman who occupied this suite?"

"Yes, sir."

"Could you describe her?"

"She was pretty."

"I need something more than that."

"She was slim and nicely dressed."

"What about eye color, or hair?"

"I'm not sure about her eyes. Most of the time she wore dark glasses."

"Even inside?"

"Yes. I saw the lady once in the restaurant, and again in the Rendezvous Room. Both times she had sunglasses on."

"Did you ever see her without them?"

"Yes, but I was too far away to make out her eye color."

"Where was this?"

"Outside, in the hallway – just for a moment, as she popped her head out."

"Why did she do that? Had you knocked on the door?"

"No. I was down the hall – delivering the afternoon paper. I'd just placed it under her door. She was retrieving it."

"When was this?"

She thought a moment.

"I believe it was three days ago."

Her answer was vague, but then she added more assuredly, "Yes, that's right. It was just before the big snowfall – Wednesday afternoon."

I decided to shift gears.

"What about her hair color?"

"That's easy. It was red."

I exchanged glances with Rollins, and then continued, "Did you ever see her with anyone?"

I think I struck a nerve because I saw her stiffen. After a long pause, she replied, "Yes, sir – but, I rather not speak about it."

"Why is that?"

"We're not supposed to gossip about the guests. It's against hotel policy."

"I think in this situation you needn't worry," I offered gently. "We're investigating a crime, and any information you can provide would be beneficial."

"Does this have to do with the person who was pushed off the cliff?"

"Yes."

She still seemed hesitant.

"What I have to say, do you think it could be important in your investigation?"

"It could be."

She took a deep breath.

"There was a man I saw her with – very nice looking. Tan, dark eyes, and curly black hair. Maybe foreign…"

"Foreign? Why do you say that?"

"Something about his clothes. He didn't dress like a tourist."

An idea struck me. I reached into my jacket pocket and produced the bandana.

"Have you ever seen this?"

"Yes," she responded, her eyes widening. "That's what I meant by his dress. He looked like a Spaniard, *a vaquero*. I saw him wearing this around his neck many times."

"When in the company of the lady?"

"Yes, and a few times when he was alone."

"How long has he been a guest?" Her answer was a blank stare, so I rephrased the question. "Did he arrive at the lodge earlier, later, or at the same time as the lady?"

"He came earlier."

"How much earlier?"

"I'm not sure."

It was an acceptable answer for now – something I could check with the front desk later. I continued: "During what occasions did you see this man and woman together?"

"You know – dinner, walking…"

Her response was vague – purposely so, and I noted that she couldn't meet my eyes. I decided to press her.

"You're holding something back." She blushed and looked away. I adopted another approach, more direct, and less tactful. "Would you say their relationship was friendly, or intimate?"

She stalled for several seconds, tugging at the edge of her white apron. Undoubtedly she was struggling with the decision to either remain discreet or tell me the full story – particularly since it might have some bearing on the murder. Her conscience finally won out.

"The evening before last, I saw this lady entering the gentleman's room. It was very late, and I could tell by her manner that she was trying not to be seen."

"How late?"

"Perhaps one or two o'clock in the morning."

"Did she see you?"

"No. I don't think so. I was at the end of the hall – it was dark there."

"Why were you here so late?"

"I was stranded by the storm. Normally I go back to the reservation after my shift – I live with my parents – but that night there was a heavy snowfall which closed the roads. I had to stay at the lodge. I tried sleeping in the lounging room, but it was uncomfortable, and I became restless. I started pacing the halls, and that's when I saw the lady sneaking into the man's room."

"Did you see her again after that?"

"No."

"Are you sure? What about the following morning?"

"No."

"What about the man? Did you see him the next morning?"

"No, sir."

"Is he still staying at the hotel?"

"I don't know."

"Have you cleaned his suite?"

"It's not a suite. It's one of the single rooms."

"Then," I corrected, "*have you cleaned his room?*"

"No, not within the last couple of days."

"Why not?"

"There's a 'Do Not Disturb' sign on the door."

I leaped off the arm of the settee.

"Could you show us this room?"

"Of course, sir. It's just down the hall."

The room was several doors away and across the corridor. As the young maid had described, there was a 'Do Not Disturb' sign on the knob. At my encouragement, she knocked and announced, "Maid service." There was no reply. She repeated the procedure again and then used her passkey.

"Looks like he's flown the coop," Rollins commented.

That was pretty evident. Drawers left open – empty, same for the closet, and there was no luggage. It was also cold in the room. A draft of freezing air blew through a window left open. I walked over and looked out.

"He didn't leave by this way," I commented. "Too high and nothing to hold on to. No ledges, drain pipes, or…"

Something caught my attention below. I called Rollins to the window and pointed it out.

"Do you see that?"

"Yes. What is it?"

"I don't know, but it's worth going down and finding out."

The grounds at this corner of the El Tovar were overgrown with shrubbery and covered by drifts of snow – at some places four feet high. Within one of these mounds, directly below the window, I saw something buried. I couldn't tell what it was because only a corner of it showed. It took Rollins and me a couple of attempts before zeroing in on the area from below. Once we did, however, the mound was easily recognizable, as was the portion of something blue that contrasted against the white snow.

We wasted little time in digging it out. The action left our hands numb from the cold. The discomfort, however, was worth it, for not only did our efforts uncover a woman's dress, but bundled with it, a red wig, undergarments, and a ladies wallet. And thanks to the ID inside this billfold, we now had definite proof their owner was Norma Daniels.

There was still one other detail I needed to check before breaking for lunch at noon, and that was back upstairs in the room we had just left. The maid was still there when we returned, and watched – as did, Rollins, with interest, while I did my Sherlock routine. As silly as I may have looked crawling along the floor, looking behind furniture, and digging through the trash, I did succeed in finding another vital clue. It was the note-pad supplied by the El Tovar, and I discovered it where it had fallen (or was tucked) between a side table and the mattress of the bed. A few seconds work on its surface with the side of a lead pencil brought out the written impression from the removed page: *Răzbunare Este Sigur.*

7

ALL THE WORLD'S A STAGE

*The Harvey chain of restaurants was
famous for serving excellent meals prepared
by capable chefs. Fred Harvey started his
company in 1876 with the opening of two
railroad eating houses located at Wallace,
Kansas and Hugo, Colorado on the Kansas
Pacific Line. These cafes closed within a
year, but Harvey, convinced of the viabil-
ity of high-quality food and service offered
at railroad stops, eventually contracted
a system-wide operation of eating houses
along the Atchison, Topeka, and Santa Fe
Railway. Initially, they were set up on an ex-
perimental basis beginning in 1878, but by
the late 1880s, his restaurants were deemed
an unqualified success, with a Fred Harvey
Restaurant located every 100 miles along
the AT&SF.*

"Excuse me?" A man approached us the instant we stepped out into the hallway. It was a stranger – likely a guest of the hotel. He began by addressing Rollins. "Are you a policeman?"

"No," Rollins returned with a mischievous grin. "But, I've played one on stage. A constable really – in the chorus line of the *The Pirates of Penzance* – Royale Theater, 1926 – no, '27."

The fellow was stunned to silence, so Rollins added with a laugh, throwing a thumb in my direction, "However, this guy is the real McCoy. You might want to talk to him."

"Can I help?" I queried.

"Are you investigating that incident yesterday?" His eyes searched my face earnestly. "That guy who was pushed into the canyon?"

"Yes, I am." Again I didn't bother to correct the assumption of the victim's gender. "Do you know something about it?"

"I may." He pointed to the room we had just left. "Do you think the fellow who occupied that room might have something to do with it?"

"It's a strong possibility."

"Then, "he replied more assuredly. "I have something for you."

I motioned that he follow us, and after dismissing the maid, led him and Rollins back to the Miwok suite.

It felt warm in the sitting room, so I asked Rollins to keep the door open. After we took our seats, I indicated that the man proceed.

"That morning," he began, "the day of the incident, my wife and I were getting ready to leave when we heard loud voices coming from the next room. We could only make out bits and pieces, but it was pretty evident that there was a big blow up of some sort going on."

"Men's voices? Women's voices?" I asked.

"Both – a man's and a woman's."

I was curious. From his earlier question, I knew he thought a man was pushed off the cliff; so where did he think this woman fit in?

"What makes you believe," I asked, "that this argument is somehow connected with the death that occurred yesterday?"

"It's what I put together from those bits and pieces."

"For example?"

"I heard the man say: 'What were you thinking,' and 'You cheating little tramp.'"

"And the woman?"

"There was a lot of sobbing, and then she said, 'I don't love you anymore.'"

"Anything else?"

"Yes," a woman's voice cut in. It was the man's wife. I hadn't noticed, but she had joined us in the suite. "There were some foreign words spoken. It's what started the argument."

"Foreign?"

"It was a language I wasn't familiar with," she offered. "Delivered more like a shout than conversationally."

"OK." I added this to my notebook. "What about what was said in English?" I directed this to her. "Did you hear anything different than your husband?"

"No, but it sounded pretty serious. I was afraid they might come to blows."

"What happened afterward?"

This time the husband spoke.

"Concerned, I opened the door into the hall. Just at that moment I heard a door slam and saw our neighbor – the male – running for all he's worth down the corridor. Immediately I thought of the lady inside. Did she come to some harm? I knocked, and when she answered, I asked if she was OK. She replied yes, so I left it at that."

I inquired next for a description of the male, and both painted a picture of him which tallied with the maid's. I also asked about the female, but neither had seen – but only heard her.

"So getting back to this argument's connection to the incident on the cliff," I continued, "you believe this man may have confronted this woman's lover, fought with, and pushed him over the cliff? Correct?"

"Yes, and for a good reason."

"Why's that?"

"Because, a short time after – as we were leaving the hotel – and coincidentally, right at the moment of the murder – while others were running toward the scene, we saw him high-tailing it the other way."

Now, there was some interesting information, and it fit the circumstances. It wasn't another male lover this couple's neighbor had met, but the same woman they heard him arguing with next door. The motive – the oldest one in the book – jealousy – a spurned lover. Or was it? Some pieces of this puzzle didn't fit, and I decided to leave those aside for now.

"How soon after the argument upstairs did this happen?" I asked.

"I'm not sure."

"Take a guess."

"Perhaps fifteen minutes, maybe twenty. Certainly no more than thirty minutes later."

I wrote this down.

"For the record," I continued, "may I have your names?" I nodded toward my notebook.

"Jefferson," he replied. Alice and Tim Jefferson."

"Thank you, Mr. and Mrs. Jefferson, you've been very helpful. We're waiting on the arrival of local law enforcement. It may be anytime now. I'll be passing this information on to them, and they may want to question you further. Will you be available?"

"Yes. We're planning to stay a couple more days." He gestured in the direction of the hall. "Room 102."

"Perfect. Then I'll pass this along."

"What do you know about the guest in room 104?"

Rollins and I had made one more stop at the registration desk before breaking for lunch. Tennyson was still there. He must spend twenty-four hours a day at his post. I asked him about our mystery man, and he consulted the guestbook.

"Checked in on Monday – registered as a Mr. Joe See from Los Angeles."

At the mention of our mysterious guest's name, Rollins snickered at my side. I turned toward him.

"What's so funny?"

"Sorry," he apologized. "It's just that – well, it could be my imagination – either that, or our friend has a sense of humor, or imagination, or both." He added quickly. "And then again, maybe it's just coincidence."

"What are you going on about?" I asked with mounting frustration.

"His name – Joe See. Do you see?"

"No, I don't see."

"There's this romantic comic operetta about a violin player that the daughter of a local landowner is attracted to at her engagement party over the objections of her fiancé – a man more of her stature. It was a revival. I played a minor role…"

"So?" I encouraged.

He then attempted to explain: *"The violin player's name was JÓzsi."*

"You say that like that it's supposed to mean something," I responded unconvinced. He then attempted to explain:

"The spelling, 'Joe See' is a variation of it."

"OK. But I still don't see the connection."

"This character *JÓzsi* – the violin player – was *a* *Gypsy*. The operetta was called, *Gypsy Love*."

"Finally," I returned in exasperation. "You could have something there, even though it seems a bit of a reach – and it took you forever to explain it."

He smiled.

"Tell me," I added with a grin. "Is there anything on stage that you weren't a part of?"

"*Naughty Marietta*."

"You weren't in *Naughty Marietta*?"

"No, I performed in it – at Erlanger's Theatre in 1931," he said. "I just didn't play Marietta."

I gave him a double take, and then commented dryly, "Very funny."

Figuring we needed to move on from this Burns and Allen moment I turned my attention back to Tennyson.

"Do you recall what this Joe See looked like?"

"Sure. I saw him around the hotel from time to time. Tall – I'd say about your height. Thin. Dark complexion. Black hair. Handsome features. And he was foreign."

"What makes you say that?"

"He had an accent that I couldn't place, and his dress – he didn't wear a tie, only a cravat. I particularly remember that because there was some 'to do' over him not having a tie to dine in our restaurant. It's a requirement for dinner."

"What color was this cravat – or was it a scarf? They can be one and the same, can't they?

"Yes."

"Then, what color was it?"

"Red."

Rollins and I exchanged glances. I had another thought.

"Do you keep records of room reservations?"

"Yes. We have a dedicated log."

"Could you check it for me, please? See who made the reservation and when."

"Sure. It will take a minute. The book is in the back."

I nodded, and he disappeared through a door off to the side of the desk. He returned a short time later with a large book. He set it down on the counter in front of us and turned it so we could read the relevant page.

"Mr. See made the reservation himself about two weeks ago," Tennyson said, tapping his forefinger on the entry in the log. "But, notice this…" His finger slid down to the next column. "Notice the time that the next reservation arrived, about five minutes later, and look at the name."

"Miss Lydia Roberts," I read.

"Interesting, wouldn't you say?" He moved his finger along the column to the 'Comments' section. "She asked for a suite on the second floor and specified the same wing as Mr. See – not mentioning him of course – just the location."

"Suggestive," I commented.

"Sorry," Rollins interrupted. "But am I missing something here?"

"It hints at the possibility that Mr. See and Miss Roberts' encounter wasn't a casual one, but previously planned," I explained.

"Right," Rollins replied, nodding knowingly. "Just like *JÓzsi* in the *Gypsy Love* having a secret assignation with the girl, *Zorika* during her engagement party."

"Can't you explain anything without bringing the stage into it?"

"Shakespeare said, 'All the world's a stage.'"

"Yea," I replied. "*But I'm not just a mere actor.*"

I turned to Tennyson.

"Rollins and I are going to lunch in the restaurant. If anything important comes up let us know."

He agreed, and we turned toward the dining room, stumbling a moment later upon the girls returning from shopping. I suggested that they join us.

The restaurant was located in a large Norwegian styled room. Six huge log trusses supported the roof, and a dozen or so electric chandlers hung from its rafters. There were twin stone fireplaces at either end of the room. Plate rails along the wall displayed old brass pots and antique English and Dutch platters. The table and chairs could best be described as the finest examples of arts and craft furniture. The tables were laid with blindingly white tablecloths, and set with china plates, glass goblets, and ornate silverware.

The maître d' escorted us to the table nearest one of the fireplaces. As we sat down, a Harvey girl, looking smart in her white, nicely starched uniform poured water into our goblets and left us with menus.

"Lunch is on us," I announced, noticing the pained-look on Rollins' face as he glanced over the menu. He started to remonstrate, but I checked him with a raised hand. "No, I insist, Jim. Besides, it's not coming out of my pocket. The trip's expenses are being paid by the owners of the El Cabana Hotel in San Diego."

"How's that?" Rollins asked.

"It's a long story…," I began, but Rita cut in, mainly addressing Liz.

"It has to do with that murder I was telling you about. The management of the hotel offered to pay all expenses for another honeymoon if Tom would take up their case…"

"Let's not bore the Rollins with details," I interrupted. Then, indicating the paper bag at her feet, I tactfully re-directed the conversation. "So, did you buy that Tomahawk you mentioned earlier, or was it a bow and arrows?"

"Neither," she replied. "I bought a Navajo hand-woven placemat."

"Just one? You're not trying to tell me something are you?"

"Don't be silly. It was expensive."

"How much?"

"Two dollars."

"I think you can go back and buy a second one. We don't want this one getting lonely."

"How about you, Liz?" Rollins asked.

"Just a couple of postcards," she replied. "Although this silver and turquoise bracelet, which we can't afford, caught my eye."

At that moment the waitress returned to take our orders. We all ordered the "Blue-Plate Special," a significant cut of chicken fried steak, covered with country gravy, and served with sides of mashed potatoes and fresh string beans. A green salad, roll, and an ample piece of berry pie completed the meal, which we washed down with plenty of strong, black coffee.

Between bites, we continued our conversation.

"You asked about our day," Liz began. "What about yours? Did you catch any bad guys?"

"It doesn't happen that fast, Liz," I chuckled. "Although I think we have a clearer picture of what might've occurred."

"Oh, do tell!" She leaned forward with her elbow resting on the table and hand supporting her chin.

I decided to pass the buck.

"Jim, you're the student. Explain it to the little lady."

"Hey," Rita interjected. "I'm interested too – count me in!"

"OK," Rollins said, pulling himself straighter in his chair. "I'll give it a go." I nodded, so he began, "Well, it's pretty safe to say that Miss Lydia Roberts and Miss Norma Daniels are one in the same. All the evidence seems to suggest it. And from what we learned it looks as if she came to the canyon to be with someone – a fellow registered under the name of Joe See, which could also be an alias, but then again, maybe not."

Rollins looked at me for confirmation, and I nodded again, so he continued. "We got a description of the guy from multiple sources which indicated that he was tall, dark, and foreign. This seems to fit with the 'Gypsy' references that seem to keep popping up in the investigation." He looked at me again, and I encouraged him to continue. "This couple arrived separately, trying to be discreet – attempting to hide that this was planned as a romantic interlude. It could've worked; however, they didn't count on a snowstorm which left a hotel maid stranded, and as a result, wandering the hotel late at night, and subsequently stumbling upon Miss Roberts sneaking into Mr. See's room. In any case, something must've gone wrong because the next morning the guests next door to Mr. See's room heard an argument between See and Roberts – suggesting, perhaps, that the relationship had suddenly gone cold. Mind you; this was on the morning before the murder. And interestingly enough, this same neighbor reported witnessing Mr. See fleeing the room in the midst of the argument and later – and more significantly at the scene of the crime.

"This suggests that the argument must've picked up outside on the canyon's rim – a fact confirmed by another witness – and in the course of the argument, this Mr. See pushes Miss Roberts, or should I say, Miss Daniels, over the edge to her death."

"I'm not sure I'm following," Liz said with a frown.

"I agree. Could you summarize for us?" Rita asked.

"Right. The couple – Miss Roberts and Mr. See arrived here expecting to share a romantic encounter, but something changed, resulting in an argument. There were words overheard by the witnesses that indicated the cause might've been jealousy – perhaps another lover. In any case, See goes into a rage and either accidentally, or on purpose pushes Roberts into the canyon."

As Rollins concluded, he smiled broadly. "Did I miss anything, teacher?" I nodded my head, and his grin faded. "What did I forget?"

I explained. "When constructing a scenario, you have to take the facts and place them together like a jigsaw puzzle, *using all of the pieces – not just some.* You also need to be sure that every item you discover will fit perfectly; otherwise, your picture could become skewed. In other words, if something is missing, or doesn't fit, then there's a good chance that you've gotten your scenario wrong."

"So what did I leave out?"

"Discovering the bundle of her clothes beneath the room's window for one. It's safe to say she didn't throw them there, and Mr. See's the likely culprit, but why? Another thing, what made him run from the room in the middle of the argument? If she had been killed in his room, that might make sense, but she wasn't. Also, why did See take the risk of removing his suit of clothes from her body? It's reasonable to assume that it was See's suit of clothes Roberts had borrowed from his closet after her clothes had been disposed of. So why take the chance – particularly since there was nothing on the labels, or in the pockets to identify it as his? And finally, why did he leave that note, and what does it say?"

Rollins started to respond but was interrupted by Tennyson, who came rushing up to their table. He seemed agitated.

"I'm so sorry to disturb your lunch," he quickly apologized, "but Sheriff Jerrod has just arrived, and he's extremely anxious to talk with you."

"Finally," I replied, rising from my chair. "Come on, Rollins. Let's hand this mess over to the authorities and let them worry about it from here on in. I'm ready for a real vacation."

8

*A Motive for Murder? "If you don't behave
like gentlemen, you can't stay here, and you
can't come again. Now put up your guns
and take a drink with Fred Harvey!"*

—Fred Harvey

The sheriff was waiting for us in the Roosevelt Room where we interviewed the Harvey girl that morning. Tennyson did the introductions. Sheriff Pete Jerrod looked as if he'd stepped off the cover of a Western pulp. A tall drink-of-water, pencil thin, with broad shoulders, narrow hips, and bow legs. He was in his late 50s. An assumption based upon his tanned, leathery complexion – weather-worn from countless hours outdoors – and his snow-white hair, which showed from under his ten-gallon hat. He also had a mustache – tobacco stained, bushy, and drooping.

"I figure you know why I've been held up – damn snow." he offered while firmly shaking my hand. "Elsewise I would've been here sooner. All the roads from Flagstaff have finally cleared, but even then it was slow going." He spoke with a drawl, which only amplified my Hopalong Cassidy impression of him. However, his uniform was twentieth century; although the boots and finely tooled gun belt, slung low on his hip spoke Wild West. The police revolver was modern, and I wouldn't be surprised if it had a few notches on its handle.

"A bit unexpected, I gather – such heavy snowfall so early."

"It happens, but not often."

Jerrod looked toward Rollins, and I caught his sharp profile. Indian blood – Cherokee? Perhaps.

"You a lawman too?" he asked Jim.

"No. You might say I'm an understudy."

"Not sure what that means," he laughed, his pale blue eyes twinkling, "but I assume you are assisting him?"

"He was," I interjected. "He's been a big help."

"Good." He returned his attention back to me. "Tennyson says that you're a PI, operating out of Los Angeles."

"I have an office in Hollywood."

"What are you doing here?"

"Honeymoon – or, some semblance of it."

"You'll have to excuse me," he continued, "but Tennyson only briefly filled me in. He asked that you start the ball rolling until I arrived. Correct?"

"That's right."

"And this fella?" He indicated Rollins. "How did he become involved?"

"Mr. Rollins and I became acquainted during the investigation, and he offered his help."

"I see." He walked over to the table, settled himself on a corner, and then asked with folded arms. *"And what have you discovered?"*

Before I could begin, we were interrupted by the appearance of a second uniformed man. This one was a park ranger. He was young, with wavy brown hair and dark brown eyes. He also had a mustache, trimmed in a Gable-style.

"Sorry to interrupt," he said from the doorway. "I hope I'm not too late?"

"This is Dave Brown," Tennyson said. "He's our local ranger. Has an office at the South Rim station. He's been away searching for that missing child on the North Rim."

"Any luck?" I asked Brown.

"Unfortunately not. It's been too many days. The longer it takes, the less hope we have of finding him alive – especially with the storm, extreme cold, and all."

"So sorry to hear it. Let's hope for the best."

He nodded, although his solemn expression said otherwise.

After a respectful pause, Sheriff Jerrod suggested that we be seated, and then repeated his request to brief him on our investigation. I spent a good hour and a half giving him all the details. I started from the moment I was made aware of the crime, took charge, and followed through on it up to the present. Referring to my notebook, I repeated witness statements and my observations regarding the body. I also mentioned the victim's final words, 'The Gypsies,' and handed over the note left with her corpse. The Sheriff took copious notes, only pausing at times to ask a question or clarify a point. When I was through, he closed his notebook, and placing it in his breast pocket along with his pen, said, "You've done a thorough job. It certainly makes my work a lot easier."

"Well," I replied modestly, "I couldn't have covered as much as I did without Rollins help."

"Thank you both." We nodded, and he continued. "Now, about the body. I've called in the coroner. He should be arriving soon." He looked at Tennyson. "Could you send someone down to direct him to the ice house?"

Tennyson answered in the affirmative and rushed out of the room.

"So what do you make of this, Mr. Logan?" The Sheriff asked, his eyes searching mine keenly.

"Not sure what you mean," I answered.

"Do you think this boyfriend of hers killed her?"

"I could see where others may think so." I was being vague – purposely so. I wanted him to draw his own conclusion. He caught on to my ploy real quick.

"You're interested in what I think, is that it?"

I nodded.

"I believe he's a possibility, but not a surety."

"I'm impressed."

He smiled. "I'm not like those police portrayed in detective stories. In fact, most of us aren't. They like to make us look dumb, so the PI, or whoever's the hero in these stories, seems exceedingly bright. It's one of my pet peeves when it comes to the pulps."

"I wouldn't take you as being dumb, Sheriff," I offered. "In fact, I've already pegged you as a sharp guy. I was just curious – or, perhaps better said, *I was seeking confirmation* that your conclusions agreed with mine."

"And do they?"

"They do."

"There are certainly some questions that still need answering," he readily admitted. "Blanks to be filled in. Hopefully when we catch this Mr. See, if that's his name, we'll get an explanation. For now, he's a 'person of interest,' and that's how I'm going to phrase it in the APB."

"There's also that other witness," I reminded him. "The one Miss Iverson thought she saw standing close to the murder scene. He or she hasn't come forward. You might want to put out a request and see if you get a response. Also, I didn't get around to interviewing Rebecca Stewart in the curio shop. You might want to check her story with Iverson's."

Sheriff Jerrod was silent. I could see his wheels turning, and sense what was coming. After a long pause, he started slowly, "I couldn't talk you into being deputized and lending a hand, could I?"

I was ready for him. "Sheriff, I stated earlier that this was my honeymoon. That wasn't accurate. This is our second attempt at one. The first was interrupted because of a situation similar to this. I promised myself when I tentatively agreed to help out on this one that it wouldn't happen again. That once you had arrived, this whole enchilada would be handed over to you. With due respect, Sheriff, I'd like to help, but I've had my fill of being Johnny-on-the-spot for the present. I'd like to spend the last few days with my bride in peace, and start enjoying the beauty of the canyon."

"I guess, I can see that," Jerrod acknowledged. "However, if you happen to change your mind…"

"Not a chance," I interrupted, then handing him my business card, added, "but if you have any further questions here's where I can be reached after we leave."

"How much longer do you plan to stay?"

"We have two more days left."

"Then go off and enjoy them," he concluded.

That was music to my ears.

The following day Rita and I were up early. We had a quick breakfast and then walked to an excellent vantage point on the rim to watch the sunrise. A description of a Grand Canyon dawn is difficult to put into words. It is as if the Creator had taken every imaginable color on his palette and splashed it along the canvas of the canyon. Shadows and light, playing across the steep rock walls, created a kaleidoscope of patterns that cannot be matched anywhere. Next, we took a casual stroll along the rim trail. The clouds had lifted last night, and the sky was a vivid blue. Walking along the path wasn't a problem, for with the clearing weather, also came the warmth of the sun melting the snow and ice rapidly.

We visited Lookout and Kolb Studio, a couple of structures perched on the edge of the rim. I marveled at their constructions. We also stopped at a few of the lookouts with interesting names like Trailview Overlook, Maricopa, and Powell Point, each of which offered differing perspectives of the canyon. The sheer size, grand plateaus, and vibrant colors had to be experienced in person to be fully appreciated – and from a safe location, not dangling over the edge as I had three days earlier. As we stood at the lookout, Rita's hand in mine, I never knew such peace and contentment. We couldn't have been further from murder, killers, and victims than we were at that moment, and I was enjoying every minute of it. Even as we passed the cliff where the woman had been pushed, I stifled Rita's reference to it with a quick, but satisfying kiss. Nothing was going to ruin this moment.

In the evening we had a romantic dinner, and even a more sensual night. I was making up for lost time.

Afterward, I slept like I never slept before, and so, I imagine, did Rita. She seemed fresh and invigorated the next morning for a repeat of the previous day's activities, only this time we attempted the Bright Angel Trail. We didn't descend too far into the canyon, just to a point beyond the natural tunnel and back again. A hearty lunch followed, and then more hiking until sunset.

We ran into Jim and Liz at the lookout we selected to watch the sunset. It was an area directly across from the El Tovar, at the rim, in an open space complete with a flagpole. After the last rays of the sun disappeared behind the western canyon walls – again, a spectacle one needs to witness in person – Rita and I settled on a swing built for two and the Rollins selected two rocking chairs on the El Tovar's porch. We talked a bit before agreeing to have a farewell dinner together inside.

Tennyson hailed us from the reception desk as we were walking to the restaurant. He had a couple of envelopes for Jim and me. They contained our wages for the investigation. Jim was pleasantly surprised. He tried to wave it off, but Tennyson insisted. I wasn't as modest as Rollins. Never mind the work done on the investigation, just the necessity of rappelling down the canyon wall was worth every dollar in that envelope.

The maître d' sat us at a table at the center of the room, and after we had ordered, I rose a glass in a toast. I would've preferred champagne, but considering prohibition had only ended a few months ago, it was taking time for some establishments to stock fine wines. I raised a glass of house Burgundy instead.

"Here's to new friends, and success as a detective on stage, Jim. Hopefully, you've picked up a few pointers?"

"I did. I only wish we could've seen the case to its conclusion."

"Yes," Liz piped in. "I would've liked that too!"

"I double that," Rita exclaimed. "Or is it, 'triple that?' Anyway, I would like to have known who done it as well."

With a pained expression, I quoted Shakespeare to Rita: "'Et tu, Brute?'"

They all laughed.

"In my defense," I continued, "this case is more complicated than it seems. It may take weeks, or even months to sort out. If the sheriff and his officers, and the ranger and his crew haven't reached any conclusions by now – and I'm sure we would've heard if they did – then what makes you think we could have solved it over these last two days?"

"Because you're sharper than the rest of them," Rita offered proudly.

"Now you see why I married her," I said, including both the Rollins in my gaze.

They laughed again.

"So," Jim began, addressing me. "What time do you two leave tomorrow? We're going to miss you."

"We'll miss you too. The train departs early – six in the morning. What about you? I supposed it's back to New York."

"Actually, no. We leave Sunday for Los Angeles."

"Los Angeles! That's great. We'll have to get together. How long will you be staying there?"

"Three weeks. My agent wanted me to pay a visit to some of the studios. I wasn't keen on it, but actors do what agents want – especially if you want to stay employed. He set up an interview with RKO and Warner's – possibly, Universal. He also found a place for us to stay with a relative – at the La Leyenda Apartment Hotel in Hollywood. That way it won't cost us."

"We're practically neighbors. My office is on Hollywood Boulevard – the 'Commercial Building' – Hollywood and Gower. We'll have to meet for lunch or something. Deal?"

"Deal."

On the way back to our room we had to pass the desk. As I picked up our key, the young man on duty handed me a note from our mail slot. I didn't bother to look at it then but waited until we reached our room. It was from Sheriff Jerrod and read: 'Just as a professional courtesy – I wanted you to know the results of the autopsy. The coroner made his report today, and the cause of death is not surprising. It's consistent with a fall. Simplifying all the medical jargon: her neck was broken. As expected, there was some bruising on her arms, neck, and face that can be attributed to the fall, but interestingly enough, he also found indications of past injuries – several mended broken bones, burn scars, and such. Possibly abuse – what do you think? He also discovered something even more significant. She was pregnant. Three months. Here we might have a motive for murder. It's starting to lean fairly heavily in the boyfriend's direction. Anything else you have discovered might shed more light on this? Appreciate your thoughts.' It was signed, Sheriff Pete Jerrod.

I took a pen and jotted at the bottom: 'Nothing more to add. Good work, and good luck.'

I would drop it off at the desk on the way out tomorrow. I wasn't about to get caught up in this any further. I was burnt out.

I had walked away from solving one murder in San Diego to stumble onto another at the Grand Canyon. It had been non-stop. Granted, the last two days provided some solace – and I certainly wanted to see justice in this case, but I'm not the only detective in the world – aside from what Rita believes – and we had a little over a day traveling and one full day back home before I had to even think about work. Damn, if I'm going to muck it up worrying about someone else's case. I'd done my duty. I was finished – or so I thought. 'Logan's Intuition' was telling me something different, and 'Logan's Intuition' was rarely wrong.

9

A NEW CLIENT

"Tip the world over on its side and every-thing loose will land in Los Angeles."

—*Frank Lloyd Wright*

Hollywood, California, four days later.
I was back in my office on the sixth floor of the art deco building at Hollywood and Gower. It was hot – the type of hot that you could easily fry an egg on the sidewalk at noon. Quite a contrast to the freezing temperatures at the Grand Canyon. I'm not sure which type of weather I detested more: freezing my tail off, or cooking like bacon in a pan. I'd slid the window open behind me, but the paltry breeze offered little or no relief. It did increase the traffic noises from the boulevard, and filled the office with smells from an adjacent restaurant. Its roof vent was directly below, and whenever there was a slight breeze, the smell

of cooking – chiefly, frying hamburgers – drifted up to my window. You'd think that would be appetizing, but I've eaten at that joint, and honestly, I'm surprised it hasn't been shut down by the health department.

It had been a slow morning. Most of it I had spent behind my desk throwing a paper airplane and seeing how far it would travel along the breeze created by my portable fan sitting next to my blotter.

"I see you're keeping busy," Rita chided, leaning into my office through the outer door.

"I checked on you a few minutes ago, doll, and you didn't look any busier." She had been at her reception desk in the connecting office, lost to the world, with a book in her hands. "What were you reading so intently? You didn't even look up when I peeked in."

"It's Agatha Christie's latest Poirot novel – *Thirteen at Dinner*. I can't put it down!"

I shook my head. *"You really are insatiable, aren't you?"*

"What do you mean?"

"I mean, how many murders does it take before you're satisfied?"

"You make me sound so beastly," she scolded. "I'm not heartless. I care for the victims. It's the puzzles that interest me."

I heard loud snoring in the next room. It was our Cocker Spaniel, Buddy. He was asleep in a cardboard box we had set up for him, complete with a blanket.

"Doesn't seem Buddy shares your enthusiasm. He's the smart one – bored by it all."

"He's just saving his energy for our next case."

"Our next case?"

She ignored my jibe. "There has to be one soon."

"We've just got back," I responded. "And quite frankly, I'm enjoying the break. It has given me time to catch up on things."

She pointed at my airplane. "Like being a junior pilot? That's a real constructive use of time."

"Hey, it tests my flying skill."

I'll admit as a comeback it was pretty lame, and I wasn't surprised that it didn't impress her either. "I think I'll get back to my book, Mr. Lindberg. When Buddy wakes up, he may need a trip downstairs."

Buddy was being cared for by the Clancys while we were honeymooning at the Grand Canyon. Knowing Red and his wife, our Cocker was most likely spoiled during our absence. Nevertheless, my canine pal was extremely happy to see Rita and me on our return. He barked, wagged his tail, and jumped up and down like he'd gone mad. I bent down to pet him and he almost leaped into my arms, while planting wet slobbering kisses upon my cheek. He finished this joyous display by peeing on my cuff. I appreciate affection like the next man, but there is such a thing as too much love – and this was it. Fortunately, it occurred on Red's driveway and not in his house.

The little guy woke up ten minutes later. Attaching his leash (and collecting the obligatory small bag), Buddy and I made our way out of the building. Nick, the young elevator operator, always began our journey with a friendly pat to Buddy's head before pulling the lever which brought us to the ground floor. Nick was growing up fast – too fast. Besides the latest edition of *The Black Mask* lying on his stool, he'd added a second – the pulp, *Spicy Romances,* apparently a new reading interest. I've read a story or two from that magazine – purely for research, of course – and figure he was seeking a broader education. It might even deepen his voice.

Buddy completed his business in his usual spot – an alley alongside the building, and after picking up after him, we returned to my office. The management has been pretty good about allowing Buddy into the building. Generally, pets were not permitted, but the Manager, Williams, liked dogs, and especially, Buddy. He told me that as long as Buddy didn't bother the other tenants, we could keep him here during business hours. Since Buddy seldom barked, is house trained, and mostly slept in his box during the day, this was no problem. We had the same arrangement at the apartment, however, there, the manager required a little something extra besides the monthly rent to seal the deal.

As we approached my office, I saw the open door, and a man speaking to Rita. They turned as we neared.

"This is Mr. Grey," she said. "He's interested in acquiring our services."

I transferred Buddy to Rita and indicated to Grey that we step into my private office. Offering him a chair, I walked around the desk and took my own facing him. There was a long pause after that – each waiting for the other to begin. The lull allowed me time to size him up.

He was short, stout, and as colorless as his name suggested. Cursed with a pale, pudgy face and small, close-set gray eyes set on either side of a flat, snout-like nose, he reminded me of a pig. A bald dome and sparse fringe of dull brown hair completed the illusion. His attire, however, was something else. He wore a first-class dark gray suit and Homburg hat – expensive, nicely tailored, and immaculate.

"I'm not too sure how to begin." His voice thin and indecisive.

"You could tell me why you want to hire me."

I was only stating the obvious, but he seemed to be having trouble with it.

"That may not be so simple."

"Why's that?"

He hemmed and hawed for a few moments and then finally answered, "I'm not asking your help for myself, but for my employer."

"And who's that?"

"I can't tell you that either."

"So let me get this straight: you want me to do a job for a man, who doesn't want his name known, and doesn't even want me to know what he wants done?"

"Not exactly."

"Then, why exactly?" He chewed on that as well, until I finally said, "Look, I don't work this way. Either your employer comes clean from the start and gives me the full picture, or he finds himself another PI."

"There's good money to be made. My employer is extremely rich."

"Money's not an issue when it comes to my scruples. I only take jobs that are legit, lawful, and don't jeopardize my license. Your inability to be upfront with me suggests that one or all of the above do not apply."

"No, it's not like that," he objected. "It's just that my employer stipulated you first accept the job before I can reveal more about it."

"Isn't that like placing the cart before the horse? How do I know that I'm not signing on to something shady?"

"No, I promise this is all above board."

"Then spill the beans, Grey. Who wants my services and why?"

He pulled a handkerchief out of his breast pocket and started mopping the sweat now beading profusely on his forehead. He spent a moment doing this, and then, after seemingly making up his mind, replaced the silk cloth neatly into the same pocket, and requested the use of my telephone.

"Do you mind…?" The receiver was halfway to his ear. "Could I have some privacy?"

I was losing my patience, but held my tongue as I retreated into the outer office and softly closed the door behind me.

"What's up?" Rita asked, gazing up from her novel. She looked guilty.

"You tell me?" I replied. "You were listening, weren't you?"

"Was not."

"Were so."

"What makes you think so?" she asked, growing more defiant.

"Two reasons. One: I could see it all over your face."

"Your imagination," she scoffed. "And two?"

"You're holding your book upside down."

She didn't reply, but glanced at the open page in front of her, snorted, and slammed the book closed and onto her desk.

Never one to let sleeping dogs lie, I added, "I rest my case," and punctuated that with a smug smile.

"Mr. Logan – thank you." It was Grey. "I've concluded my call."

I returned to my office, and not a moment too soon. Smoke was starting to pour from Rita's ears.

"So?" I inquired, after taking my seat.

"My employer agreed to reveal himself, but only on the condition that you promise to keep what I tell you a secret – even if you decide not to take the case."

"Does that go for family members?" I said it loud enough so Rita could hear in the next room.

"Yes, of course." He then added: "He's especially concerned that it not become public."

"I don't have a problem with that. The Press and I aren't exactly pals anyway."

He then said something unexpected.

"That could prove unfortunate. My employer – the man who's asking for your help is, none other than Charles W. Randolph."

"Not *the* Charles W. Randolph," I responded in amazement. I heard Rita gasp in the next room.

"Yes, the newspaper publisher," he confirmed matter-of-factly.

Stating that Charles W. Randolph was a newspaper publisher was like saying the Pope was just a priest. Randolph is *the* owner and publisher of thirty newspapers in major cities across the United States with an overall circulation of 20 million. Over the last ten years, he has been busy successfully building not only this chain of newspapers, but other media sources as well, including a motion picture company, several magazines, a newsreel production outfit, and at last count, twelve radio stations. These enterprises, under the banner of 'Randolph Communications,' has netted him a fortune – easily in the multi-millions. He had also delved into politics; serving as a Mayor and Governor in Chicago, and two terms in the House of Representatives. Why this powerful, media tycoon with many influential friends would need my help was beyond understanding.

I had to ask: "What is it that Mr. Randolph wants me to do?"

"He wants to tell you that himself." Then added: "That is, if you're interested in the job?"

"Yes." I tried not to sound too anxious. "But, could you give me a hint?"

"I suppose it would be OK – as long as this is all confidential?"

"Of course. Fire away."

"As you can imagine, Mr. Randolph – in his position – can at times, ruffle a few feathers. He has had many critics in his lifetime, the majority of which he ignored, and they simply went away. However recently he's come across one he feels he cannot turn a blind eye to and believes you can help."

"Is he being threatened? "He will tell you that himself."

A non-answer, which said to me that I was correct.

"Why me?"

"I don't know."

"I'm sure there are hundreds of private investigators he could have chosen. I can't believe he just opened the phone book and randomly selected my name."

"Again, I couldn't say."

"Then I guess I'll have to ask him. When and where does he want to meet?"

"His office, the *Los Angeles Herald* building, at three o'clock."

My watch said a quarter past two. Tight, but I could make it.

"Please tell Mr. Randolph I will be there."

"Be on time," he warned, "Mr. Randolph is a stickler for punctuality. He's planning to travel to his ranch up the coast, and doesn't want to leave any later than three."

Charles W. Randolph had spared time from his busy schedule to meet with me. That said something about the case. Randolph's not the type of guy who ducks under his bed covers whenever someone yells 'boo.' If he felt this was serious enough to warrant attention, then I better be prepared for trouble. In 45 minutes I would find out.

10

CHARLES W. RANDOLPH

*"There's no such thing as a no news day. If
nothing's happening – create something."*

—*Charles W. Randolph*

I waited less than five minutes before grabbing
my hat and heading out the door. Rita wanted to
come along, but I convinced her that she should
stay and mind the office. Naturally, I had to promise
that I would fill her in on the details when I returned.
That is, whatever I could share. Randolph cherished
his privacy, and even though his fortunes were made
exposing other people's secrets, he was paranoid
regarding his own.

"While you're gone," Rita shouted waving her
notepad, "I'll telephone Dr. Klaus at the University
of Southern California's Language Department and

see if he can make sense of that note you found on Daniels' body."

"Right," I replied, not letting on that it had slipped my mind. Fortunately, I had a wife who can function as the other half of my brain. "I was going to ask you to do that."

๛

Lester, the parking attendant, retrieved my car, a 1930 Ford A Tudor Sedan, from the lot. I bought it used a year ago to replace my 1925 Packard Coupe. Its tan paint was chipped in places, and a few dents adorned the body; still, it has been reliable and a damn sight better than depending on public transportation – even though gas these days cost ten cents a gallon.

The Herald building was located on the Southern end of Broadway and Eleventh Street. I usually could make it in twenty-five minutes, but not knowing the traffic, decided to leave with time to spare. Since 1924, when they had banned horse-drawn vehicles from downtown, the number of cars registered in Los Angeles County has risen from 161,846 to 806,264. Traffic was something new, but now necessary when factoring time and distance traveled. The rise in popularity of the automobile was also why I had to circle the block several times looking for a parking space before deciding to fork out ten cents at the car park adjacent to the building.

Architect Julia Morgan designed the Herald building to the exact specifications of Charles W. Randolph. This massive, three-storied Mission Revival Spanish Colonial with a crowning tower provided a perfect monument to the man who ruled a media empire; a castle fit for its king. He had many more across the country, but none as grand as this, except the structure he calls 'his ranch' on the Central Coast. But that didn't count. This was his business, and the ranch was where he lived. According to Grey, Randolph would be traveling there after our meeting – hence my urgency to arrive on time.

The lobby was as ornate as the building's exterior, incorporating many Spanish, Italian, and Moorish touches. Carved wooden panels, hammered iron grills, white marble, lustrous gold, and hand-painted tile flooring lent their palace-like impressions to the interior design. The vast lobby bustled with activity. I found Grey waiting for me at the large reception desk which ran the length of an entire wall.

"Good," he began in a clipped, efficient manner. "You've made it on time. Mr. Randolph is waiting upstairs. I'll escort you."

He led me through an archway to the right of a large elevator, and up a marble staircase to the second floor, home of the newsroom and private offices. People scurried in and out of office doors and along the hallways carrying files or news copy in one hand and mugs of coffee in the other. Many had cigarettes dangling from the corners of their mouths, trailing smoke like runaway locomotives.

The shroud of smoke was even thicker in the newsroom. I almost choked when we entered. The room was large and spacious, spanning nearly half of the entire second floor. It was also neatly planned, with workspaces evenly arranged in four rows about its center. Every desk we passed was occupied by a reporter who was either busy on the phone, pounding a typewriter, or scribbling on a notepad. Bright lights hung from the ceiling and daylight poured in from the broad, arched windows. No one bothered to glance up as we walked among them; and by the time we'd traveled midway, the din from this caffeine/nicotine driven crowd had grown unbearable. It was almost as bothersome to my ears as the smoke was to my sinuses. It was a relief when the doors of the private elevator at the far end of the newsroom closed behind us.

"Is it always this hectic?" I asked once quiet had finally enveloped us.

"Are you kidding?" Grey replied, "this has been one of our slower news days." He said this with a straight face, so I figured he wasn't pulling my leg.

This was one of those new automatic elevators that were slowly being introduced into buildings. Grey merely had to push a call button to open the doors, and once inside, push another button on a panel to send us up to our floor. No need for operators. I expect in time, my building's elevator boy – good ole, Nick, would be looking for other employment.

With a subtle jolt, the elevator came to a halt one floor up, and the doors slid silently open. Grey gestured that I proceed, and once doing so, heard the door snap closed behind me. When I looked back, he was gone, or in aristocratic parlance, 'had quietly withdrawn.' In any case, I was now on my own.

A tall silhouette gazed out of one of many tall arched windows that surrounded the circular enclosure. The building's tower served as a luxurious office. Several of the dark, wood-paneled walls were covered by fifteen foot high shelves of books – an enormous collection of leather-bound tomes covering everything from business to history. There were large dictionaries too, some open on their portable stands. Classic Renaissance oil paintings, Italian and Greek marble statuettes and a few Remington sculptures were arranged about the office. Before me stood a long, elegant oak boardroom table, solidly built with heavy legs. A score of newspapers was open upon it – many belonging to Randolph's press, but some from his competition as well. There was also a personal desk in the room; again oak, massive, and solid. It sat at the end of the room, in front of the figure near the window. As I cleared my throat, he turned to face me.

"I'm sorry, Mister... Logan isn't it?" He had a deep, authoritative voice. "I didn't hear you come in. Please..." He waved a hand for me to join him. As I traversed the plush, Persian carpet that protected a substantial area of the highly polished, honey-colored oak wood flooring, he continued, "I get lost in my thoughts quite often." He made a vague gesture toward the window. "When you work in an ivory tower it always helps to remind yourself who your readers are. Those people down there, Mr. Logan – without their two-cents – the hard earned money they shell out every day to read my paper – I wouldn't be sitting in this office enjoying my good fortunes."

Good fortunes indeed, he was born into wealth. His father was a millionaire – a mining engineer in Nevada, who, between his rich goldmine and subsequent years in the U.S. Senate, had made a fortune many times over. And as an only son, Charles Randolph was given the best of everything. That included a top-notch education that landed him in Harvard College. There he scored high marks, not only scholastically, but in sports as well. He was a member of Delta Kappa Epsilon, the Harvard Business Club, and for fun, the Hasty Pudding Theatricals. At Harvard, he was also credited for the creation of the school newspaper, *The Harvard Gazette* – a first-class journal, and perhaps a foretaste of things to come.

After graduating with a Journalism Major and a Minor in Political Science, Randolph was handed his first job – management of *The San Francisco Bulletin*, a newspaper his father received as repayment for a gambling debt. Charles took to the news business like a duck to water, and soon he was dreaming of creating a chain of papers that would span the entire nation.

Supported financially by his family, he began by purchasing a failing East Coast newspaper, *The New York Journal*. By hiring well-known, gifted writers, he subsequently turned *The Journal* around to the point that it became real competition for Joseph Marshall, the owner and publisher of the leading newspaper at the time, *The New York Sentinel*. A circulation war followed, with *The New York Journal* coming out as the clear winner.

More newspaper acquisitions followed – Chicago, Denver, and Santa Fe, to name a few, and usually by following the same pattern: an impoverished paper purchased for a reasonable price and then capital poured in to elevate it to higher standards through hiring of the best staff, including intuitive managers, keen reporters, and excellent feature writers. Repeating this formula, Randolph saw great success, earning him awards in the process, and ultimately achieving for him the title of the nation's most celebrated newspaper publisher. But that wasn't enough. Pulps, magazines, a newsreel production company, and a movie studio were soon added to Randolph's empire (not to mention his forays into politics) making Charles W. Randolph the most powerful media mogul in the nation, and some would say, the world.

"Could I offer you a drink?" he asked, shifting gears.

"I prefer not to drink while on the job." Not entirely accurate, but a resolution I've been trying to keep. In any case, I thought it could score a plus in my favor, and I was correct.

"Good for you. I'm a teetotaler myself."

He reminded me of an austere minister or stern schoolmaster. He was a big man, about 6'3 or 6'4 in height, well-proportioned with broad shoulders and a narrow waist. His dark blue pin-striped suit was tailored and expensive. It was cut from wool and made me sweat to look at it, especially with the scorcher we were experiencing. However, there wasn't a drop of moisture anywhere on his person. Not on the firm chin of his long face, nor above his tight, thin lips, or along the prominent nose and beetle-like brow. To Randolph, sweat was a form of weakness; something he would go to great lengths not to display. His father taught him that. Randolph Senior was also a master of not showing his emotions.

"I'm Charles Randolph," he began as if an introduction was necessary. He offered his hand, and I shook it. The handshake was firm and dry.

"Please make yourself comfortable," he continued, indicating a seat in front of his desk. He stepped forward and sat down facing me in a large, brown leather chair with plush cushions and a high back. Its price tag was probably several months of my wages during a good year.

"I don't have a great deal of time, Mr. Logan. I believe Mr. Grey has already explained I need to travel to the ranch tonight. It's a long drive, and as it is, I will be arriving there late." I nodded. "So, I think it would be best if I quickly explain the matter at hand."

"Please do," I offered meekly, suddenly feeling intimidated. His deep-set, hazel eyes, searching unblinkingly into mine, caused me to direct my gaze to his broad forehead, or at the part along the center of his tidy, barbered, red hair. I forced my attention back to his face, noticing how close together his eyes were set, and the dark circles and puffiness below them. He had the look of a deeply troubled man.

"I've received a threat. Not to me, mind you. If it were, I could handle it, but to my companion. I assume you've read about Miss Rogers and our friendship?"

'Friendship' was putting it mildly, most of the rag sheets had spelled it out in no uncertain terms. She was his mistress.

Randolph had a wife, Sarah Jane, living back east. Sometime during the mid-1920s, they separated. He stayed in California, and she moved back with her family in Boston. Soon after, during the summer of 1925, Randolph met Alice Rogers. She was a leading actress in a silent comedy his studio was producing, and from their initial meeting, he fell head over heels with her. For her part, it wasn't so much love, but his wealth and power that attracted her. There was over thirty year's difference between them – a real May to September romance. In time she had grown to love him, at least that's what the rags led the public to believe. In any case, he'd been living openly with her for around seven years.

Again I just nodded, deciding discretion was called for, and he continued: "This morning I received a note delivered here to my private address…"

"Private address?" I asked, interrupting.

"Yes. I have a business post office box and a private box, each with its own address. The business box address is widely distributed, but the private is strictly maintained, so only a select few have access to it."

"How select?"

"It's hard to say. Like everything else, a secret isn't a secret for long. My private address could've been leaked. However, as a whole, only those who are, or have been close associates would have it."

"And this note – it was threatening Miss Rogers in what way?"

"Here," he said, removing an envelope from his inside jacket pocket. "Read it for yourself."

I took it with my handkerchief, although the precaution was probably futile. By this time any evidence – prints or otherwise – was likely contaminated by haphazard handling.

Removing the note from the 4 ⅛ x 9 ½ inch envelope, I began to read: YOU TREASURE THAT LoLLiPOP

OF A GIRLFRIEND. WOULD YOU STILL LOVE HER WITH HER BEAUTY SCaRrED UP?

As if reading my mind, Randolph commented, "If you're wondering, the words were cut from my newspaper. We use a special type. I recognized it immediately. Also, the words – there was a piece about Treasure Island in San Francisco, a beauty pageant in Texas, and a fellow locating his girlfriend – a long-lost love after many years. Hence the words TREASURE, GIRLFRIEND, and BEAUTY. The other words are common enough, except lollipop and scarred, which were composed of partial letters."

"You sure you need a detective?" I laughed.

He ignored my jest.

"The paper on which the letters are glued is from my company's stationery, as is the envelope. There's (obviously) no return, and my address is crudely written upon it with ink. The writing resembles a child's, no doubt to disguise the perpetrator's own handwriting."

Randolph was a shrewd guy. He wouldn't be where he was today if he weren't. Still, I had to add something to show I was up to the task.

"Which makes me wonder, Mr. Randolph – why bother about the handwriting? The knowledge of your private address, the use of the company stationary, and the letters cut from your own paper point to someone on the inside. So, how come this person was careless about everything else – except the handwriting?"

"My thoughts exactly. Either this person is foolish, or…"

"Very cagey," I finished.

"That too. Or insane. That's what got me worried. In this business you make a lot of enemies – it's inevitable. I've received threats in the past and even a few attempts at blackmail, but they were directed at me, and usually I knew what they were about, or who might've been making them. But this is something different – a threat coming from within *and directed toward of all people, Alice.* This has never happened before."

"Perhaps this person is using Alice as a means of getting to you."

"Which would work. But, why? There's no clue in the note."

"There's another possibility," I offered. "Does Miss Rogers have any enemies?"

"No. Well, at least no one who would go to these extremes. A few of Alice's acquaintances have demonstrated petty jealousies, but nothing that would amount to this."

"What about your wife?"

"Sarah Jane? No, I don't think so."

"Did you tell Miss Rogers about the threat?"

"I hesitated at first – didn't want to frighten her. But, I eventually called her at the ranch. She has a right to know so she can protect herself until I could join her. That's why my urgency to return to the ranch."

"How did she take it?"

"Better than expected."

"Can I hold onto this?" I asked, indicating the note.

"Sure, but, I'd appreciate if it goes no further than your person."

"No problem." I tucked it into my jacket pocket. "Did you call the police?"

"No. I contacted you. Alice and I agreed not to involve the police. In fact, she was more insistent on that than I was. We don't want the publicity. The gossip columnists on my competitor's papers would have a field day with this. Besides, we wanted someone who can devote full time to the investigation – and do so, discreetly. Hiring you made sense."

"Then, my next question is: why me? Why not someone closer to home. Your ranch is located two hundred miles up the coast…"

"Actually, two hundred and forty," he corrected.

"Right. I realize the town of San Sebastian is small, but what about nearby San Luis Obispo? Couldn't you find a detective there?"

"Alice particularly asked for you."

"For me?"

"Yes."

"But, how did Miss Rogers know…?"

"You'd have to ask her," he interrupted. "However, I wouldn't want to disappoint her; she seemed very adamant that I hire you."

"Nevertheless, the logistics of the investigation…"

Here he interrupted again.

"Mr. Logan, I will definitely make it worth your while. Money is not an object, and I have a guest house where you can stay – and my staff would provide all your meals."

"My wife…"

"Bring her along. There are plenty of activities to keep her occupied – tennis, swimming…"

"But we also have a dog…"

"Bring the dog along. There are many other animals on the ranch. We have zebras, lions, giraffes – a whole darn zoo."

I still wasn't convinced.

"The investigation could take some time. The guilty party may not be that easy to flush out."

"Actually, Mr. Logan, I have some ideas about that…"

I'd heard rumors that no one says no to Charles W. Randolph. I was beginning to believe them.

11

RANDOLPH'S PLAN

"By failing to prepare, you are preparing to fail."

—*Benjamin Franklin*

Keeping one's enemy close at hand, in theory, seemed reasonable, but problematic when applied to the real world. This thought was going through my head as Randolph outlined his plan.

A week from tomorrow was Halloween, and Charles Randolph and Alice Rogers had organized a costume party that they hoped would outdo last year's lavish affair. Randolph planned to use this gala as bait, to, in his own words, "attract the rat," and allow me, as the "ferret," to hunt him down."

"We've sent out announcements," Randolph explained, "and I've included at least a half dozen invitations to people with grudges big enough to send a threat like this."

"But, will they all accept?"

"No one has ever dared turn me down."

Randolph's statement wasn't pure bluster. An invitation from him was a privilege not to be ignored. To snub Randolph was unforgivable, a sure way to become *persona non-grata* in social circles.

"How many guests are you expecting?"

"Forty."

I grimaced, and he asked:

"What's the matter?"

"Forty is a large number for one man to keep an eye on. If this was a routine investigation, I could manage it, but it's the threat that concerns me. Something doesn't add up. I can't put my finger on it, but I feel something's missing. Even though Miss Rogers is the implied target, that could be a ruse – it could be you instead. In any case, I can't be at two places at once, and logistically the setup itself is a nightmare: people in costumes – party going on – lots of distractions. And I imagine your guest's movements are not restricted?"

"They're allowed to wander wherever they wish. It's a large place, and I encourage them to treat it like their own home."

"My point, precisely."

"You could use some of my household staff."

"Perhaps," I replied, but I wasn't convinced. The threat had come from the inside – all indications pointed in that direction. It could be a personal acquaintance of Randolph's or a business enemy, but it also could be someone from his household. At this juncture, I couldn't say, and I wasn't about to be care-less and show too many people my hand so soon.

"However," I continued, "I'd prefer working with someone *not* connected to you."

"No police," Randolph reminded me.

"It would be the simplest solution."

"No. I'm sorry, that's out of the question."

"Having police presence I wouldn't have to play bodyguard, which would free me up, so – using your own words – I'd be able to 'ferret out this rat' of yours."

"My guests usually arrive a day or two before the party and leave several days after. That would give you will plenty of time to observe, question, or whatever it is you do to suspects during an investigation."

"Nevertheless," I persisted. "At the party, I can't watch over you and Miss Rogers at the same time."

"Then protect Miss Rogers – I can look after myself."

"I don't work that way."

"You're acting very…"

"Wait," I interrupted, holding up a hand. A word he just said ignited a spark of an idea. "What if I found a friend to give me a hand? Would you approve of that?"

"If that friend could be trusted to keep quiet about what goes on here."

"Actually, it would be another couple, and I'm not sure they will be available. But I guarantee they can be trusted."

"Then, sure, I'm willing to hire them on."

"Good. I'll ring you once I get their answer, and we can discuss any other arrangements at that time."

He gave me his private telephone number at the ranch, which I jotted down in my notebook.

"Probably best if you call me at noon tomorrow," he explained. "I'm driving straight through, but even so, won't be arriving until early tomorrow morning."

I wished him a safe trip and left him gazing again out his office window.

Randolph's persona, however, wasn't the only lasting impression I took away from the meeting. Just before I reached for the elevator call button, Grey stepped from the shadows close by. Had he been there all along? Could he have been eavesdropping on what we'd been discussing? Instantly the thought crossed my mind, here's another person I may need to keep an eye on. He escorted me out the rest of the way.

"So what's Randolph like?"

I'd no sooner entered the office than Rita asked the question.

"First things first," I replied. "How did you make out with that note?"

"I got the lowdown from Dr. Klaus, and I was right about it being written in Gypsy..."

"Romany," I corrected.

"Romany. Roughly translated it reads…" Here she referred to her notepad. "'Revenge is sure.'"

"Interesting," I responded. "The question is; revenge for what? Was it in regards to Daniels' death, or because of it? Motive or response?"

We both fell silent for a moment.

"You've got my report," Rita began again. "Let's get back to Randolph. What's he like?"

"He doesn't have horns, a tail, or breathe fire as the rags would lead you to believe; but he does radiate an aura of power and money."

"So, did you decide to take his case?"

There was a momentary breathlessness as she awaited my answer. Not wanting her to keel over, I responded quickly, "Yeah, doll, I took the job."

"Wonderful, Tom," she exclaimed. "I was praying you would. This could help our business."

"Or hurt it."

"What do you mean?"

"I may've bitten off more than I can chew. I'm going to need help. Which reminds me, have we gotten a call from the Rollins yet?"

"No."

"I was hoping they'd already arrived in town. Do you remember where they're staying?"

"Yes, the La Leyenda Apartment Hotel in Hollywood."

"Good. Could you look up the number?"

I noticed her hesitate.

"What's wrong?" I asked.

"Tom, there's something I've meant to talk to you about."

"OK, I'm all ears. Fire away."

"First off, I'm correct in assuming that you're going to ask Jim Rollins for help?"

"Yes…yes, I am."

"Well, that's just it. I was hurt when you pushed me aside at the Canyon. I could've assisted you as well as Jim…"

I tried to interrupt, but she continued, "I know it's not male ego; you're not like that…"

Again I tried to cut in, but she was too set on her course to be detoured now. Speaking faster and more animated, she persevered: "And, I understand that you're trying to protect me. You've reminded me of that over and over whenever this topic comes up – how you felt during that Gertrude Hurd case when I was kidnapped, and you thought that killer had snapped my neck. And I also…"

This time I didn't allow her to finish but smothered her words with a kiss. During the stunned silence that followed, I finally got a word in edgewise.

"If you would've taken a breath," I gently admonished, "I would've explained that I need your help, as well as Jim's, and even Liz's on this case."

"Really?"

"Yes. I've thought long and hard about including you in my work for something other than reception – although," I quickly added, "you've been of immense help, and I will still need you to continue that as well. However, I have to admit that I've been overprotective, and that hasn't been fair to you. I do realize that you can take care of yourself, and aside from that, you're smart, intuitive, and resourceful – everything a good detective needs. And look, we've been equals in marriage, so there's no reason that couldn't apply to business as well."

For once, Rita was stuck for words. After a long pause, she leaned over and kissed me long and hard on the lips.

"Now," I continued, after first clearing my throat. "Could you check on the Rollins for me?"

"With pleasure, darling," she responded.

And at that instant, I knew that I was indeed married to a gem.

"Tom, you've must've been reading my mind," I heard the familiar voice of Jim Rollins say on the other end of the phone line. "I was just thinking about you."

"When did you get in?"

"Last night, and I've been running around all morning doing interviews. My agent must think I'm a dynamo. Three studios today – two tomorrow, and maybe another the day after that. The good thing is, after Thursday, Liz and I will be free for the remaining two weeks of our vacation to do whatever we like."

"Which is why I called."

"We're still on for lunch?"

"Sure, although that isn't why I called. I have a proposition for you."

"You want me to play detective again." He said it in jest and was surprised when I confirmed it. There followed silence on the other end, which encouraged me to explain further.

"There's cash in it, and a chance to rub shoulders with some big movers and shakers that could benefit your career."

"How's that?" he asked, taking the bait.

"I'll need you to keep this under your belt, but my client is Charles Randolph..."

"The newspaper tycoon," he breathed.

"Yes, and he's having a party at his ranch at San Sebastian – it's about 240 miles North of here on the coast. If this party is anything like the others I've read about, there will be actors, actresses, producers, directors – Hollywood types – and newspaper people too: critics, columnists, and that sort."

"I've read about those parties too, and descriptions of his ranch," Rollins replied, with an exciting edge that told me I'd piqued his interest. "But it's not so much a ranch, but a grand castle. Although, they say he doesn't like it referred to as such."

"In any case," I continued. "He's having a Halloween party a week from tomorrow and asked that I keep an eye on things during the event. He's expecting forty, not counting staff – that's a lot of people for one man to cover."

"He's hiring you for security? I didn't know you did that kind of work."

"I don't," I replied, debating about how much I should – or could, tell. I decided to go for it. "But, I do provide protection for individuals, and there's good chance that Miss Rogers – his companion, or even Randolph, might be in danger."

"Alice Rogers the film actress?"

"Actress/comedian she likes to be billed. However, she hasn't been working lately. Not as much as she did before the talkies."

"Who would want to harm little Alice Rogers? She's just a slip of a thing."

"That's what I'm hoping to find out."

"And where do I come in?"

"I'll need a pair of eyes on her while I'm watching him."

"I'm sure there'll be a lot of eyes on her as it is," Rollins commented with a smile in his voice. "She's a looker. So, let me get this straight, you want to pay me good money to keep company with Alice Rogers for the duration of the party – to stay glued to her side."

"Yes, something like that."

"Hell, most men would offer *to pay you* for an opportunity like that!"

"I don't want to steer you wrong, Jim, it could be dangerous."

"How so?"

"I can't say for certain. There was a note threatening her; it could be real, then again, maybe not. It also may be a way of getting at Randolph, but I cannot say for certain about that either."

"So it sounds to me like you're not sure about anything."

"That's exactly the case, and why I want to err on the side of caution. I just wanted you to know what you'd be getting into."

"And the pay? You said it would be considerable?"

"Randolph has opened his wallet for our services."

"It sounds tempting – *real tempting*, but to be fair, I'll need to discuss it with Liz. Is it just for a day or longer?"

"I'd figured on picking you up at your apartment next Sunday the 29th – we'll take my car – stay overnight in Santa Maria, and then drive the rest of the way to San Sebastian, arriving late morning at the ranch Monday the 30th – a day before the party. And depending on how things go, stay a couple of days after. But, regarding Liz – the invitation from Randolph also includes our wives."

"Then that's a whole different kettle of fish. I know she'll jump at the opportunity. However, that danger you mentioned…"

"We won't expose the girls to anything risky," I quickly interrupted, curtailing any reservations he might have. "At the most, I'll have Rita acting as a social butterfly at the party trying to pick up any gossip she might overhear – and be another pair of eyes to catch anything I miss."

"Liz could do the same."

"Wonderful. I was hoping you would say that."

"However, it wasn't danger to her that I was referring to. I was talking about myself."

"I don't follow."

"Me, hobnobbing all night with Alice Rogers while my wife's in the same room..."

"Then you can have Randolph," I interrupted, laughing, "and I'll take Rogers."

"No way. I'll take my chances."

❧

I telephoned Randolph as requested the following day at noon and explained that everything was set to go. When I mentioned that we planned to stay in Santa Maria, he suggested the Inn that bore the city's name and offered to cover the costs. In fact, he told me all the expenses from the moment we left Los Angeles would be covered under our agreement. I didn't argue. He had bigger pockets than me. He also offered the services of his private plane to fly us from Santa Maria to the airfield on his ranch. At first, I rejected his offer because we didn't want to inconvenience him. He insisted, saying that there would be other guests he'd be flying up to the ranch from Santa Maria as well. In the end, I accepted his offer.

"I'll have a car waiting at the Inn to pick you up at nine Monday morning and drive you to the Santa Maria airfield. You can leave your car parked at the Inn. Afterward, I'll have you flown back. Sounds good?"

"Yes, sounds fine. See you Monday."

I signed off but didn't immediately hang up. There was a click, followed by silence, and then a second click. Someone was listening.

12

FILLING OUT THE WEEK

"Nothing was truly finished until all the questions have been adequately answered; then the obscure could be put to bed."

—*Anon*

The heat wave continued throughout the week, which might be why I wasn't getting any new clients. Considering the one I had already landed, I wasn't nervous about paying next month's rent, or for that matter, the one after that. Besides, I didn't want to pick up anything new because starting this weekend I had a job that would be consuming all my energy and time.

I wanted to use the current week constructively, so one morning I concentrated on the note I'd taken from Randolph, analyzing it using my fingerprinting kit. I would have preferred running the note through the police laboratory, but Randolph's stipulations about keeping it private prevented me from doing so. I also had reservations about how useful dusting would prove. Randolph hadn't been particularly mindful about handling it back at his office. However, I decided to give it a shot. My procedure was rather primitive. The kit came with a tin of black powder – a mixture of rosin, black ferric oxide and lampblack – a small brush, and several lift cards. Carefully opening the note paper, I poured a portion of the powder along its edges and with a combination of brushing and blowing off the excess materialized a few latent prints.

As predicted, there were many large fingerprints, which didn't take an expert to attribute to Randolph, considering his stature and proportionally big hands. To be sure, I would need to collect his prints and compare them. That could be a future consideration, and why I lifted several more prints with adhesive tape and secured them on the convenient lift cards. A white, 3 x5 inch lift card has a gloss-coated front for latent lifts and a documentation form on the non-gloss reverse side. Their design was convenient for photographing and storing of prints.

What I figured were Randolph's prints dominated the note's edges. However, there were a small number of impressions within the page – near and between some of the glued letters. Principally, a partial, three smudged ones, and one complete, all of which I lifted from the note. These were noticeably narrow and tinier than the other prints – maybe a woman's, a child's, or even a small man's. I also preserved these on lift cards.

Toward the middle of the week, I got a phone call from downtown. The switchboard identified the party as Detective Sean Clancy from Homicide Bureau, Los Angeles PD. This wasn't going to be social.

"You've been a busy man lately, Thomas," he observed, his Irish brogue thicker than usual. "How come ya didn't mention dat murder case at the canyon when ya returned?"

"Embarrassed I guess," I replied. "Bad enough spoiling my first attempt at a honeymoon, but twice…"

"Ya don't have to worry about my impressions, me boy; it's dat bride of yars dat I'd be worried about."

"Rita? You know Rita, she pretty much pushed me into it."

"Then as I suspected," he laughed, "ya two are perfect fer each other."

"So, how did you find out?"

"I just got a call from Coconino County Arizona – a Sheriff Pete Jerrod asking about a suspect – a Mr. Joe See. He wanted to know da usual: If we knew of him? Did he have a prior record? All dat stuff."

"And naturally you asked why," I interjected, "and he gave you an account of the canyon murder, which included a mention of a certain gumshoe from LA who happened to step in and help with the case."

"Something like dat. He was very complimentary, Thomas – said ya were very helpful – and indicated dat I contact ya if I needed more information. I didn't mention, by da way, dat we're old friends. I wanted to keep it professional."

"Thanks," I said dryly.

"So?"

"Frankly, Red, I think Jerrod is barking up the wrong tree. This Joe See, which incidentally I believe is an alias, has plenty of marks against him, but there were other inconsistencies – mostly in his actions – that makes me suspect that he's not our killer."

"Then who do ya suspect?"

"That's the problem. I don't know. A Mister X, I guess. But there's no real evidence to support that. In fact, what little we have still seems to lean toward the boyfriend."

"Then ya have nothing new to offer me."

"There's the possible motive." "Da baby."

"Yes."

"But dat points to her boyfriend as well."

"True. But there are other possibilities."

"Like what?"

"Daniels' husband? They're separated, and jealousy could be a factor."

"Jerrod's already followed dat line of investigation and came up empty. Daniels' husband was in San Francisco during da time of da murder. He has a witness to back it up."

"Then I don't know, Red. I wish I could help, but I can't. If you try looking for Mr. See, I'm positive you'll find that he doesn't exist. I assume Jerrod gave you his description?"

"He did, as well as his location – the hotel register listed it as Los Angeles. Dat's why he contacted me at da department."

"His description isn't going to help. There's a hell of a lot of guys in this town that it could fit, and the location – it's probably a blind."

"Any more encouraging words ya can give me, Thomas?"

"Again, Red; sorry, I wish I could."

"Thank God, it's actually Jerrod's worry," Red concluded. "But I'll go through the motions and do wat I can."

An idea suddenly struck me.

"Red, you might check for any Gypsy caravans in town. There's a chance – perhaps a slim one – that See might be found hiding among them."

"Ya think he's a Gypsy?"

"Daniels' dying words mentioned Gypsies, and there are other indications that might suggest it as well. It's worth a try."

"Thank ya, Thomas. I'll check into it."

Regarding the public, the details of the Daniels' murder were slow in coming. There was only a mention of it on page three of the *Los Angeles Herald* when I'd first checked at the beginning of the week. But even that was pretty sketchy, with the identity of the victim incorrectly listed as Miss Lydia Roberts of San Diego. Faulty reporting, I believed, wasn't the issue here, but a careful censoring of the facts by either law enforcement or the powers-that-be at Norma Daniels' studio – or perhaps both. In any case by Friday, when Rita and I met the Rollins, the full story had already dominated headlines for two days.

I'd chosen the Musso and Frank Grill for our reunion. It has been around since 1919, serving excellent food and providing outstanding service for the past fourteen years. In the beginning entrepreneur Frank Toulet teamed up with Oregon restaurateur Joseph Musso and French chef Jean Rue to create the Grill, which boasted a menu that drew Hollywood celebrities and literary types alike. It was a colorful place, and why I chose it to treat the Rollins for lunch.

After being seated, the four of us reminisced about our adventures at the canyon and discussed the events of the past week. I asked about Jim's interviews at the studios, which he downplayed, and he, in turn, wanted to hear about my week, which eventually led to the Randolph investigation, a topic on everyone's mind.

"So," James Rollins began after we'd placed our orders – hot pastrami on rye, all around, with coffee – "could you tell us something more about this case you're getting us involved in?"

"For instance?"

"What roles do we play? I assume we don't walk around introducing ourselves as detectives."

"True. I figured we'd represent ourselves as partners in a business – an advertising firm that's interested in getting a contract with Randolph's news agency."

"Do we use our own names?"

"Yes. It's one less thing we have to worry about screwing up. For good measure, I'm having some phony business cards printed with our names on it. They should be ready by tomorrow."

"And what about us?" Rita and Liz inquired almost in one voice.

"You have a more difficult role."

"What's that?" Liz beat Rita to the question, her eyes shining.

"You'll be playing our wives."

"That's no fun," Rita piped in. "Couldn't we be mistresses or something? Wouldn't that be more appropriate for a setup like this?"

I looked at Jim, and he shrugged his shoulders.

"OK, by us," I agreed with a smile.

"Wonderful," Rita squealed. "Liz, we need to go shopping tomorrow and get something sexy."

Looking at Rollins, I stated flatly: "Jim, I hope we haven't started something."

"Actually," he returned with a smile, "I'm kind of hoping we did!"

Once the snickering faded, I continued to address Liz, "As I mentioned over the telephone to your husband, I'll need you and Rita to circulate among the party crowd and somehow gauge the attitudes of the other guests toward either Charles Randolph or Alice Rogers."

"You mean, 'dig up the dirt?'" Liz offered.

"Precisely – but, don't be too obvious. Take particular notice of anyone who might have a gripe or an ax to grind with Randolph or Rogers."

"I can do that," Liz answered, and then noticing Rita's enthusiastic nod, added: "We both can."

"Good," I acknowledged. "And if, and when, you do learn something you are to immediately pass it onto us."

"And what will you two be doing?"

"Keeping tabs on Randolph and Rogers."

The sandwiches arrived, and for a few minutes, we ate in silence.

"What time should we be ready Sunday?" Jim asked, again taking up the conversation.

"I was thinking 7 AM in front of your apartment – pack light, there's not a lot of room for luggage in the car."

"That may be a problem." I noticed him looking at Liz. It reminded me that this could be an issue with Rita as well. Not that I'm criticizing, but I could get by with only the suit on my back and a paper bag filled with a couple of changes of shorts and socks. However, this affair was something different – just about as high-class as you could get.

Which also reminded me: "Do you have a tux, Jim?"

"No."

"You'll need to rent one. Don't worry, it'll be covered on the expenses. I'll have to get one myself."

"But regarding the luggage…" he began.

"Don't sweat it. I'll work it out. Probably strap whatever won't fit on the back of the car or onto the roof."

"I can help with the driving," he offered.

"Not a problem. I'm comfortable with long hauls, and there's a change. We won't be driving the second half of the trip. Randolph will have a plane waiting for us in Santa Maria to fly us up to the ranch."

"Oh," Liz exclaimed. "This just keeps getting better and better. How exciting."

I seemed to recall that she found murder exciting too, not a comforting thought. There was something about this case that troubled me. I couldn't put my finger on it, but it was there. Like a calm surface that hides the dangerous undercurrents of the sea. Nothing seemed to add up. And not only this case, but the Daniels' murder was bugging me as well. I hated leaving things half done. Those inconsistencies in her case were still dogging me, and I was having trouble letting go. Red's call had reminded me of that and the adage that I've learned to live by: 'nothing was truly finished until all the questions have been adequately answered; then the obscure could be put to bed.'

13

STORMING THE CASTLE

"The use of traveling is to regulate imagination by reality, and instead of thinking how things may be, to see them as they are."

—*Samuel Johnson*

When we finally arrived, the sight of the Santa Maria Inn was like a fertile oasis after crawling through an endless desert. The drive had been slower and more difficult due to unexpected beach traffic. The unusually hot weather had people inland scrambling for the cooler temperatures along the coast, causing backups and delays that I wasn't counting on.

We'd met the Rollins in front of their apartment precisely at 7 AM, and after some challenging re-arranging of luggage – some strapped to the roof of the car, others to the back, we piled into the overloaded vehicle. I drove, Rita sat up front with Buddy between us and Jim and Liz took the back seat. It was a cozy setup – for the first fifty miles. Besides the traffic, there were the inevitable stops – sometimes for Buddy and other times for us, and gas station hopping and breaks to eat. Rita also experienced motion sickness. We figured the winding roads had led to that.

I first headed west out of Hollywood along Sunset, then reaching Highway 1, continued north until we reached Santa Maria. Highway 1 took us through many cities and townships lining the coast; Santa Monica, Malibu, Oxnard, Ventura, Santa Barbara, Lompoc and finally our destination. Some sections of the road were paved, and others were not, which made for rough going as well.

Santa Maria is a small town with a population of just over 7,000. Oil put it on the map, with thousands of wells, dug and pumping in the nearby Solomon Hills and Cat Canyon. Union Oil owns a number of these wells, the rest belonging to smaller, private companies. Each one creating much-needed employment for local job-starved men and women still suffering the effects of the recent depression.

The Santa Maria Inn was the jewel of this township. Proprietor Frank J. McCoy opened it in May of 1917 with only 24 rooms, a kitchen, and a dining room. By 1930, however, it had grown to 64 bedrooms and a coffee shop had been added. This two-story, quaint, English-style hotel had surrounding gardens of colorful flowers, clinging rose vines, thick shrubs, and patches of well-tended, vibrant, green grass. Even though steps from downtown, there was something very isolated and serene about a stay here. No wonder it had become a favorite stop for weary travelers and celebrities alike.

President Herbert Hoover and William Jennings Bryan had been guests, as were actors, Charlie Chaplin, Douglas Fairbanks, Mary Pickford, and Rudolph Valentino. While filming his 1923 epic, *The Ten Commandments*, Cecil B. De Mille and his crew enjoyed the comforts of the Inn after hours spent at the magnificent sand dunes located near the town of Guadalupe.

Not surprisingly, Charles Randolph also had guests stay here on their way to his ranch. The accommodations were excellent, the restaurant's food, first class, and the service, like nowhere else.

Jim and I signed the register and collected our keys at the front desk. A bellboy took our luggage. We were given rooms next to each other on the ground floor of the north wing.

Before separating, we made plans to meet at five for dinner in the Inn's fine dining room. I was exhausted, and at the moment, nothing mattered, but the promise of some much-needed rest. I spotted a big overstuffed chair next to our bed as Rita and I entered. I dashed for it, supposing it the perfect place to stretch out and catch a few winks before the events of the evening. Buddy must have had the same idea because it became a matter of who would get there first. He beat me, but being the master, I had the last say. Scooping him up, I laid him softly on the floor and then threw myself into the chair. Not five minutes passed before I found myself drifting into a deep, untroubled sleep.

"I thought you might find this interesting," Rollins said, handing me a newspaper he'd been carrying under his arm. Rita and I had just approached him and Liz, standing in line to be seated for dinner. There were a few couples ahead of us, which gave me time to unfold the newspaper and read what he'd indicated.

Daniels' Boyfriend Sought in Her Murder! screamed the headline.

"He's going out on a limb," I commented dryly.

"Who?" Rollins asked.

"Sheriff Jerrod. I thought he was smarter than that. I didn't think he would go so far as to accuse See of murder. Questioning him is one thing – makes plenty of sense, but to accuse him of murder..."

"Who else could he blame?" Rollins interrupted. "See was the only man left standing."

"Still," I began, as the maître d' caught my attention. It was our turn to be seated.

The spacious dining room featured a large number of windows which looked out into the Inn's garden. Flowers were everywhere, not only outside, but in vases set artistically around the room.

As we followed the maître d', I noticed small table lamps being lit by busboys to offset the approaching dusk, the illumination from their flickering candles casting a warm glow upon the starched linen tablecloths, bone china plates, crystal glasses, and polished silver utensils.

After being seated at a window table, I took a moment to observe the other diners before turning to the leather-bound menu presented by our waiter. The patrons were a classy lot – wearing suits, sports coats, and neckties. Rita had woken me up in time to splash water on my face, and put on a fresh shirt, jacket, and tie. Good thing, because with this crowd, I would've felt out of place.

Rita and I ordered the restaurant's specialty, prime rib, mashed potatoes, and baby carrots. The Rollins chose roasted duck with orange sauce, whole grain rice, and broccoli. Salad and dessert came with the meal, and we picked a bottle of California Rosé to complement our entree selections.

I picked up on our earlier conversation as we waited for the salads.

"Aside from making the charges against Mr. See official, there's not much new about the case in today's paper."

"I noticed that too," Rollins admitted. "However, I found amusing the amount of "I's" Sheriff Jerrod used in regards to the investigation. You gave him everything he claims to have discovered. Yet he doesn't once give you credit, or even mention your name to the press."

"It happens all the time. I'm used to it. The only reason cops might throw out your name is when an investigation sours – then it's your fault, or if they're suspecting you of the crime itself – then they're only too eager to let the press know about it."

"You're kidding."

"I wish I was. However, don't get me wrong, there are a lot of good cops – many of whom I've worked with. They'll give you a fair break. But professional jealousy is still an obstacle of the trade."

"Then I better stick with stage acting," Rollins concluded ruefully. "No matter how small the role, we're still guaranteed billing."

Our salads arrived, and as we were picking at them, Liz changed the subject.

"I took a walk around the Inn earlier and overheard some excitement from the staff. It seems some celebrities arrived."

"Who?" Rita asked, sitting upright in her chair.

"I only caught a couple of names – Karloff and Lugosi."

"What are they doing here, I wonder?" Rita mused.

"Probably guests like us of Charles Randolph," I offered.

"We might be spending Halloween at the castle with them," Rita exclaimed. "What fun!"

"Sort of scary to me," Liz replied. "Spending the night with both the Frankenstein Monster and Dracula at an isolated castle – gives me the chills."

"Come on, Liz," Rollins admonished. "They're actors like us."

"I know, Jim," she said with a nervous giggle. "But, especially that Lugosi with his frightening appearance, those piercing eyes, and unusual accent – it turns my blood to ice water."

"Then eat plenty of garlic," Rollins offered, but quickly relented. "On second thought, do not. I don't want you ruining our evenings. Just wear your crucifix."

"You're being silly."

"Exactly my point."

With our entrée came another surprise that had the diners murmuring excitedly amongst themselves. A third motion picture actor and his female escort were being ushered to a table. It was Claude Rains and his wife. I recognized her from a picture I saw in a magazine.

"Looks like the Invisible Man has joined the party as well," I commented out of the corner of my mouth. "Randolph doesn't spare the horses when it comes to his soirees."

"Is Rains playing the lead in the film?" asked Rollins.

"Yep," I replied. "Trade papers say the picture will be in theaters next month."

"He doesn't look invisible to me," observed Rita.

"Nor do those rocks his wife's wearing!" Liz added.

"Well, let's hope those rocks don't disappear during the party," I said sarcastically. "I have enough on my plate as it is, without robbery."

We finished our meal with sherbet and coffee and then agreed upon a short stroll before bed. We ambled around the Inn's gardens, but finally directed our steps toward downtown. Most of the stores were closed, but that didn't prevent us from window shopping, and eventually stumbling upon the brightly lit foyer of the Santa Maria Theater. The feature presentation on the marquee was, *I'm No Angel*, starring Mae West and Cary Grant. More interestingly, the second movie on the bill was an earlier silent comedy, starring Alice Rogers entitled, *The Dutch Mill*. I minutely examined the illustrator's image of her on the film's poster, noting the round, girlish face, short-cut, blonde curly hair, and large, wistful blue eyes. The painted, pouting lips below her pert, upturned nose projected innocence with a hint of allure. The artist was good, but I expected the real thing would be better.

I heard the girls talking behind me.

"This was her last picture before retiring from films and moving in with Randolph," said Liz.

"What was it about?" asked Rita.

"She was a Dutch miller's daughter who wrote love letters to herself to make her boyfriend jealous. A bunch of silly mishaps and misunderstandings occur because of it. Pretty funny."

I was awake at five the following morning, which gave me plenty of time to shave, shower, and get dressed. As arranged, we joined the Rollins at the coffee shop at six-thirty for a quick breakfast and then we both returned to our rooms to pack. By half-past eight we had checked out and were waiting in front of the Inn for the car to take us to the airfield.

Precisely at nine, a black, 1932 Packard 901 Sedan pulled up, and the driver helped us load our luggage onto the car's rack. A ten-minute drive took us north to Hancock Field and the waiting Ford Tri-motor 5-AT airplane.

The "Tin Goose," as it was affectionately named, was constructed of corrugated aluminum. The 5-AT had three powerful Pratt & Whitney Wasp radial engines that would make for a noisy, but safe and reliable flight. It was owned by the Randolph Company, as evidenced by its logo painted on the gray fuselage to the left of the passenger door.

The interior was cramped, but not uncomfortable, with wood paneling on the cabin walls, tied beige curtains at each window, and equally spaced lamps mounted along the ceiling. We took the two padded seats offered toward the front – one on either side of the aisle – with the Rollins' directly behind. Buddy sat on my lap.

When it comes to traveling, Buddy was a pleasure. He wasn't demanding and usually slept. Rarely did he bark, and that was only when food was close by. He was so quiet in fact that there were times I forgot that he was with us.

Two other couples were seated at the rear of the plane; the Karloff's, and the Rains.' Lugosi was on his own. I tried to act nonchalant at their presence. Just a short acknowledgment with a casual nod of the head. Rita, on the other hand, wasn't quite so poker-faced. After a gasp, she took her seat, reached across the aisle and slapped me on the wrist.

"Do you see who's sitting back there?"

"Yes, and don't make a fuss, it's embarrassing."

An attendant leaned toward us.

"Is there anything I can get you two?"

"How about an autograph from the back of the plane?"

"She's joking," I interceded quickly. "We're just fine."

After taking on some bundles of newspapers, I assume for Randolph, who liked to check out his papers, as well as the competition, we took off.

The weather on the thirty-minute flight was perfect, the ride smooth and devoid of jolting air pockets. The pilot flew as the crow flies, north along the coast with the golden brown mountains out my window on the right side, and the blue Pacific on Rita's left.

The plane made a full circle over the castle as we approached the ranch's airfield – a single graveled strip with a maintenance hangar. From the air, I could see the castle, with its guesthouses, grounds, and a large pool. A road snaking up the hill toward it buzzed with traffic; trucks mainly, with some cars. It looked like they were storming the castle.

For whatever reason, we made two passes, then landed with a couple of bounces onto the runway. We had arrived.

14

AN UNEXPECTED TURN OF EVENTS

"Nobody knocks here, and the unexpected sounds ominous."

—*D.H. Lawrence*

The limo waiting at the airfield was identical to the one that had picked us up at the Santa Maria Inn. Randolph must have a fleet of them because there were three more lined up behind. It looked as if each party would have their own car, and since the four of us were first off the plane, we were given the first car in line.

Again, our luggage was hoisted aboard, and in no time we were being driven off the field and onto a gravel road. There was a caterpillar gate which blocked the way. Here the chauffeur got out, raised it, drove through, and then closed it behind him. A sign next to it warned: 'Beware of Animals.'

"Randolph keep guard dogs?" I asked the driver as we resumed our journey up the hill.

"No guard dogs, just a couple of Dachshunds," he replied over his shoulder. "Why do you ask?"

"I was just curious about the sign back there."

"He has a whole menagerie of animals – Rocky Mountain elk, wild goats, llamas, white fallow deer, Barbary sheep, and sambar deer. Not to mention the zebras, polar bears, lions and what have you at his zoo."

"Any get loose?"

"The lion did once and killed a couple of deer. But he was caught before he could do more damage."

We passed buildings on either side of us, and I asked about them.

"Chicken ranch on the right," he answered, "and the cattle ranch proper to the left."

"He's got some setup."

"This is only a portion. Mr. Randolph has some 83,000 acres which include the castle and the ranch. But, don't let him hear you call it a castle. To him, the entire property is 'His Ranch.'"

"Yes. I've heard that."

The journey up to the castle took about twenty minutes. The road was steep and winding with several hairpin curves. Monterey pine, coastal oak, and sage scrub could be seen along the hillsides bordering the way, while opposite, a vista of chaparral and grassland spread out toward the ocean. Colorful seasonal wildflowers were in abundance everywhere.

"Here we are," the chauffeur announced after rolling to a stop and engaging the brake.

He dropped us off at a level parking lot below one of two cement staircases that led up to the north terrace of the property. As we exited the limo, I noticed three trailers, a truck, and one horse-drawn Shepherd's Hut parked at the far side of the lot.

The chauffeur must have perceived my curiosity because he explained, "Gypsies. Mr. Randolph hired them as entertainment for the party."

As our driver was talking, a couple of young, black-haired, darkly tanned men appeared and began unloading a large box from the back of the truck.

I felt a hand grip my arm. It was Rita.

"Tom, *those are Gypsies!*"

"I know, doll. Don't make a fuss." I turned again to the chauffeur. "Entertainment? What kind?"

"Palm reading, Tarot cards, séances – and music. I figure it's atmosphere for the party. Mr. Randolph usually has a theme for his parties, and this year is 'Monsters from Film.'"

That explained Karloff's and Lugosi's invitations. Karloff's *Frankenstein* and Lugosi's *Dracula* were big hits two years ago, in '31, and both actors have been associated with these characters ever since. Rain's *Invisible*

Man was new – Universal Pictures plans to release it in November, and based on its hype, its legacy was also a foregone conclusion.

"Excuse me." I felt a tap on the shoulder and turned to see a gentleman brandishing a clipboard. "You are the Logan and Rollins parties?"

"Yes," I replied.

"Great." Using a pencil, he ticked off our names from the list and then waved over four young men who started collecting our luggage. "Would you please follow me."

I had to hand it to Randolph, from what I'd seen so far, he had a very competent, well-oiled operation. Everyone knew their job, was in their place and executed their responsibilities with maximum efficiency.

Our guide led us up the steep staircase to the North Terrace. The rest lagged behind, but Buddy pulled me along on his leash, taking each step by leaps and bounds, which got us there ahead of the rest. To my horror, Buddy decided to leave his calling card on the terrace next to a marble statue whose scantily clothed woman had an expression that hinted this might have happened before. Quickly I removed a bag from my pocket and snatched up the evidence. Hopefully, with no one the wiser.

"Tom," I heard a voice from behind and jumped. Turning, I realized it was Rita.

"Yes."

"What's the matter?"

"Nothing. Why?"

"You look guilty."

"No. You were going to say?"

"About those Gypsies…" she began.

"Let's discuss it later," I replied shortly. Noticing that our entourage had gotten ahead of us, I threw a thumb in their direction. "We better catch up."

Nevertheless, I did shoot a glance back down toward the driveway and the Gypsies unloading their truck. One of them, a tall, swarthy looking young man had stopped working and started gazing keenly in our direction.

"Excuse me," our guide shouted. I turned. "Could you please follow us? I apologize for the rush, but we're on a tight schedule – we're expecting the other guests from the plane shortly. They're staggering the arrivals, so we're given only limited time to show each party to their rooms."

"Sure. Sorry," I responded, the image of the Gypsy still lingering on my mind. We immediately rejoined our group.

The guide led us past the outdoor pool – immense in size, lined with white marble tiles accented by green trim. Marble columns and capitals from the first through the fourth century Roman Empire stood at the far end. I'd read that Randolph had purchased these from an antiquities dealer in Rome. The water filling the pool was turquoise blue and inviting, especially under the blazing sun.

We were taken up another flight of stairs that led past one of three guesthouses. Small compared to the castle itself, but grand by any other standards. A garden of roses surrounded the elaborate courtyard entrance to this building, which was decorated with Persian tile and accented by ornamental grills. On a tan concrete wall above the door and just below the orange tiled roof, '*Casa del Norte*,' the 'House of the North' was painted in a bright blue script.

The other two guesthouses – the one facing south and the other west – were respectively called '*Casa del Sur*' and '*Casa del Oeste*.' These residences were reserved for celebrity guests like the Karloffs, the Rains, and Lugosi. We were led instead to the castle itself, which resembled a grand Spanish cathedral.

'*Casa Encantada*' was a four-storied, concrete building designed in the Mediterranean Revival style with two bell towers on either end. The façade was extremely ornate with an entrance flanked by bas-reliefs of knights, and a carving of the Virgin Mary holding the infant Jesus in a niche above the massive main doors.

Numerous bronze carillon bells could be seen through double-arched windows where they hung in the tower's belfry, and its spires were crowned with decorative mosaic tiles of blue and gold. The entire surface of the structure's concrete was painted a stark white except for the cornice below the central peaked roof which was overlaid with carved Siamese teakwood. *'Casa Encantada'* was dazzling to the eyes and impressive on many levels.

The interior was just as opulent, although since our guide was rushing us along, I hadn't time to take it in. Our entourage was hurried through the Assembly Room with its large French mantled fireplace and Flemish tapestries, into the Refectory – a romanticized version of a medieval castle's dining room, past the Gothic Morning Room, informal Billiard Room, and a short hall before reaching the staircase which led us up to the guest rooms on the third floor. Here we and the Rollins were given adjacent accommodations. The décor was not as elaborate as the rest of the castle, but comfortable and practical. Each room had its own bath, twin beds with soft mattresses, and plenty of solid oak furniture – chairs, tables, a desk, and padded sofa – everything you'd need for a restful and satisfying stay.

As the young men placed our luggage next to a chest of drawers, our guide informed Rita and me that cocktails would be served at seven and dress would be formal.

"If that's a problem," he continued, "Mr. Randolph has tuxedos from which you can choose."

"No," I answered, reaching into my pocket and extending some bills. "I've brought my own, thank you."

He held up a hand.

"Tipping is not allowed. It's Mr. Randolph's rule, but thank you just the same."

After a short bow in our general direction, he headed toward the door, and with an exaggerated flourish, shut it firmly behind him.

"What a fantastic view, Tom," Rita announced from the other side of the room. She was standing near a window facing north revealing a vista of rolling hills.

A door to her right led outside to a covered balcony/walkway that ran the length of several guest rooms. I stepped out onto it, took in a breath of clean, fresh air and let it slowly out with a long sigh.

"Now, this is what I call living."

"Well, don't get too used to it," Rita admonished, joining me. "Once this job is over, it's back to our modest little apartment."

Her mention of the job sent my thoughts careening back to the moment and again searching out the Gypsies near their caravan parked below.

"It couldn't be coincidence – these Gypsies showing up here." Rita commented as if reading my thoughts.

"It could be," I responded. "But I wouldn't put my money on it."

"So you think there's a connection?"

"I wouldn't venture to say – time will tell."

"Do be careful, Tom – remember Daniels' last words were a warning about Gypsies."

"That's not totally true, sweetheart. She just said, 'The Gypsies' and died. She gave no indication *how or if* they were involved in her murder."

"Still, watch yourself.

"I plan to, and you do the same. No playing detective beyond the task I asked of you. Wander about the party guests..."

"And act as an extra set of eyes and ears," she finished, dryly. "I've got it."

"And if you do stumble on anything, don't follow it up yourself. Pass it along to Jim or me."

"OK, but..."

"No buts. It's not that you can't take care of yourself, but this new development – these Gypsies – is worrying me. I'm beginning to suspect that there's more to this case than I was led to believe. Until I can figure out what, we need to stick to our plan."

I felt a nose sniffing at my heels. Buddy had followed us out. I didn't want him wandering loose on the balcony, so taking him by the collar, I led him inside. Rita followed.

"Tom, I think I'll take a nice warm bath, it'll help me to relax. Care to come in and scrub my back?"

"In a minute," I returned with a smile. "Although I think the experience might do the opposite for me." She giggled. "Let me get Buddy settled first."

As she disappeared into the washroom, I pulled Buddy's blanket from our bag and set it on the floor in the corner of the room. He made a dash for it and after turning this way and that, sank into its folds, his head resting between his paws.

"Take a nap, little guy," I said leaning forward toward one of his floppy ears. "I think we're in for a busy stay."

Rising, I caught sight of something I hadn't noticed earlier. On the desk nearby was a small envelope leaning up against the base of a table lamp. As I drew near, I could see that it was addressed to me.

"Must be a welcome note," I thought as I ran a convenient letter opener along its sealed flap.

"Tom, I'm almost ready," Rita called. I could hear her turning on the tap.

"Just give me a sec," I returned.

The note inside was written as meticulously as the script on the envelope. Its content, however, was not what I expected. It said, *"Expect danger. Will tell you more, tonight, after dinner,"* and it was unsigned.

"Is everything all right, Tom?" Rita shouted above the noise of the running water.

"Yes, sweetheart," I lied, and then folding the note, returned it to its envelope, and placed it snugly into my pant pocket.

15

RANDOLPH'S SUSPECTS LIST

"It is not for me to suspect but to detect."

—*Anna Katharine Green*

"Sorry, boy," I said to Buddy, as I poured a handful of dog food into his travel bowl. "They didn't invite you tonight. You'd probably find it boring anyhow. Cocktail parties usually are – even for some humans."

"You say something, Tom?" Rita called from the bedroom.

"I was talking to Buddy."

"What did you tell him?"

"Nothing. Just that cocktail parties are usually boring."

"I'll bet this one isn't."

I left Buddy munching away in the washroom and joined Rita.

"I'll take that bet," I answered in a feigned whisper. "But I didn't want to disappoint him."

"You're being silly. I don't believe he cares one way or another. But, you know what…"

"What?"

"I think you're just projecting your feelings on to him."

"So, you're a psychoanalyst now."

"Well?"

"True, I'm not crazy about wearing this monkey suit," I admitted, indicating the tux.

"It looks very handsome on you. I can't remember the last time I've seen you so dressed up."

"It's been a while," I conceded. "I believe it was on our first date at the Coconut Grove after that Hyland case."

Whoops. Bad call. Mattie Hyland was still a sore spot, even though three years had passed. I decided to change the subject.

"Speaking of appearances – you look beautiful in your new dress!"

And she did. The gown shimmered in black silk charmeuse from the scooped cowl neckline down to the flowing hem with overlapping bands on the waist and hips, which accented her figure.

"Thank you," she responded coolly. "But don't change the subject."

I thought I'd directed her away from the subject of Mattie, who she perceived as her perpetual rival for my affections – but apparently, I didn't – or so I believed, until she added, *"You don't enjoy cocktail parties, do you? Admit it."*

Breathing a sigh of relief, I responded: "Dressing up, talking to a bunch of rich snobs, and trying to seem interested – no."

"Then, Tom, I rest my case."

"However," I continued, "this party is different. It presents an interesting challenge."

"So you're convinced someone's planning to harm Miss Rogers?"

"Someone's planning something. The question is who, what, and when." I indicated the door. "Are you ready?"

"Sure," she replied after a last minute check of herself in a full-length mirror. Then starting for the door, added, with a cat-like grin, "We can discuss your old girlfriend, Mattie Hyland, later, after dinner."

The party was held in the Assembly Room. It wasn't hard to find. We just made our way towards the din of laughter and conversations that could be heard throughout the castle. This particular area served as Randolph's living room, a place where guests could gather and socialize before dinner. It was the first room after the main entrance foyer. Guests gaining access from inside the castle entered through a door off the dining hall. It was disguised to look like a wall panel when viewed from the Assembly Room side.

Randolph had quite a few hidden doors in the castle – some obvious, some not. Many came off secret passages that only Randolph and perhaps a select few knew. It was a well-known chink in this king's armor that he was overly sensitive about other people's opinions of him. So at times, it wasn't above him to hide behind one of these panels and listen unobserved to guests' comments.

I took a quick look along the length of the room the instant we entered. The Rollins were already about the various duties I had assigned them – Liz mingling with a circle of guests at one end, and Jim sticking close to Alice Rogers at the other.

Miss Rogers was every bit as beautiful in person as I had imagined. She was undeniably the 'Queen of the Manor,' dressed in an elegant floor-length evening gown of star-studded midnight crepe, highlighted by a draped arm treatment. Counter to this vision of sophistication was her perky personality, as evidenced by the antics Rogers displayed to those gathered around her. She appeared comical, carefree, and a bit ditzy. As I watched more closely however, I caught something else; a haunted expression that would cloud her eyes when conversation wandered away from her and not clear until a casual remark had again been tossed in her direction. There was something troubling going on here.

"Mr. and Mrs. Logan." Randolph, suddenly appeared at my elbow. "How good of you to join us."

"Thank you, Mr. Randolph," Rita replied with a blush. "It's such an honor to meet you."

"The honor's all mine, Mrs. Logan, and please don't be so formal, everyone around here calls me 'CW.' That is, except my employees. They usually call me 'Chief' or some other term not fit for a lady's ears."

We politely laughed, and he continued: "Now, if you don't mind, I have something to say to your husband in private."

"Yes, of course," Rita replied, excusing herself with an awkward curtsy.

A curtsy for crying out loud. Randolph was no more royalty than I, but this grandiosity was affecting her. He was a publisher of newspapers, not a ruler of a country. Although arguably, he has influenced decisions in some countries.

"Let's step away to a place we cannot be overheard," Randolph continued.

He led me toward the room's centrally placed marble fireplace with a 16th-century French mantel of intricately carved figures, and after taking a quick look over his shoulder, touched something that opened a door in a nearby wall panel. Quickly he guided me through and closed it behind him. The chamber was pitch-black as we entered, but with a click, was bathed in harsh light from a bare bulb hanging by a cord from the center of the ceiling.

"It's a priest hole – or my version of it," Randolph quickly explained. "Just a whim of mine when we were drawing up the plans. I don't use it much."

The area was small, cramped, and devoid of furniture. The only residents – spiders, as revealed by the many webs hanging about.

"So, what is it that…" I'd begun to say. However, before I could finish, he'd fished out a folded sheet of paper from his pocket and pressed it into my hand.

"I've typed a list," he explained. "Six people whom I believe have grudges major enough, to attack me by threatening Alice."

I unfolded it as he explained, "There are names on this list and a sentence or two about each explaining their gripes against me. Briefly: Al Bellini, recently placed on leave from my San Francisco office, suspected of fixing the books; Cookie Clark, gossip columnist, formerly of my paper, wrote something about Alice for which I'm suing for libel; Charlie Coons, a small-time movie comedian I released from my studio for pestering Alice…"

"Pestered in what way?" I interjected.

He paused for a second, and then answered sharply, "For being flirtatious."

I waited for more, but he didn't elaborate. "Damien Price, actor, screenwriter, producer – you name it. He's putting together a film about my life, and I'm trying to stop it."

"Getting back to this gossip lady," I said. "What did she write about Miss Rogers?"

"A whole lot of garbage – calling her a no-talent and how she was using me for my power and money."

I had a hunch there was more, so I pushed further, "Is that all?"

Again he seemed reluctant to answer, but eventually added in a terse way, "Some nonsense about Alice and Coons, but there's nothing to it."

OK, time to move on, I thought.

"Who else is on the list?"

"Carol Keen and Anthony Wells. Keen is an actress who's being re-cast in a film that's shooting at my studio. Alice has shown interest in the part. She's a bit bored at the moment, and believes this could be a new start, so the studio has agreed to give her the role."

"And Keen's not happy about it?"

"She thinks she's being forced out to make way for Alice. It's not the truth – she just wasn't right for the part – but, unfortunately, it isn't the way she's taking it. She's making a big to-do, and hiring a lawyer over it."

"What about Wells?"

"Wells is a piece of work. He *was my lawyer*, but I recently learned he wasn't taking my interests as seriously as his own. He'd been charging me for work he'd never done, or over-billing me for what he had, and selling my private information to anyone willing to pay."

"Like who for instance?"

"Business competitors, gossip columnists…"

"This Clark woman perhaps?"

"Perhaps."

"But, you're not sure?"

"No. But it's possible."

"And these six," I said. "They're at the party?"

"Four are – Clark, Price, Coons, and Wells. Keen and Bellini indicated that they would be joining us tomorrow for the Halloween celebration."

"Good." I slipped the list into my tuxedo's pocket. "I'll pass this information along to the others. They're out mingling with the guests now. I'll tell them to concentrate on those you've listed particularly."

"And what about you?" he asked warily. "You're still not planning to act as my bodyguard?"

"That was my idea."

"It's a bad one," he returned. "I can take care of myself. It's Alice that I'm worried about…"

"Jim's watching her. I have every confidence…"

"I'm sure he's capable," he interrupted.

"And the ladies will be observing and reporting on those you've singled out."

"Hey, I'm not questioning their abilities. It's just that I'd prefer you direct all your resources to protecting Alice. That means you, Mr. Logan, personally getting out there and finding whoever it is that could do her harm. You can't do that handcuffed to me all evening."

"But this threat to her could be a blind. Back at your office, I warned you could be the actual target."

"No matter," he argued. "I'm paying you to protect Alice, and that's what I'm expecting you to do – nothing more – nothing less."

His resolve indicated that further pursuit would be useless. I shrugged, "It's your money. I can't tell you how you spend it."

Needless to say, I'd already made up my mind that no matter how much he might disagree, I would at least cast one wary eye in his direction. I don't suffer fools gladly, and this idiot was taking too much for granted. Randolph may be an expert when it comes to the newspaper business, but detecting was my beat, and my instincts were telling me that something wasn't adding up. I felt that earlier, and even more so now.

Randolph wasn't used to having someone speak to him as I had. I could tell by the way his lips tightened, but to his credit, he held his tongue.

"I think we'd better return to the party," he suggested abruptly. "They may be wondering where we got to."

I turned toward the door and then paused as another thought struck me.

"Did you leave a note in my room?"

"No. Why?"

"Probably nothing. Don't worry about it."

It wasn't his worry. It was mine. The note warned of danger, and yours truly and Randolph's friends were not excluded.

The Assembly Room was more crowded than when we'd first stepped out. Every antique chair was taken, even those around the tables set up for checkers, chess, cards, or putting together jigsaw puzzles. The plush rose-colored sofas placed back to back – one facing the fireplace and the other toward the center of the room – were crammed with guests, cocktails in hand, chatting gaily with their nearest neighbors. Where there weren't chairs, people stood in groups or leaned against tables, walls, or the mantelpiece. Considering the number of priceless art treasures displayed throughout the room, I was surprised at how unconcerned Randolph seemed to be about having such a large number of guests jammed into one place.

I headed to where Jim Rollins stood.

"How's it going?" I asked.

"Not bad. Did you know that Randolph set a one limit cocktail for his guests?"

"You're kidding."

"Nope. Not that I care, but Miss Rogers has been having a young waiter sneak her a few extra since I've been watching."

"Have you introduced yourself?"

"No. I was waiting to ask you if I can."

"Can't see why not, I'm sure Randolph has told her his plans. But if not, she should know that we're here to provide protection."

She was only a couple of feet away but engaged in a conversation with an elderly couple. I added, "But let's wait until she's alone and avoid the risk of being overheard."

"Where's Randolph now?" Rollins asked.

"Playing host over by the foyer. We had a heart to heart just a minute ago."

"What did he have to say?"

"Just that we concentrate on Alice and forget he's even around."

"That's taking an awful risk."

"You're telling me – but try to convince him."

I noticed the elderly couple stepping away from Rogers. Nudging Rollins' arm, I announced, "Here's our chance."

Rogers turned in our direction. Her wide, deep blue eyes narrowed as we approached her. Her beauty was intoxicating, the scent of her expensive perfume – distinctively sweet and strong – only intensifying the aura of allure which had seemed to surround her.

I quickly introduced us.

"And how do you know CW?" she asked once the formalities were completed.

I carefully surveyed the space around us before answering: "We were hired to protect you."

"From what?"

She laughed when she said it, but the merriment didn't extend to her eyes.

"You're not aware of the threat sent to Mr. Randolph?" I responded, trying not to sound too incredulous.

"Regarding me?"

"Yes."

"Oh, that's sheer nonsense – the fellow referring to me as a 'lollipop!' It's surely a prank."

"Mr. Randolph didn't think so."

"CW is overly protective, especially towards me. Too much so. And very gullible."

"He did tell you about it?"

"Yes, he telephoned me from Los Angeles."

"What did he say?"

"Just that he'd received a threatening note about me."

"That all?"

"Yes."

"Did he read it to you?"

"No."

"Why not?"

"He probably didn't want to frighten me."

"Weren't you curious?"

"Not at all. This may seem odd to you, Mr. Logan, but CW is a very rich and powerful man. There are a lot of people out there who could only wish to be as wealthy and influential as him. That breeds contempt, jealousy, and threats. It's a common occurrence in our world. I quit taking them seriously long ago."

"Have you discussed this note with Mr. Randolph or any other person since the phone call?" I persisted, purposely ignoring her previous argument.

"No. We've been busy planning the party. Really, Mr. Logan, I'm certain there's nothing to it. Don't waste your time hanging around me. Enjoy the party, and at the end, collect your fee. I won't snitch to CW, so nobody will be the wiser."

"I wouldn't take this too lightly," I tried to warn her again, but she wouldn't listen.

"Believe me, Mr. Logan, if I thought there was even the slightest chance that I was in danger, I would be the first to call upon you, but honestly, I don't see it. Besides, I'm not as frail as CW makes out. I can take care of myself."

First Randolph, and now Miss Rogers proclaiming they didn't need me. I was getting an inferiority complex. However, they weren't changing my mind. Both were being foolish. No matter which way you looked at it, the conclusion was clear, something very definite was being orchestrated here. What exactly I couldn't say, but we needed to find out. That meant staying on our toes and taking nothing for granted. Like for example, the fellow who had suddenly materialized from nearby — so close, in fact, that he could've overheard us. Who was he? How did I miss him earlier? And was he there by accident, or interested in what we had to say? It was just another piece to this evolving puzzle.

16

DINNER AND HATE

"Beware of snobbery; it is the unwelcome recognition of one's own past failings."

—*Cary Grant*

I left Jim watching Rogers. Although Rogers said she wasn't crazy about this arrangement, Randolph was paying the bills, and that decided it for me. Rita and Liz were talking together near the exit leading into the foyer. I joined them.

"You two learn anything?" I asked in a voice just above a whisper.

"Nothing yet," Liz answered, following my example.

Rita shook her head, but added, "We've only just got started, Tom!"

I smiled to temper her objection.

"I know, doll – just curious – that's all. Perhaps hoping we might catch an early break."

"I don't think it'll be that easy," she said.

"Never is," I returned. I drew closer to them. "Randolph gave me four names of people at the party now. He believes they could be likely suspects: Cookie Clark, Damien Price, Charlie Coons, and Anthony Wells. Have either of you crossed paths with any of them?"

"I talked to a woman who introduced herself as Cookie," Liz said.

"Good. Could you point her out?" I asked, and then quickly added, "Discretely, of course."

"Sure. She's that tall, attractive redhead over by the corner of the couch. She's talking to that fellow who looks like George Zucco. The stocky guy, balding, with a prominent nose, beady eyes and wearing those thick lens peepers."

I noted them.

"How about Price, Coons, or Wells?" I queried. "Coons shouldn't be difficult to recognize…" I turned to Rita. "Remember, sweetheart; he was the lead in that comedy we saw at the Rialto a few months back."

"I don't recall…" she responded vaguely.

"You, remember," I insisted. "The moving picture about the tramp who's mistaken for a rich eccentric. I believe it was called, *Mistaken Mayhem*."

"That's right," she recalled. "Small, wiry guy, with dark features and a funny mustache twisted at the ends."

"I believe the facial hair was fake, but the rest fits. Either of you sighted him?"

Liz shook her head, and Rita said, "No."

"And you're sure you haven't crossed paths with Price or Wells?"

"Damien Price, I'd recognize in a minute," Liz interjected. "He's done some stage work in New York."

"I'd recognize him too, Tom," Rita added. "His picture has been in all the papers regarding that proposed Randolph biopic."

"Then that leaves Anthony Wells – Randolph's ex-lawyer. Did you come across him?" They both shook their heads. "OK," I concluded. "Then get out there and see if you can engage any of those guys in conversation. In the meantime, I'll introduce myself to the redhead."

As I turned, I heard Rita utter under her breath: "Men – they're so predictable."

❧

"The tapestries are all Flemish," I heard the man described as resembling the actor George Zucco say to Cookie Clark as I'd approached them. He hadn't noticed me, as he was gesturing toward the enormous hangings on the room's walls. She did, however, and was giving me the once-over.

"They depict Rome's 3rd-century's victory over Carthage," he continued, not aware that her interest was now focused elsewhere.

"Who's this lovely man?" she purred as I walked up. That directed her companion's attention from the tapestries and unapprovingly in my direction.

I smiled at them.

"Logan, Tom Logan."

I handed them both a card from my billfold, the same phony business cards I had printed before we left. The name and phone number were real, but the advertising agency was one I'd picked at random from the telephone book. I made up the same prop for Jim as well – only with his name printed on it.

"You're Cookie Clark, aren't you," I continued.

"Yes, dear boy," she replied beaming from ear to ear. "And how, may I ask, do you know that?"

"I inquired, and someone pointed you out. I was a big fan of your column."

"Oh, really." The glee in her voice, indicating how flattered she was. "Nice of you to say so."

"But, you're not with the *Los Angeles Herald* anymore?"

"No. No, I'm not," she responded. Her smile didn't fade but became more forced.

"I can't see why," I returned, pretending not to notice the change in her demeanor. "Your writing was brilliant. You didn't mince words, got right to the point, and weren't afraid to call it like it was."

"Perhaps, too much so," she said, somewhat introspectively. "I'm working for another paper – *The Daily Letter* – a small publication, but soon to be a rising star among the others in its class."

I'd heard of *The Daily Letter*. It was a cheap rag sheet, and I doubt it was ever going to become any more than that. I figure it was the only paper that would hire her.

Once you get on Randolph's wrong side, competitors take notice.

At this juncture, I thought I'd drop the subject and turn my attention to her companion.

"I don't think I caught your name?"

"Todd, Todd Butcher," he stammered. He may have looked like Zucco, but his voice was not as smooth and cultured. It was thick and particularly guttural.

"I happened to overhear your comments about the tapestries," I said. "Very interesting. How do you know so much about them?"

He'd seemed cross earlier, but now that I'd given him the floor, his countenance brightened.

"I worked with CW on the plans for the ranch from the very beginning. The buildings and grounds were inspired by CW's travels abroad. This structure, *Casa Encantada*, for instance was designed after a 16th-century Catholic church he'd visited in southern Spain."

"Is that so," I responded, trying to sound interested.

Unfortunately, that only encouraged him.

"Yes, yes indeed. When CW and I started drawing up the plans, this was just a bare hill with an old cabin and spaces for a few tents. *Colina de Magia* – Magic Hill, the family called it. He used to camp there as a boy. Fell in love with the place and promised himself that he would make it his permanent home someday."

"It's stunning," I commented politely.

His tour guide routine was starting to wear thin; I had other fish to fry. I glanced at Clark, and she raised a sympathetic brow. "You're such a storehouse of knowledge, Todd," I continued, smiling. "We'll have to talk more later."

I was hoping he'd take my not too subtle hint, but unfortunately he did not.

"Speaking of storehouses," he droned on. "I also helped CW with the interior design. Would you believe he has several warehouses crammed full with artwork, antiques, and such, all collected from his visits to Europe and other foreign places, still crated up. In fact…"

Thankfully he was interrupted by the dinner gong. I quickly excused myself and followed the crowd filing through the panel door into the dining hall.

The dining hall, or 'Refectory' as it was called, seemed like something out of the 'Knights of the Roundtable,' only instead of a circular table, there was one long one situated lengthwise in the center of the room. There were forty padded antique chairs, twenty on each side, paired with name cards and place settings laid out on the table. On the surrounding walls hung Gothic-style tapestries from the Flemish period depicting scenes from the Old Testament. The Refectory's ceiling was from the 16th-century. It was adorned with exquisite figures of the Virgin Mary and various saints carved on each panel. Cathedral-style windows were spaced at regular intervals high up near the ceiling and hung between them, banners designed after those displayed at the *Palio delle Contrade* in Siena, Italy.

I made my way along the table searching for my seat. Massive silver candelabras, also rare antiques from 18th-century Spain, were placed strategically on the table to provide candlelight. But not so many as to ruin the ambiance created for the diners by the staff. I would've preferred that they concentrated less on the mood and furnished more illumination. Even with my excellent vision, I was having trouble reading the gold script on the name cards. They were arranged boy-girl, boy-girl, and I'd assumed Rita would be seated next to me. I was therefore surprised to find that wasn't the case. Instead, I was sitting at the far end of the table with Alice Rogers at the head to my right, and in defiance of the seating rule, the man who had materialized earlier from the shadows, sitting to my left.

Nodding politely to both, I pulled out my chair and caught sight of something falling to the carpet. Trying not to seem too obvious, I bent down, and in one smooth motion snatched it up. The item was a white envelope with a note partially sticking out. I shoved it into my jacket pocket and then glancing around the table, checked to see if anyone had noticed. Most eyes were engaged elsewhere, except for the stranger to my left. When our eyes met, he looked away.

I'd been aware all evening that my mysterious correspondent had said he or she would make themselves known, but had filed it to the back of my mind due to my other concerns – like the arrangements regarding Randolph and Rogers. I figured when the time arrived, my mysterious contact would make his or her move. Still, I didn't expect it this way. And although I was anxious to see what the note said, I decided to wait until I was alone.

The celebrity guests arrived late. Randolph had reserved the chairs nearest him for their parties. While the Karloff's, Rains,' and Lugosi took their seats at the other end of the table, I caught Rita's eye from where she sat near the Rollins' about midway. I could tell by her expression that she was curious why we had been separated. My only response was a slight shrug of the shoulders.

The first course was a Caesar salad or cup of minestrone soup. A glass of red wine was then poured by the wine waiter, whose job was relatively easy. Once he'd completed a round, his duties were finished. As with the cocktails, Randolph only allowed a glass per guest. Hot rolls were also offered with small squares of creamy, yellow butter.

A quartet of string instruments began playing softly from the balcony above the entrance to the Morning Room. This added even more elegance to the already refined atmosphere.

"Are all your meals so elaborately presented?" I commented to Rogers while picking at my salad.

"No," she answered. "Only when we have guests."

Her response was cold, her manner, stiff and unfriendly. Nevertheless, I persisted.

"Do you have guests often?"

She remained the Ice Queen:

"Not as often as I'd like."

At that, she turned rudely away and began an earnest conversation with the gentleman next to her.

Rogers' body language said it all: "If you don't play the game my way, then expect to be badly treated." I couldn't help it if Randolph were over-protective. If he tells me to watch her, I watch her. Let Rogers give me the cold-shoulder if she liked, she wasn't the one who'd hired me.

Rogers' reluctance to make conversation, however, left me with a more important opening. I was curious about my other dinner companion, so turned to him instead.

"I don't think we've been introduced?"

"Introduced?"

He acted as if I startled him.

"Your name," I explained.

"Steve… Steve Gregg," he mumbled.

"How do you know Mr. Randolph?"

"I'm one of his Auditors."

"For his businesses?"

"Yes," he responded, then quickly corrected, "Well, primarily for one of his newspapers."

"Which one? I believe he has many."

"His San Francisco publication, *The Bulletin*."

He appeared uncomfortable by my questioning, which got me curious. But before I could continue, I was interrupted by the gentleman across the table, the same one who Rogers turned to after scorning me.

"And what do you do, Mister...?"

"Logan. I'm with an ad agency."

"No he's not," Rogers cut in. Undoubtedly the alcohol was talking. "He's a shamus who's sticking his nose where he oughtn't."

I ignored her, which wasn't easy, and continued, still directing my conversation to the gentleman, "I don't believe I caught your name?"

"I don't believe I pitched it," he answered with a smile. It wasn't sincere. I waited a moment longer for a response, but soon realized it wasn't coming. The main course arrived at this point and provided a much-needed diversion for what had become an uncomfortable situation.

I remained silent for the rest of the meal, which consisted of a thick rib-eye steak of Angus beef bred at Randolph's ranch, pan-fried sliced potatoes, and string beans. Afterward came a tasty dessert, chocolate pudding with whipped crème and a vanilla wafer. All of this was washed down with ample black coffee. Thankfully we weren't limited to one cup.

Aside from his aversion to alcohol, there was another eccentricity of Randolph's that I observed during the meal. Although he had the table set with the finest of china dishes, formal crystal glasses, and sterling silver flatware, they were offset by paper napkins, and accompanied by plain bottles of catchup, mustard, and other condiments.

I rejoined Rita and the Rollins after dinner in the adjacent Morning Room.

"What's the deal? Why were you seated next to Rogers?" Rita asked upon my approach.

"I don't know," I replied. "But, for whatever reason, it was done at the last minute."

"What makes you think so?" Jim interjected.

"The arrangement was all wrong. Aside from the fact of us being separated, it was evident that the seating pattern was designed to be boy-girl, boy-girl, except in my case. I believe someone re-arranged the place cards."

"But who?" Liz asked.

"I can't say for certain, but I have my suspicions."

"Who, Tom?" Rita said.

I didn't want to tell her about the notes – the one I'd found earlier in our room, nor the other I'd just discovered in the dining hall. Perhaps I was being a considerate husband, and didn't want to worry her, or I was afraid she'd want to get involved, which might put her in danger, or maybe it was a bit of both. In any case, I avoided answering her by changing the subject.

Turning toward Jim, I said, "Rogers spilled the beans on our cover at dinner."

"Why did she do that?"

"I have no idea. Maybe too many martinis. In the meantime, walk softly."

"I will."

Addressing the girls, I said: "Either of you two make contact with those guests I mentioned earlier?"

Rita was the first to answer.

"I spoke with Wells. He was a real bore. Tried to impress me with the fact that he was a successful lawyer. Went on endlessly with his legal mumbo-jumbo."

"What did he look like?"

"Tall, thin, youngish, with pale blue eyes and bushy, pre-mature graying hair. And oh," she quickly added, "terrible skin – very pitted."

"What's your initial impression of him, besides being a bore?"

"That he could've climbed out from under a rock."

I smiled at her response, and then continued, "What about Coons and Price?"

Rita shook her head, but Liz replied, "I came across them both. Coons flirted with me and Price – well, Price was too full of himself to notice anyone but himself."

"Tell me more about Price."

"Both he and Coons don't look any different than when you see them on stage or in pictures, except Coons doesn't wear a mustache."

"I don't mean physically. I mean personally."

"It's what I said. Coons is a flagrant flirt, probably regards himself a ladies man."

"And Price?"

"Self-centered. Considers himself an intellectual."

"Did any of them," I included Rita in this next question, "express any dislike to our host? Perhaps make any negative remarks?"

Both shook their heads.

"How about Miss Rogers? Anybody make any statements regarding her?"

Again nothing.

The room was starting to get crowded, and I was concerned that we might be overheard. I steered the conversation toward something more conventional.

"So, what's next on the evening's agenda?"

As if in answer to my question, there came a general announcement by our host.

"If you will all follow me, I have a surprise."

We were ushered into the Castle's movie theater where Randolph was screening one of Miss Rogers' old silent comedies. After my brush with the lady in the flesh, I doubt that she would seem very funny up on the screen. Brash, spoiled, and a snob perhaps, but never funny. I guess that's what made her a good actress. Nevertheless, we had a job to do, which meant keeping a close eye on them both – so it was off to the movies.

The movie theater was located in the North wing. The auditorium was as large as any respectable movie house found on Broadway Street in Los Angeles and as fashionably gilded. The seats were plush, high-backed and covered in soft, red velvet. Gold-leaf statues of partially clothed women stood almost floor to ceiling at intervals along the walls. Their extended hands were cradling large frosted glass globes which cast ample light throughout the auditorium.

We picked four seats within view of Randolph and Rogers. They had the celebrities surrounding them, so I wasn't necessarily worried about their safety. Still, it was wise to stay vigilant.

Once everyone had settled, the lights went down, and a 'Randolph Newsreel' was presented. Through short film clips accompanied by staccato delivered narration, we were shown the news of the day. A report on how Albert Einstein was settling into his new home, the United States; an update on the jail breakout of John Dillinger by his gang; and a story about the progress of the Norma Daniels' murder investigation.

Upon the screen, big as life, only in black and white, were the familiar vistas of the Grand Canyon we'd recently visited, and with them, some staged investigation footage of Sheriff Jerrod and his men scrutinizing the crime scene. I know it was staged because they were obviously playing to the camera. As far as the reporting, there was nothing new. Jerrod was still seeking the mysterious boyfriend, Mr. See, beating that old horse to death.

A series of sports segments, including the Berlin Olympic Committee voting to introduce basketball in 1936, and Primo Carnera beating Paulin in 15 rounds for the heavyweight boxing title, ended the newsreel, and a Disney Silly Symphony, 'The Three Little Pigs,' followed. At the cartoon's completion, the Alice Rogers' feature, *The Dairy Maid*, was finally screened. It looked dated, especially now, after the advent of sound. Even the live organ music that accompanied it couldn't clear the cobwebs. Randolph seemed to be enjoying it, however, and when he laughed, so did the audience – minus one.

About a quarter of the way into the film I leaned over to Rita and told her that I needed to find a washroom. It wasn't, however, for the usual reason, although I didn't tell Rita that. I was curious about the note, and not being a patient man, the substance of its contents was praying on my mind. A staff member directed me to a washroom down the hall. Once inside I turned on the light and locked the door.

Upon removing the note, I immediately noticed that like the first, it was handwritten and again unsigned. It read: *Meet me at the indoor pool tonight – midnight. Come alone.*

My next move was to remove the earlier note from my pant pocket and compare them. Aside from a few letters, the writing looked identical. However, on second glance, something else struck me. On the latest note – the 'N,' 'M,' and 'E' appeared somewhat child-like in their execution and similar to the same written letters on the envelope containing the threatening note targeting Rogers. The same note I'd examined in my office and later fingerprinted.

17

IN THE DARK

"Understanding can overcome any situation, however mysterious or insurmountable it may appear to be."

—*Norman Vincent Peale*

We returned to our room around eleven thirty. The timing proved convenient. Buddy required a walk before bed, and if I stalled twenty minutes, it would bring us to the indoor pool close to midnight. It also took care of any curiosity Rita might've had about my sudden need of a nocturnal outing.

Partway down the hall, I paused in front of the Rollins' door, tempted to knock and ask Jim for backup. However, as Buddy pulled on his leash, I let the idea go for two good reasons. One, the note was specific that I come alone, and two, I didn't want to expose my friend to any danger.

There wasn't a soul once we left the castle, and had taken the cement stairs down to the lower terrace. The murmurs of the guests who remained in the Assembly Room could still be heard, although muted in the distance. Light from the downstairs windows cast little or no illumination along the lower terrace; and if it wasn't for a sliver of a moon acting as our guide, I'm sure I would've stumbled several times along the path. There were stars, visible in the velveteen sky, more than I ever saw in the city, and a movement of warm air that made them twinkle like sparklers on the fourth of July. It was indeed a beautiful night.

Eventually, we wound our way down to the building housing the indoor pool. I checked my watch. It was just midnight. The entrance to the pool was as inviting as an ancient tomb, and perhaps a little grimmer. Even Buddy started pulling away as I tried the door handle, which yielded to my touch. With me tugging on Buddy's leash, we entered.

There were no lights inside. The Stygian darkness overtook us the moment we crossed the threshold. It was oppressive too. The lack of air, mixed with the smell of pool chemicals weighed heavily on my chest.

"Hello," I called softly, after first transferring Buddy's leash from my right to my left hand. My right now cupped firmly around the handle of the .45 which I had the sense to bring along.

I met with deafening silence.

"Hello," I cried again, slightly louder.

Nothing. Just the whimpering of Buddy by my side. He sensed, what I was now conscious of – Death. Death was in the room.

Feeling along the wall with the hand holding the leash, I located a panel and switched on the lights.

The pool ran the length of the building, approximately 84 feet long and 40 feet wide – large enough to accommodate the two full-sized tennis courts on its roof. Thousands of mosaic tiles, cobalt blue and gold-leaf decorated the pool from floor to ceiling, lending a stark contrast to the white marble ladders, alabaster lamps, and classically inspired Roman god's and goddesses' statues placed about the room.

The main section of the pool had a consistent depth of ten feet with a centrally placed alcove with a side pool approximately four feet deep. Above the entrance to this alcove was an open balcony and diving platform, fashioned for the more daring of Randolph's guests.

Buddy started for the edge of the pool and then froze dead in his tracks. His body language, saying it all, and the implications sent a shiver up my spine. Dropping the leash and slipping the safety off my .45, I cautiously moved toward the pool, my eyes darting everywhere. Although my senses were on full alert, their feedback was telling me nothing.

Nearing the pool's edge, I caught sight of something. Blood, and lots of it blossoming out like an oriental fan from a body of a man floating in the water. I waited until convinced that danger no longer presented itself before holstering my gun and searching for something to drag him in.

Using a convenient swimmer's hook, I caught a section of his clothing and pulled him closer. He was face down in the water, but by his dress his identity was clear. It was Gregg, and after performing the usual checks, I confirmed that he was dead.

There was an intercom connecting the pool to other locations around the property. I pressed the button labeled 'Main House,' and was greeted by a person from the night staff. He was caught off-guard by my persistence to summon Randolph, indicating that Randolph had already retired and was not to be disturbed. After my further insistence, he relented and connected me.

"What is it, Mr. Logan?" answered Randolph. He sounded tired.

"I think you better get down to the indoor pool," I responded.

"Has something happened to Alice?" he asked sharply.

"No, Mr. Randolph. It's something else." I heard an audible sigh of relief on the other end.

"What is it then?" he asked.

"It seems one of your guests has met with an accident."

"What kind of accident?"

"I think you better come down and see for yourself."

"I'll be there in fifteen minutes."

"And," I added, "I suggest that you send along some staff. I may need a hand or two."

"You got it."

After replacing the receiver, something strange attracted my attention. I hadn't noticed it before, but a robust flowery scent lingered in the area where I stood.

It took a couple of minutes to pull the body out of the water. Two men had to strong-arm it from the pool and heft it up and over onto the edge.

By this time Randolph had joined us and was overseeing the operation.

"It's Gregg, my auditor," Randolph said, peering down at the body. "What the devil do you think happened?"

I indicated that Randolph follow me and led him a few steps beyond earshot of the others. In a low voice, I answered, "It looks like he was murdered."

"Are you sure?" he responded loudly. I motioned that he lower it a few decibels. "Couldn't it have been an accident?" he continued more softly.

"It's no accident. Didn't you notice the bruise on his forehead and the gash across his left temple?"

"Yes, But couldn't he have gotten that stumbling into the pool?"

"That could've happened if the injury was to the back of the head, but not the front. And besides, notice the floor halfway between the entrance and the edge of the pool – it's hard to see because of the color of the tile, but there's a splattering of blood. It's where I believe he was attacked."

"Yes," he said, straining his eyes in the direction I was pointing. "It doesn't jump out at you. How did you see it?"

"Experience. I made a careful examination before you, and your men arrived."

Actually, Buddy deserved the credit. His curious sniffing of the area drew my attention to the blood stained tile. Presently he was tied up to an alabaster lamp – napping, which I should be doing about now.

"So based on that, you believe it was murder?" Randolph stated. It seemed he needed more convincing.

"What else could it be? He didn't hit himself on the head, and there's nothing between the door and the pool he could've walked into."

"Then what do you think happened?"

"It's anybody's guess. I can only state the facts. He was attacked by someone and subsequently tossed into the pool. Whether he was dead before hitting the water, or afterward, I couldn't say. The coroner will have to answer that."

"So my next question is, why was he here? Or, for that matter, why were you?"

"I can't answer for him. Maybe he was planning to meet someone. Maybe he was hoping to talk to me."

"To you?"

"That note I'd mentioned earlier – I received a second at dinner. It asked that I show up at the indoor pool at midnight. It also warned of danger. Somebody may have found out about this meeting and gotten here ahead of me."

"Why didn't you tell me?"

"I figured it was smart not to. The note stressed that I come alone – the sender was anxious to keep it private."

"So let me get this straight, you think someone murdered Gregg to prevent him from speaking with you?"

"That could be true, although there's a second and more sobering possibility."

"What's that?"

"Perhaps the killer was really after me, but mistook Gregg in the darkness."

The two helpers, soaking from their ordeal, timidly approached us.

"I'm sorry to interrupt, Mr. Randolph," began the tallest of the pair, "but what would you like us to do now?"

"We'll need to store him somewhere..."

"Aren't you going to call the police?" I interjected.

Randolph indicated that the men wait, and after waving them off for privacy, answered: "Not until after Halloween." He saw my jaw drop. "It's not that I'm worried about ruining the party," he continued. "I'm afraid that the police presence will ruin our chance of discovering who's threatening Alice."

"You don't know that," I said. "It may aid us."

"You think so? San Sebastian doesn't have a police force. It's too small. Officials will have to be called from San Luis Obispo. And once word gets out that there's been a murder at the ranch, my competitors in the press won't be far behind. It'll become a circus, with cops and press crawling all over the place. Alice's tormentor would have no other choice but to lay low and wait for another day to get at her."

"There's a second possibility to consider," I suggested.

"What's that?"

"The murderer and author of the note are one and the same. We can follow up on that. If you figure out the one, you'll catch the other."

"And what if they're not?" he returned. "Then we hit a dead end. Besides, I believe our plan will work. Keeping a low profile and waiting for our prey to trip up is the best course of action."

"I still have a couple of objections," I persisted, and then added hastily, "actually more than a couple, but let's focus on these two. Murder is murder, and not reporting it will get us into trouble…"

"Dammit, I'm Charles W. Randolph!" he exclaimed. "If anybody can fix it, I can." Taking a breath, he continued less passionately: "However, if it'll make any difference, I'll take all responsibility. It's *my* home, *my* party, and *my* decision. You're totally out of it."

"Fine, but don't tell me later that I didn't warn you," I conceded "Now about my second objection, or perhaps it's not really an objection, but something to be considered. If the murderer and note writer are one and the same, wouldn't he or she already be on guard, waiting for us to discover the body?"

"Not if we let it be known that we believe Steve Gregg's death was accidental. Tomorrow, before dawn, I'll have my staff transfer Gregg's body from the house to a car and then to the airfield. My plane will fly him down to San Luis Obispo and a waiting coroner, who will temporarily list him as 'John Doe.' I'm good friends with the coroner, so that won't be a problem. Then, later that morning I'll announce to the guests about this poor man's unfortunate accident and how he would want us to go on with the festivities. This should buy us time to flush out the guilty party…"

"And if we don't," I interrupted.

"I'm sure *you* will," Randolph replied with emphasis. "I have every confidence in you."

I wasn't so sure.

He continued: "But if by chance you don't, I promise within 24 hours, 'John Doe' will be listed as Steve Gregg, and the police will be handed the case – with my apologies, of course."

I let out an audible sigh, and concluded, "It's your funeral, Mr. Randolph. But, since you're willing to take responsibility…" He nodded. "And I can't convince you otherwise." He shook his head vehemently. "Then I guess I have no choice, but to go along. However, I do have a request."

"What's that?"

"Give me a few minutes with the body before you take it away."

Randolph agreed.

"Also," I continued, "I'll need some index cards, a pencil, and a pad of ink."

Randolph waved the two helpers over and repeated my request. The shorter of the two hurried off to retrieve them. I went on: "And could your other man," I threw a thumb at the remaining helper, "get a flashlight and make a careful sweep around the area, inside and out, for an object, yea big," I indicated a length about the size of a baseball bat, "and with something sharp projecting from its surface. It could be a tree branch, or something made of metal, anything that seems discarded, out of place, and could've been used as a weapon."

The second fellow exited to leave Randolph and me alone.

"Now, Mr. Randolph, if you don't mind, I'd like you to be a witness as I search the body."

Very carefully, with the aid of a handkerchief, I started going through the victim's pant pockets. His wallet didn't tell me much, only who he was, which I'd known, and that it wasn't robbery, which I'd already suspected. Other than that, there was some loose change, a monogrammed handkerchief, and a set of keys. His inside jacket pocket, however, did yield something of interest – a folded piece of soaking-wet notepaper.

I wasn't sure what I expected as I separated the dampened folds with care, but was nonetheless intrigued by the penciled scribblings, which yielded three names: Dr. Jean Boucher, Shirley Lake, and Dick Pratt.

Who were they? Could they be somehow connected to Gregg's death? Or might they have no connection at all? I showed the list to Randolph.

"These names mean anything to you?"

"No."

"Are you sure?"

"Yes, I'm positive."

The fellow who had gone off to find the materials I requested, returned. On one index card I recorded the items found in the victim's pockets, and on another copied the list of names I'd just discovered. Finally, using the ink pad, I took impressions of the victim's fingerprints by pressing each digit against the blank surface of the final two cards.

"What do you plan to do with his fingerprints?" Randolph asked, curiosity getting the better of him.

"Background search," I replied.

"Jeff Layton might be able to help you there."

"Layton?"

"My manager at the *San Francisco Bulletin*. He hired Gregg, so he must know something about him."

Layton, the name struck a chord with me.

"Wasn't he married to Norma Daniels?"

"Yes. Very tragic. He and Gregg were working on an audit at the paper when the news reached them."

"I'd like to talk to this Layton guy," I said. "How could I reach him?"

"He's a guest at the party. I'll introduce you."

"Great. Still, I'd like to run these prints and see if Gregg had any priors."

"A criminal record!" Randolph exclaimed. "One of my employees."

"Just procedure," I explained. And don't worry, my contact at the Los Angeles Police Department will keep it confidential. I want to send the prints and a copy of that list. It may, or may not yield something."

"And you say this contact is trustworthy?" Randolph asked seeking reassurance.

"He's an Inspector in Homicide whom I've worked with many times, and also a good friend. He won't breathe a word."

"Very well. I could arrange to have the prints and list delivered personally tomorrow. The messenger can fly out in the morning with the body. After they drop it off, I'll instruct the pilot to continue to Los Angeles. Your inspector friend should have it by afternoon."

"Great. Here's where you can find him." I wrote the address. "I'll also give him a call in the morning."

I checked with the taller of our two assistants before leaving. He hadn't located the weapon.

"Tom, thank God you're OK!" exclaimed Rita as I entered the room with Buddy. "You've been gone so long I was beginning to worry."

She was in night dress and robe and looked as if she'd been pacing the floor.

"Sorry, sweetheart, but I ran into some trouble."

"What kind of trouble?"

Briefly I explained about stumbling upon the body at the indoor pool and what followed. I conveniently left out why I was there in the first place, and fortunately, she didn't ask. I believe it was because she had news of her own and was anxious to share it.

"You'll never guess who paid us a visit tonight?"

"Who?" I asked, the Cheshire cat-like grin on her face piquing my interest.

"Alice Rogers."

"Rogers? For what reason?"

"She said she was checking to see if we were settling in OK, but frankly I don't believe her."

Neither did I. Rogers didn't seem the type to care about anybody but herself – and that, plus the uncivil way she treated me at the dinner table, told me her visit had to be for something else.

"What time was this?" I asked.

"You missed her by maybe ten minutes. She didn't stay long. After I answered her knock, she stepped into the room, looked around, and asked if everything was OK? When I said, yes, and that you were out walking the dog, she nodded and left. Funny thing though, she had this strange, vacant look on her face when she walked out."

18

SEEING THROUGH THE MIST

*"If you can't dazzle them with brilliance,
baffle them with bull."*

—*W.C. Fields*

We awoke the next morning to the roars of lions and other big beasts. The sounds were coming from Randolph's zoo. Buddy had disappeared from the corner where he was sleeping, and it took a few moments to locate him cowering under our bed – not exactly his finest moment. After much coaxing and some persistent, but gentle tugging at his collar, we finally got him out. Bribery also helped in the form of his favorite biscuit. When it came to food, not even the threat of danger deterred Buddy from accepting a treat.

Rita decided to join me on Buddy's morning walk, so after we freshened up and dressed, I snapped on Buddy's leash, and we headed out the door.

"Up early this morning," Randolph greeted us from the bottom of the stairs. Two Dachshunds were running loose at his feet, yipping at Buddy. "Beautiful dog," he continued, indicating our Cocker. "What's his name?"

"Buddy," I answered, as we completed our descent and approached him.

His two dogs were playful, and ours was pulling at his leash to join them.

"Mine are called Weiner and Schnitzel. Weiner is the small one. Anyway," he continued. "Let them have some fun. Don't feel like you have to keep Buddy on a leash. I don't with mine. Give him some space to run around and enjoy himself."

"I don't know if that's a good idea," I began, but he didn't let me finish.

"Nonsense. This place may look like a palace, but at heart it's just a ranch, and animals belong in a ranch. Any damage these little critters might do can be easily fixed. Let him loose."

It was difficult not to succumb to Randolph's generosity, and not wanting to seem hardnosed, released Buddy from his restraint. Almost immediately I felt some reservations as I saw the three of them bounding off and rough-housing with one another down an adjacent hall.

"I have some information," Randolph offered.

Because my attention was divided between him and the antics of the dogs who were now tearing up the hallway, I didn't catch what he said at first. I asked him to repeat it.

"I have some news. We didn't locate the object you were seeking, but just before sunup one of my staff was preparing a fire in the Morning Room when he noticed the fireplace poker missing."

He now had my full attention.

"Aren't there glass doors in that room that lead to the outside?"

"Yes, that's correct."

"Then, if someone was looking for a weapon," I reasoned, "all he or she would have to do is nab the poker and walk a few short feet to the exit, minimizing the chance of meeting anyone in the process. And if it were snatched when we were in the movie theater last night, its safe removal would've been guaranteed."

"My thoughts exactly, Mr. Logan. So, I now have the staff searching the house and the grounds specifically for this poker."

Immediately after concluding this statement, Randolph whistled for his dogs, and they came running. Then excusing himself, he left with them for their walk.

"Are you sure this poker is the weapon?" Rita asked soon after they had departed.

"Nothing's a surety, sweetheart. But the victim's blunt force injuries – the bruising and cut at the temple – would be consistent with such an object."

"Excuse me, sir." An old servant had approached from behind. His hail, momentarily surprised me. "Is that your dog?" he asked drolly, his slightly shaking, gnarled, index finger, pointing in the general direction of the hallway.

To my horror, Buddy was dragging his butt along the length of an expensive looking Persian rug, which ran clear down the hall. Thinking quickly, I indicated Rita with a flick of my thumb and responded, "No, it's hers," and ran for the hills.

※

Rita caught up with me later, outside on the patio. She had Buddy in her arms. Without a word, she snatched the leash dangling from my hand and placing Buddy on the ground, attached it.

"Sorry," I responded.

I saw the signs. Rita's Irish was up – face, red, and jaw tightly clenched, Buddy wasn't the only one in the dog house.

After a quick intake of breath, she finally uttered, "Coward," and stormed off with Buddy in tow.

I was still looking after them when for a second time I was surprised by a servant, only this one was young, female, and attractive.

"Mr. Logan?"

"Yes," I answered with a smile. My eyes darted between her and Rita, who had just disappeared around the patio wall with Buddy. "What can I do for you?"

"My mistress asked that I give you this."

She handed me a note. Lately, I was getting a lot of these; only this one wasn't anonymous. It was signed by Alice Rogers and asked that I come up to her room immediately.

"I'm to escort you," she further explained, as my eyes met hers after I'd finished reading the note.

"Great," I responded. "Lead the way."

Deep in thought, I followed, but only after first tucking the note securely into my jacket pocket. I was on the verge of discovering something. The mist was starting to clear, and when I realized what that 'something' was, it brought a smile to my face.

Alice Rogers' room turned out to be a sitting parlor on the top floor of the castle, Randolph's and Roger's private living quarters. Their separate bedrooms and baths were located across from each other.

An elevator in the North tower took the servant and me up to the floor, and a short hallway from there led to the sitting room.

"I appreciate you coming so quickly," she greeted me as I was escorted in.

Rogers was stretched out on an antique settee, dressed in a rose-colored, silk dressing gown trimmed in Ostridge feathers. Her pose was something out of a glamor magazine; cheesecake for the susceptible male, of which, I'm sorry to say, I was a member. The hem of her gown was drawn back far enough to expose two shapely legs, which I had trouble keeping my eyes off of. I kept reminding myself that I was here in a professional capacity and that I was happily married, and would like to stay that way.

"Why don't you take this chair." Rogers waved to a seat opposite.

"Mary, that will be all," she directed her servant. "You may leave us."

"Yes, Ma'am," the young girl returned primly, and with a curtsy, exited.

An awkward silence followed as we stared at each other for what seemed like an eternity. Rogers, I imagine, sizing me up, and I, waiting to hear what she had to say. In the interim, I examined the room.

The living quarters was a miniature of the Morning Room on the first floor, gothic in design, but not as impersonal as the latter, enlivened by touches that were uniquely Randolph and Rogers. Photographs of his family for instance and Hollywood-like images of Rogers displayed in silver frames on tables, hung on walls, or placed in the niche of bookcases. Trophies and awards were also abundantly exhibited, and above the fireplace hung a large oil painting with Randolph seated and Rogers standing behind with one hand on his broad shoulder. It was an excellent likeness of both.

My eyes wandered back toward the woman.

"Could I interest you in a drink?" she asked suddenly. It was odd, but she was civil, not at all like the spoiled snob of the night before.

"It's a little too early for me," I replied. I noted her disappointment.

"I really don't like drinking alone, so perhaps you'll make this one exception?"

"I haven't had breakfast," I said.

"Please," she insisted, licking her lips. "What I have to say requires fortification."

"Sure."

"Thank you. There's whiskey over on the bar, and some soda if you'd like. I'll take mine straight."

I walked over and poured the drinks. As instructed, hers was straight, three fingers, and mine cut with soda from the siphon – more soda than bourbon. Returning to my chair, I handed her the glass. In one mouthful, she downed it and then indicated I fill it again. I repeated the process, this time, however, she only took a sip, and then we got down to business.

"To begin with," she started timidly, "I want to apologize for the way I treated you last night. The rudeness was an act – a part of my scheme..."

"Like that threat against you," I interrupted.

"Yes," she replied with evident surprise.

"And the other notes."

"Yes, but how do you know?"

"It was all too theatrical, like something from one of your moving pictures. *The Dutch Mill,* for instance. Girl composes phony letters about herself to fool her boyfriend."

"You concluded all this based on one of my movies?"

"Not exactly. From the start, I suspected an amateur had composed the threatening note. The haphazard way it was delivered, obviously by someone in the know, someone on the inside. The handwritten address on the envelope – a seasoned professional, would've used a typewriter. Also, the wording was curious, and no demands were made. It seemed pointless. Overly dramatic, but with no sense of purpose other than to elicit a response. What exactly that response was, however, remains a mystery."

"It was to get us to this moment, but I'll explain in a bit. Is there more?"

"Much more."

"Do tell," she said leaning toward me in anticipation. "I find this fascinating."

"You left a fingerprint on the envelope. Professionals use gloves: a single print – a partial, but enough to test for a match if that proves necessary. And your attempts at disguising your writing wouldn't even fool a five-year-old. The threatening note, the anonymous notes I've received since I'd arrived, even the note you wrote asking me to come to your room just now, all have similarities that told me they were from the same writer."

"I guess I wouldn't make a good criminal," she commented with a chuckle.

But I wasn't finished. "However, the dead giveaway was a statement you made last night. When we first discussed the threatening note, you said that you were unaware of the actual contents, nor were you interested in them, and that Randolph never read the note to you. So how did you know that it referred to you as a 'lollipop,' unless you wrote it yourself?"

"Very good," she admitted, applauding.

When she finished clapping, I stated pointedly, "So, that's my story, what about yours? Why the deception?"

"I didn't want CW to know what I was up to. But I need to give you some background for this to make any sense."

She paused as if to ponder her next words, taking a deep breath in the process. "When I first started in the moving picture business," she began finally, "I roomed with another girl who was also interested in making it big in movies. She was pretty green like me, so we hit it off famously. At first, she was fairly guarded about her background, but I guessed from her strange accent, and especially her name, that she was foreign. Nadya Jeneko was what she called herself then. It was only after the studio hired her that she changed it at their insistence. Over time we became close, and as luck would have it, we ended up working for the same studio and went through the similar paces together."

"Paces?" I asked, interrupting.

"Learning the ropes in the industry," she explained. "Anyway," she continued, "She was a beautiful girl – she had this exotic look about her – dark, doe-like eyes, pale, velvety skin, long, silky black hair, and full, pouting lips, that she usually painted a blood red. In appearance, she was perfectly suited for the screen but was a diamond in the rough when it came to her manners. The studio sent her to classes to teach her finesse. During this time she confided that she was a Gypsy born in Romania."

More mist was starting to lift. I was beginning to see where this was all leading. However I didn't interrupt, I let her talk.

"You'd think the publicity boys at the studio would've used this background to enhance her mystique, but for whatever reason, like her name, they went the Americanizing route, and she became little Norma Daniels from Sarasota, Florida."

"Which now explains why I'm here," I added dryly. "Somehow you found out about my involvement with the investigation of her murder. Correct?"

"Right. I know the assistant manager at the El Tovar. When the news of Norma's death first came out, the details in the press were rather vague. I contacted him hoping to get more information. He put me onto you using the contact information listed on the business card you'd left him."

"Which you passed along to Randolph after creating this whole cock and bull scenario beginning with the threatening note," I concluded. "Or was Randolph in on this with you?"

"God, no. He didn't want anything to do with Norma's murder. I asked him to look into it, but he brushed it off. No," she corrected. "Actually he *ordered* me not to have anything to do with it."

"Any particular reason?" I asked.

"He wouldn't say. Maybe because his old friend was married to Norma and he didn't want to interfere. I really don't know."

"So, all the secrecy – the anonymous notes to meet with you and so forth, was to keep Randolph in the dark?" She agreed. "And the feigned animosity toward me?"

"Partially to fool CW, but mainly to keep Norma's killer off balance."

"You know who killed Daniels?"

"Yes."

"Who?"

"You've met him."

"I'd appreciate a straight answer, Miss Rogers. Stop playing coy."

"Sorry, I didn't mean to. I thought you might've already guessed. It was her husband, Jeff Layton."

I laughed shortly and then replied: "In case you haven't heard, Layton has an airtight alibi. A fellow named Gregg."

"Layton is lying. They both are – Layton and Gregg. Layton put him up to it."

"How do you know this?"

"I can't say." I just looked at her, so she explained further, "I promised my source that I wouldn't reveal his identity."

"His?"

She became flustered, "Please don't press me."

I decided to play along – for now.

"You say I met Layton?"

"Yes. He was sitting across from you at dinner. I arranged it that way."

That explained the place cards.

"And Gregg, Layton's alibi, you indicated was false," I stated. "Why would he do that?"

"I can't say, but Layton is a shady character. What Alice saw in him I really don't know. Their marriage was a disaster. He was insanely jealous, overbearing, and physically and mentally abusive. He was pressing her to leave her career behind. She confided that she was afraid of him, felt threatened, even believed he might go so far as to kill her, which unfortunately is what happened."

"Getting back to Gregg's motivation," I prompted.

"Who knows: promises of money, blackmail, anything like that, Layton wasn't above it."

"Still, this is all supposition, aside from this witness you're unwilling to name. I'll need to talk to him to get at the facts."

"Isn't Gregg's death all the proof you need? Layton obviously killed him – that was no accident."

"It wasn't, but we don't want that to be known just yet, so please keep it to yourself. Still, there's no evidence that Layton was his killer. That is unless you have something to offer?"

"What do you mean?"

"You were there. I smelled that distinctive perfume of yours near the pool last night."

"I'm not afraid to admit it; I was there waiting for you. I didn't enter through the outside door, but a private one located in the alcove. It was pitch black when I arrived. I heard some splashing, which ended by the time I made my way to the main section of the pool – no surprise because I took my time getting there."

"What time was that?" I asked interrupting. "I mean, when you heard the splashing?"

"Oh, I don't know exactly. Maybe eleven forty or eleven forty-five?"

"OK. Go ahead."

"When I got to the area of the pool nearest the outside entrance I saw a body floating in the water, but because of the darkness, I couldn't see who it was – for all I knew it could've been you. I heard this morning that it wasn't. I was going to use the pool phone and call for help, but hearing someone approach, panicked and left. That person I guess was you."

"So you didn't see the killer?"

"No. *But it had to be Layton.*"

"Why?"

"I just know."

"Not good enough. It could as easily been you."

"That's ridiculous. Why would I kill him?"

"Don't know. Maybe because he covered for the guy who'd killed your friend? I'm just illustrating how the police might think. Being present at the pool around the time of Gregg's death would make you more of a suspect than Layton. At present we have no witnesses to the fact that Layton was there."

"But he could've been."

"That cannot be proven. Not without a witness. Besides, how did he know to be there? Unless," I reasoned, "he followed Gregg. And for that matter, why was Gregg at the pool?" I recalled the note on my chair at the dinner table. It could've been tampered with. "The note you left me at dinner, did you place it completely into the envelope?"

"Yes."

"Then someone besides you handled it before me. When I'd found the note it was only half-way stuffed into the envelope. So, let's say it was accidentally discovered by Gregg and subsequently read by him. It would explain how he came to be at the pool. Still...

"Once you placed the envelope on my chair," I continued, "was there any time that it was out of your sight?"

"Sure, quite a bit of time. When I changed the place card, I also set the note on your chair. That was earlier in the evening. I was away mingling with the guests in the Assembly Room for a half hour after that, right up until dinner."

"And Gregg, did he arrive before or after you came to the dinner table?"

She thought for a moment and then answered, "Before."

"You're sure?"

"Positive."

OK, I thought, then it's possible he could've discovered the note and read its contents. There was plenty of time. Now, why would Layton want to kill him? Another thought struck me. "What was the idea of announcing to the table that I was a detective?"

"To keep Layton off balance, to make him slip and expose himself. I figured knowing that you were a detective might do that."

"More likely just the opposite. It usually makes a guilty party more careful. And something else, your miscalculation could be why Gregg had to be killed. If what we have conjectured so far is true, my questioning of Gregg at the table as witnessed by Layton could've made him nervous. Made him afraid that Gregg would crack and expose the truth to me. This may have been the case because Gregg was waiting at our meeting place at the pool. Perhaps he wanted to confess everything there. However, now we'll never know, and it would be near impossible to prove."

"My God," she exclaimed. "That means I was responsible for his death!"

I ignored the outcry, deciding to let her suffer the consequences of her actions, but stated instead, "There's still nothing here regarding Layton that would stand up in court. Your eyewitness, should he come forward, would be the only way of nailing him – that is, if it can be proven that he'd actually seen Layton murder your friend."

"He did."

"Then we'd be able to also pin Gregg's murder on him now that we have a motive."

"My witness will not come forward, however. I'm positive of that. He's afraid of the police and sure he'll be arrested immediately if he comes forward. The police would more likely accept the story of a seemingly solid citizen like Layton, than a...."

"Gypsy," I finished.

"But how....?"

"Did I know?" I completed her sentence. "It doesn't take a genius to figure that your witness is this Mr. See the police have been looking for. He's here, isn't he?"

She didn't have to answer. Her expression told me everything I needed to know. Moving picture actors are supposed to emote. They're trained to let their feelings be apparent on the screen. That's what makes a good actor, but conversely a lousy poker player, as demonstrated by Rogers, whose eyes now revealed every card in her hand.

I continued, "Is he among the staff?" *Slight reaction.* "Gypsies?" *Stronger.* "Then Gypsies, as I already surmised. And since you've been orchestrating everything, I'll bet you were the one who arranged for them to be here as entertainment."

"OK," she admitted. "I'm impressed by your Sherlock routine, and you're right. He's here. Earlier he came to me for help, and he's here now by my request with his clan, tribe, or whatever these Gypsies call their people. We have a plan which I'm sure will expose Alice's husband as her murderer. All I'm asking of you is to be present when he confesses to it."

"You seem pretty sure of that?"

"I am."

"But what if he doesn't?"

"Then you can talk to my witness, and we can figure something from there."

"I would still like to conduct some inquiries on my own until whatever you have planned occurs."

"Suit yourself, but make sure you're present for the séance at nine forty-five tonight, not the earlier one, but the one scheduled for nine forty-five. I included you on the attendance list. I guarantee that it should be very revealing."

19

DETECTIVE BUSINESS

*"I never forget a face, but in your case, I'll
be glad to make an exception."*

—*Groucho Marx*

"Where have you been, Tom?" Rita asked. There was panic in her voice, which led me to believe someone else had gotten murdered in my absence. Thankfully, it was less grave. The Rollins were waiting on us for breakfast.

"Sorry, doll. I got delayed. Detective business." I was intentionally being cryptic. I didn't want to confess that I'd been speaking with Rogers, *alone, and in her private quarters.* I was in the dog house as it was, no use adding more fuel to the fire. Which reminded me, "I hope you're still not mad about Buddy?"

"That wasn't very nice of you, Tom; running off like that and leaving me holding the bag. It was very embarrassing."

"I apologize, but he's still half your dog."

"Huh? I don't get it?"

"Well, as I figure it, it was your half that was rubbing his butt along the carpet…"

"Therefore I should handle it," Rita completed.

"Yes. Something like that," I replied sheepishly.

"Very funny. Just for that, I'm *not* accepting your apology."

"No, really honey, the apology was sincere. I just couldn't resist injecting a little humor."

She thought a moment, and a gleam entered her eyes.

"All right, Mister Comedian, I'll accept your apology, but only on one condition."

"Which is?"

"That lovely coat with the fox collar I showed you at Bullocks Wilshire. You buy it for me, and all will be forgiven."

I made a show of wincing in pain, for as I recalled, the coat cost twenty-five dollars. But in the end, I smiled, and said, "Deal."

That settled it.

"Where is the little guy, now?" I asked.

"*Your, dog* – correction – your half and mine, are both locked in our room where I hope he'll not get into any more mischief. He was settling into his blanket when I left."

❧

The Rollins were waiting in the Refectory. They were the only guests, seated at this unbelievably long table that made them look small and insignificant. By the Castle's standards, we were late for breakfast. Although it was just nine am, the other guests familiar with Randolph's schedule had already eaten and were now going about the activities of the day. Fortunately for us, the buffet table was still set, and the food kept warm in antique silver chafing dishes. The offerings were the usual: scrambled eggs, sausage, bacon, and toast. I helped myself to it all, washing it down with plenty of rich, black coffee. I knew this was going to be a long day and was fortifying myself for it.

"Thanks for waiting," I addressed the Rollins after we'd settled at the table. "Sorry, but I was detained by the management."

"Randolph?" Jim asked.

"No, Rogers. It seems we've been played like a fiddle."

"How so?"

Besides ourselves and a couple of waiters standing at a distance, the Refectory was empty. Nevertheless, I paused to be doubly sure before proceeding, saying in a hushed tone: "Rogers set this whole thing up. The threatening note was a ploy to get us here so we can be part of a plan to uncover the murderer of Daniels."

"Wait," Jim interrupted. "I lost you. Didn't Randolph hire us?"

"He did, but under the assumption that Rogers was actually being threatened. Rogers didn't want him to know the real reason for hiring us."

"I still don't follow?"

To answer, I related my conversation in full with Rogers. When I'd finished, Jim asked since our objective had been changed, what was now expected of him.

"She particularly requested that I attend this séance tonight; but for you and the ladies, I'd suggest continuing mixing with the guests and dig up whatever information you can on Layton – facts, rumors, and what-have-you. However, avoid Layton if you can. I want to speak to him myself."

"But, what about the costumes, Tom?" Rita asked.

"Costumes?" I replied.

"We're required to wear costumes for the party tonight," Liz explained, picking up the conversation. "Randolph rented a score of them from the Western Costume Company in Los Angeles and had them shipped here. We're to pick one out today. A storage room downstairs in the castle is where we're supposed to select one. There are all types and sizes, and staff to assist us."

With all that's been going on, I'd forgotten about the costumes, and now that I'd been reminded, I wasn't too pleased.

"You three go ahead and pick something out."

"But, what about you, Tom?" Rita sounded disappointed.

"I don't play dress up, sweetheart."

"But, you must. Randolph's requiring it. And besides, wouldn't you stand out like a sore thumb without one?"

She had a point.

"OK," I relented. "I'll meet you halfway. Pick me out a domino mask, and I'll wear it with my tux. I can be Raffles or some other master cracksman."

"But, Tom," pleaded Rita, "The theme is moving picture monsters."

"Well," I reasoned. "Jewel thieves are villains, and some villains can be monsters. So, case closed." And as far as I was concerned, it was.

We separated after breakfast. Jim, Liz, and Rita went off to select their costumes, and I went in search of Jeff Layton. He wasn't hard to find. I no sooner left the Refectory through the panel exit than I spied him seated in a large, overstuffed chair near a window in the Assembly Room. I'd recognize him anywhere. Having sat across from me at dinner, his round face, beetle brows, lantern jaw, and broad features, were unmistakably etched in my mind. What the beautiful Daniels saw in him, I couldn't even begin to guess. He was arrogant to a fault and looked dangerous. Perhaps that was it. Some women were drawn to those sorts. It gave them a thrill.

I walked up boldly and addressed him, "Good morning."

A corner of his paper dropped, and an eye inched around it.

"Oh, it's you, *the detective.*"

I was happy to discover that Layton wasn't any less odious this morning than last night. It justified my instant dislike of him. He may, or may not be a wife killer, but based on his social skills alone, I wouldn't have any problem classifying him as a first-class jackass.

I didn't bother to ask if I could join him. It would've been a waste of breath. Instead, I dropped down into an empty chair beside him.

"Sorry, Mr. Layton, I hadn't realized who you were last night," I began, ignoring the irritation that was evident in his expression. "Please let me offer my condolences regarding your wife."

The scowl instantly left his face and was replaced by a look of self-pity, which seemed somewhat rehearsed.

"Thanks. She was the love of my life. I hope they catch the bastard who'd murdered her."

"An acquaintance of hers, I'd read?"

As quickly as he'd turned on this mournful act, it was off again, transitioning into something between bitter and indifferent.

"I wouldn't know. The police tell me they're seeking a guy named See, but honestly, I don't believe Norma ever knew such a person."

"In cases of infidelity," I responded casually, "it's usually the victim who's the last to know."

"Which means?" he returned caustically.

"Sorry, but I assumed you were informed – the police think this Mr. See was your wife's lover."

"Impossible."

"Didn't you read it in the papers?"

"Yes, of course, I did. But, the papers print what the people want to see. They're looking for saucy tales and lurid acts. It's what sells. Believe me, Mister – Logan, wasn't it?"

"Yes, Tom Logan," I answered.

"Believe me, Mr. Logan," he continued, "Norma wasn't that type of woman. She'd never cheat on me. Our marriage was perfect."

"That's not exactly what I heard," I pointed out.

"And what exactly was it that you'd heard?"

He was trying to be restrained, but I'd noticed his jaw tighten and face flush.

"Word has it that your relationship was on the rocks. That you were insanely jealous, manipulative, and violent – to the point, in fact, that she feared for her life."

"If you're insinuating what I think you are, you're setting yourself up for libel. I wouldn't murder my wife, Logan. Besides, I have an alibi…"

"Yeah, but Gregg is dead."

"So I heard this morning at breakfast. CW said it was an accident. In any case, I was with Gregg in

San Francisco going over the books when my wife was killed. He's already said that to the police. It's a matter of record."

"And if Gregg's death *wasn't an accident?*"

"You saying it wasn't?"

"It's a possibility."

"No matter, as I said, his alibi is already on the books."

"That's not exactly what I'm getting at." I locked eyes with him. "Personally, you weren't feeling threatened by him were you? At the table last night, I was under the impression that you were uncomfortable with my questioning him."

"Are you saying that I murdered Gregg? Isn't it enough accusing me of killing my wife? Now, adding insult to injury, you're trying to pin the auditor's death on me as well. You're delusional, Logan. Tell me, for what possible reason would I want to kill Gregg?"

"Perhaps you were afraid he was getting a conscience, maybe planning to change his story," I suggested.

"That's nonsense," he shouted. "And you can't prove it!"

A tense silence followed, and then Layton continued more sedately, "If Gregg were murdered, Logan, I'd be looking for somebody with an actual motive."

"Like, who?" I queried.

"Al Bellini, for instance. Al would have reason to kill Gregg."

I'd remembered that Bellini was on Randolph's list, but that he wasn't to arrive until today.

"Nice, try," I responded. "But, Bellini wasn't here…"

"But he was."

"What do you mean?"

"What time did Gregg die last night?"

Here I paused to reflect. I couldn't quote an official time – at least, not until a proper autopsy was performed. But, based on Miss Rogers' story it had to have happened sometime around her arrival at the pool – eleven forty-five or eleven fifty. I told him so.

"Then that cinches it," he exclaimed, snapping his fingers. "I saw Bellini in the hallway when I returned to my room last night."

"Time?"

"It was after the movie. Eleven fifteen or thereabouts."

"Continue."

"He seemed surprised at seeing me. He didn't say a word, but nodded and continued toward the staircase leading downstairs. I remember thinking to myself that it seemed strange I hadn't seen him earlier, or for that matter, what was he doing wandering around at such a late hour."

"There were still a few people up," I suggested. "Maybe he was feeling sociable, or perhaps just searching for a glass of milk before bed."

"Bellini – drinking milk – not a chance," he replied with a chuckle. "He was up to no good. The startled look of discovery. The way he was creeping about…"

"What would be his motive for murdering Gregg?" I interrupted.

"Simple. Revenge. Gregg had found him out. In a matter of days, he was going to make official his report regarding the audit of the San Francisco office. It was definitely Bellini who was cooking the books."

"This, the same audit that you and Gregg were engaged in at the time of your wife's murder."

"Yes, of course. Bellini was suspected and on leave pending proof. Gregg now had that proof."

"It's a possibility," I had to admit. Although I wasn't going to take his word for it, but follow it up myself. "And if what you're saying is true," I continued, "you too could be on his hit list. After all, you were involved in this investigation as well."

He became thoughtful and replied, "You got a point. Perhaps I should watch my back from now on."

"Nevertheless," I stated, shifting gears, "I'll still have to ask, where were you last night between eleven forty and midnight?"

"I thought I'd already answered that. At eleven fifteen I was in the hallway leading to my room, and a few minutes after that, in my room for the night."

"You have anybody to back that up?"

"Bellini, I suppose. But he would probably deny it."

"How about someone besides Bellini?"

"Come now, Mr. Logan. I'm still a grieving widower. You're not suggesting that I'd be engaged so soon...?"

"No," I quickly interrupted. "I was just asking – well, actually, I…"

"In answer to your question," he interjected, saving me further embarrassment. "No, there's no one else who could swear that I went directly to my room, or remained there, for that matter. But, putting this all aside, remind me, Logan, why is it that you're here? Didn't Alice say something at the table last night about you protecting her?"

"Yes…"

He didn't let me finish.

"Then stick to it. No offense, but I'd appreciate you not sticking your nose into my affairs. Let's leave the murder of my wife to the professionals." He then added, as an afterthought, "And I'm sure the law around here might ask the same regarding Gregg's death as well."

I rose as if leaving, then pausing midway out of my chair, turned and asked, "Did you know your wife was pregnant?"

This caught him off guard, as I'd hoped it would. After the briefest of pauses, he cleared his throat and answered, "Yes, yes, of course. Why?"

"I was just curious," I responded with a smile and left him staring after me.

20

INTERVIEWING BELLINI

"He who dares not offend cannot be honest."

—*Thomas Paine*

Al Bellini wasn't hard to track down. I approached one of the first-floor staff whose job was to know where all the guests presently were, and he directed me to the Billiard Room.

The Billiard Room was added just in time for the party. It was smaller and more intimate than the other rooms, yet elaborate in design. The 15th century Spanish ceiling was low and painted with medieval scenes, and on the walls hung Franco-Flemish tapestries of a delicate and intricate weave. Two large, red baize billiard tables constructed of quarter sawn oak with rosewood rail tops occupied the center of the room, one of which was being played upon by the actor/screenwriter, Damien Price, and my architect friend from the night before, Todd Butcher. They were in the middle of a spirited game that was being observed by Bellini. He was standing near the Gothic fireplace, a grin of amusement frozen upon his lips.

I walked over and introduced myself, then wasting little breath, got directly to the point, "I'm curious, but considering the cloud you're under, why did you agree to come to this party?"

"The cloud I'm under?" he repeated. "I'm not sure what you're referring to?"

By the sudden tightening of his jaw and hardness which materialized in his hazel-colored eyes, I could tell he knew exactly what I was alluding to. Nonetheless, he decided to toss me the ball and see what I was going to do with it.

"I've heard through multiple sources," I began slowly, "that you were suspected of embezzlement. And that an investigation conducted at Randolph's newspaper office in San Francisco was about to conclude, confirming this fact."

"That's news to me," he retorted; the stunned look on his face reflected it. "Not the investigation," he continued, "but the results. However, I'm not surprised."

"Why's that?" I returned.

He looked intently at me for a couple of seconds, and then asked: "Why's this any concern of yours?"

"I'm not making any judgments. I'm just trying to get at the facts."

"You a lawyer or something?"

"A private investigator hired by Mr. Randolph to look into some suspicious goings-on."

"Like what for instance?"

"Steve Gregg's death for one."

"CW said it was an accident."

"That's what we're calling it, but there are a few inconsistencies that might make it something else."

"Like murder?" he asked. "Look, I'm from New Jersey. There's no need beating around the bush."

"OK. Murder."

"And what's that have to do with me?"

"Seeing that Gregg was investigating you…"

"You accusing me of killing him?" he exclaimed. "Because if so, we can settle this outside."

I looked toward the men playing billiards. Price had frozen mid-shot with his cue, and Butcher was staring with surprise in our direction. I sensed they, as well as Bellini, were waiting with anticipation for my answer.

Al Bellini was slightly shorter than I, but stocky and muscular. In a fair fight I might beat him, or at worst, we'd come out even. However, I wasn't about to let it go that far. A swollen lip or black eye wouldn't prove anything. Besides, my instincts were telling me that he could be telling the truth. He did seem honestly surprised when I mentioned the outcome of Gregg's investigation. And besides, there was something about this guy – and don't ask me what – that made me want to believe him.

"Hey," I responded, holding up a hand. "As I said, I'm only searching for the truth. I have to ask these questions. It's my job." He remained tight-lipped, so I continued, "And it's also my job to listen to your side of the story if you're willing to tell it."

"Sure, why not?" he finally agreed, simmering down some. "But, if you don't mind...?"

I followed his eyes to Price and Butcher who were back at their game, but by their silence, evidently eavesdropping on our conversation.

"Let's take this to somewhere more private," I said under my breath. "Any ideas?"

"Sure," he whispered and indicated that I follow.

He led me into an anteroom adjacent to the Billiard Room. It was perfect: small and private, furnished only by a single, cushioned bench, which we took advantage of.

Before beginning, Bellini glanced down at the colorful Persian carpet beneath our feet, gathering his thoughts. When he looked up, he continued in earnest, "I was the one who blew the whistle – the person who felt something wasn't right about the newspaper's accounts. I was assistant to Mr. Layton at the time and immediately reported it to him. He was very appreciative of my bringing it to his attention and said he would investigate it himself. Soon after, I heard that he brought in Gregg as well, specifically to examine the books. That was the last news that crossed my desk until suddenly I was being accused of the same crime that I'd brought to their attention. It didn't make sense, and Mr. Layton agreed when I confronted him. He was extremely nice about it – actually apologetic, explaining that unfortunately due to the circumstances he was forced by company policy to place me on leave pending the results. He did add that he was sure that there was nothing to it, and in a short time I would be returned to my post."

"Did he explain why you were being accused?" I interrupted.

"No. Naturally it was my first question to him, but he said he hadn't a clue. The accusation had come from Gregg, but Mr. Layton indicated that at that moment he hadn't all the details. He did promise to find out and fill me in as soon as he could."

"And did he?"

"No, and I began to wonder. From the start, I sensed a frame-up but thought it more probably Gregg than Mr. Layton. I thought Mr. Layton was on my side, that he was my protector. He certainly took every opportunity to convince me so, but now, with this information you've just given me, and knowing that I'm innocent, yet accused, I'm beginning to think that both Gregg and Layton are in this together."

"You've just provided me with your motive for Gregg's murder," I offered matter-of-factly.

"I didn't kill him," he stated. "I didn't even know the investigation's conclusion until you just told me."

"It's OK," I said, raising my hand for the second time that morning. "Let's say I believe you. However, I still need you answering my questions."

"Sure," he replied with a sigh.

I sensed resignation in his response, so I played it gently.

"Where were you between eleven forty and eleven forty-five last night?"

"I was in my room."

"And prior to that? I need times."

"Let's see. I arrived at the Castle around eight. Everyone was at dinner, and since I wasn't expected until the next day, figured it would be impolite of me to suddenly drop in. Therefore I asked one of the staff to show me directly to my room, and if it wasn't a bother, to make me a food plate to be sent up later."

"And did he?"

"Yes, no sooner than I unpacked, there was a knock on my door, and a waiter brought in a plate of rib-eye steak, fried potatoes, string beans, and a pot of hot coffee."

"Time?"

"I'd say close to eight-thirty."

"You ate it there, I suppose?" He nodded. "And when you'd finished?"

"I fell asleep. I hadn't much rest the night before. As I'd mentioned, I was planning to arrive tomorrow, but due to a scheduling mix-up had to settle on Coach and book it on an earlier train. I don't sleep well when

I travel, and riding in Coach, it is even worse. Anyhow, once I hit the pillow, I totally conked out. I remember waking and looking at my watch and being surprised that it was after eleven."

"Did you step out of your room any time after that?" I asked.

"No, I don't believe so," he replied vaguely. "No, wait. I noticed that I hadn't had the food tray picked up, and called downstairs to send a waiter. I then placed it in front of the door out in the hall."

"Did you see anyone then?"

"Yes, as a matter-of-fact. I saw Jeff Layton."

"Did you, or he, say anything?"

"No. We just acknowledged one another, and he headed downstairs."

"Wait," I injected. "Did you say he *was going downstairs?*"

"Yes."

"You sure?"

"Positive. Why? Is that important?"

"Very. What time would you say that you saw him?"

"Eleven fifteen or eleven twenty. Sometime around there."

"Then what?"

"About eleven fifty I heard some rattling outside my door and I opened it to see the waiter retrieving the tray and dirty dishes. I apologized to him for the late hour and slipped him a fin."

"Could you point out this waiter if I asked you to?"

"Better than that, I can give you his first name. It's Rafael. I've seen him around here before."

"And he can verify your story?"

"Yes. I believe so."

"Perfect. It looks like you've got an alibi."

"Thank goodness for that."

"But, I still would like you to clarify a couple more points."

"Fire away."

"Even though you were under suspicion of embezzlement, why did you accept Randolph's invitation?"

"The better question would be, why did Mr. Randolph invite me?" "You have a point."

"Since Mr. Layton was leading me to believe that he'd thought me innocent, I'd assumed Mr. Randolph was of the same mind. However, aside from that, I didn't want to offend Mr. Randolph, so I accepted."

"Final question. Earlier, when I'd started to question you, you said that you weren't surprised about being accused of embezzlement. You already explained something about that a minute ago, but could you elaborate further?"

"I naturally was stunned when you told me, but at the same time, it had been in the back of my mind that something hadn't been kosher all along. Why did Mr. Layton allow Gregg, our internal auditor, to examine the books? It should've been someone from the outside. After all, Gregg had as much opportunity to fudge the company's figures as myself or anyone else. I guess I was in denial, especially when it came to Mr. Layton. He had me bamboozled. I was leery of Gregg but thought Layton might be on the level and in the end, give me a fair break. After you told me that they now considered me guilty, it really sunk in, and I became certain that both were using me. Mr. Layton and Mr. Gregg. It's the only conclusion I can draw."

It was the only logical solution I could come to as well. But, I wouldn't be a good detective if I relied entirely on my instincts regarding the truth of a suspect's story. I have been wrong. So, even though I was leaning heavily toward believing Bellini, it would be amiss of me not to verify his alibi, and that's precisely what I did next.

The castle's kitchen and pantry were enormous. They encompassed the entire lower floor of the adjacent Service Wing. All the modern appliances were installed, as were such extravagant luxuries as copper countertops and gold faucets. The room was buzzing with activity when I entered; chefs, bakers, and their assistants preparing lunch and other foodstuffs for the party that evening.

I caught the attention of a male staff member and asked if there was a waiter named Rafael around?

"Rafael?" he repeated.

"Yes. He would've been on duty late last night – around eleven fifty?"

"Oh, yes. Rafael Contreras. He's night staff. He'd be asleep in his quarters now."

"I'd hate to bother him, but this is important. Could you tell me where his room is?"

"It would be easier if I show you."

"I don't want to take you away from your duties." I waved a hand around the kitchen. "It seems pretty busy this morning."

"All the more reason why I could use a break," he laughed. "It's not far. Follow me."

True to his word, it took only a couple of minutes and a few short corridors from the kitchen wing to reach Contreras's room. I knocked, and my waiter friend waited until a sleepy-eyed Contreras answered before returning to his duties.

Rafael Contreras was a middle-aged man, short and slightly bow-legged. He had thick, straight black hair, graying at the temples, and a full mustache that curved down at both ends. His dull black eyes searched my face as if seeking recognition.

"What can I do for you?" he asked.

He was wearing a V-necked T-shirt and striped pajama bottoms. Rumbled as they were, it was evident that I had gotten him out of bed.

"I apologize for disturbing you, but I'm a detective working for Mr. Randolph…"

"This about the accident last night?" he interjected.

"Yes, in a way," I responded.

"I was so sorry to hear about the accident," he continued. "It was very unfortunate."

"Yes, yes it was. In any case, I have a question…"

"Sorry," he interrupted again. "Would you like to come in?"

"No. This will only take a second." He nodded, and I continued, "Did you retrieve a food tray from a guest late last night?"

"Yes, I did," he replied without hesitation.

"What time would that have been?"

"Close to midnight."

"Could you be more specific?"

"Eleven fifty or eleven fifty-five."

"Are you sure?"

"Very sure. I heard the clock in the hall chime the hour after I picked up the tray."

"And could you name this guest?"

"Yes, sir. It was the Italian gentleman, a Mr. Bellini."

"Do you know Mr. Bellini by sight?"

"Oh, yes. He's visited the ranch many times."

"Great," I concluded. "Thank you for answering my questions."

That confirmed it. Layton was lying about his encounter with Bellini. It was Layton, not Bellini, who was heading downstairs prior to Gregg's murder. Therefore Rogers could be right; Layton killed Gregg, and my assumption, to hush him up, reasonable.

Likewise, Bellini thoughts about Layton and the embezzlement scheme were now believable. Either Layton was working with Gregg from the beginning, or uncovered Gregg as the embezzler, and wanted in. In either case, Layton could use this revelation to blackmail Gregg into giving him an alibi for his wife's murder. And, as Bellini suspected, he became their stooge, a means of covering their tracks. By discrediting him, he was no longer a danger to their plans. Bellini was the employee who had originally blown the whistle. His continued curiosity might expose them – what better way to be rid of Bellini than accuse him of the crime? It all seemed to fit.

The long and short of this was that Alice Rogers' suspicions regarding Daniels' murder had now gained some traction. But, the trouble was, there was still a question of proof. For my part, I had to do more digging, and in the meantime hope that whatever plan Rogers had put forward might produce the answer we were both looking for.

21

SMOKE AND MIRRORS

"What the eyes see, and the ears hear, the mind believes."

—*Harry Houdini*

The Halloween party was in full swing after dinner. The staff and Gypsies had been busy throughout the morning and early afternoon preparing for the event. Tents were set up on the terrace for holding traditional Halloween games like bobbing for apples and bean bag toss, or activities such as pumpkin carving or caramel apple decorating, and a couple were specifically erected for palm and Tarot card readings. Although the Castle had outdoor lights, they were extinguished, and for atmosphere, torches set every few feet creating a feel of Medieval Transylvania. Large bales of hay were also placed around the terrace, mostly for decoration, but some as barriers or extra seating, and for added décor, there were numerous scarecrows.

The interior of the castle was just as fanciful. Orange, red, and yellow colored maple leaves were spread lavishly on tabletops and mantelpieces, as were numerous jack-o-lanterns, ceramic witches, black cats, and haunted houses, some covered with faux cobwebs, courtesy of a special effects warehouse in Hollywood. Paper bats and foam spiders were also in abundance, mostly hanging by strings from the ceiling.

The dinner menu was also fall oriented: Autumn Greens with Cider Vinaigrette, Garlic and Lemon Roasted Rack of Lamb, Roasted Acorn Squash, Baked Sage-and-Saffron Risotto, and for dessert, Pumpkin Pie. As we ate, the same string quartet from the night before provided background music from the balcony above. Selections from Vivaldi and Tchaikovsky, again with an autumn theme.

On the bottom of the menu was an announcement that the films *Frankenstein* and *Dracula* would be screened later, and for those seeking more active pursuits, dancing to Gypsy music, and other attractions to keep everyone entertained the entire evening. And if that wasn't enough, there was always the old standby of people-watching, made even more amusing by the outlandish costumes some had selected. My group was somewhat traditional, Rita opted for a witch – although an attractive one at that, Liz was a Vampire – pale, but also stunning, and Jim decided on the Phantom of the

Opera costume, with cape and mask as worn by Lon Chaney. I still stood with my original decision to don a mask with my tux.

After dinner, and before heading into the midst of the party, I pulled the Rollins aside. It was the first opportunity I had that evening to address them in private

"How did it go today? Any interesting impressions on Layton?"

"Nothing to write home about," Jim replied. "Most of the people I came across knew of him, but not personally."

"Same here," Liz offered. "Although one guest I spoke with, that journalist woman, seemed to have some thoughts on him, but we were interrupted before she could share them."

I made a mental note to seek out Cookie Clark.

"I had an interesting talk with Layton," I offered. "And heard something very revealing from Al Bellini."

"What's that?" Jim asked.

"Briefly, that Layton's a liar, and very likely killed Gregg and his wife."

"Then you got him," Jim exclaimed.

"No, we still need proof." I turned to Rita, "What about you, sweetheart? Anything?"

"I had an impression from the few I spoke to that he wasn't really liked, but beyond that, nothing."

"Then we'll have to keep digging," I sighed. "Best if we split up for now, and do just that. Jim – you and Liz hang out here, Rita and I will cover the terrace."

As agreed, Jim and Liz wandered off to mingle with the guests inside, while Rita and I stepped out into the warm night air. Lights flickered from the torches as we strolled amongst the tents, casting our shadows in their orange glow. A gentle breeze carried the strains of a Gypsy violin playing a well-known East European tune, *Csak egy szép lány* – *Just a Beautiful Girl* when translated into English. Walking hand-in-hand with Rita, this seemed the perfect setting for romance, except that I was here on business, the nasty business of murder. Spying Layton about to enter a tent advertising 'Tarot Readings' reminded me of that.

"Would you mind being on your own for a while, doll?" I asked Rita.

"Sure, Tom. What's up?"

"I just spotted Layton. I want to openly tail him – make him aware that he's being watched. Then, after getting him really nervous, lean on him a bit."

"Do you think it will work?"

"Won't know 'til I try. At the worst, it will irritate him, but best case scenario, it could trip him up."

"Good luck." She leaned over and pecked me on the cheek. "And Tom," she added quickly. "Be careful."

The tent was rather large. It permitted a group of people just to observe the readings if they preferred. A half-dozen folks were inside when I entered, four of which I recognized: Layton, who was taking a seat at a small table, replacing a guest who'd just left; and

Charlie Coons, Damien Price, and Al Bellini, who were milling about as spectators. I nodded to Bellini and stood by Price.

An old Gypsy woman, who could've been sent from Central Casting, but was the real McCoy, was shuffling some cards. Her gnarled, arthritic hands were surprisingly adept at handling the colorful, large cards before her.

"She's good," I heard Price say under his breath.

"Pardon?" I asked.

"The old hag, she's manipulating the cards. A real professional at it."

"How do you know?"

"I'm a bit of a magician, myself – know all the tricks of the trade."

As I watched, the old Gypsy set the two decks before her, picked a card from one and placed it face up on the felt-lined tabletop.

"This represents you," she hissed. Initially, she wore a scowl, but as Layton glanced down at the card, a toothless grin crossed her face. Pictured on the card was a carefree vagabond, labeled 'The Fool.'

The audience snickered. Their amusement, however, wasn't shared by Layton, who growled and glared back at them.

The Gypsy then took the three top cards from the other deck and laid them horizontally, left to right, underneath 'The Fool' card. The first showed a man on a white horse, the second a tower being destroyed by lightning, and the third, a blindfolded woman holding scales.

"I see death in your past," she read, a frown creasing her age-spotted brow. "And danger in your present. Due to the exposing of a lie, perhaps?" Here she paused and brushed back a tuft of white hair that had fallen lazily across her brow. Before continuing, she looked up sharply, and locked eyes with Layton. If eyes were indeed a mirror to the soul, hers were on fire.

"Your future," she commenced, "indicates justice. Your deed will be uncovered, and you will pay, pay in kind as you did to another, and your soul will rot in hell because of it."

"You old witch!" Layton exclaimed, and then suddenly recalling they had an audience, addressed them with a nervous laugh, "A whole bunch of hooey this is. Just wants to scare the pants off you."

He was trying to make light of an awkward situation, but by the look on the audience's faces, they weren't buying it. After a long and painful pause, he grunted and stormed out.

Price was laughing when I looked over. I cocked my head, and he quickly explained, "That old lady certainly had it in for him. Played him for a sap. Come out, and I'll show you how." He nodded toward the exit, and I followed. But not before glancing back at the old fortuneteller who was being comforted by a young Gypsy girl who had somehow materialized from the shadows. I couldn't hear what they said since they spoke in whispers.

꩜

"Let me demonstrate how it's done," Price said, brushing the dust from the knees of his trousers as he sat upon a bale of hay, and then indicate that I join him.

It was the first time I took a good look at Price. He was much taller in life than he'd seemed on screen, and big, not only in stature but girth as well. He had a round, boyish face, with exceptionally huge, dark green eyes, which bulged slightly. A mop of unkempt brown hair gave him a somewhat bohemian look that was at odds with the costume he was wearing – a tuxedo, a century old in design, complete with top hat and full cape. Noticing a medical bag by his side, I asked, who he was supposed to be.

"Dr. Jekyll, old boy," he replied with a mischievous grin. His voice was deep, strong, and commanding. The ideal combination for performing Shakespeare, which he did on occasion. "Didn't the bag give it away?"

"You could've been Jack the Ripper," I suggested.

"True," he conceded. "But no knife, I assure you."

"So, where's Mr. Hyde?"

"In my room hiding," he returned with a chuckle. "The mask was extremely uncomfortable – one of those rubber things. This Jekyll/Hyde outfit was the only costume they had in my size. What about you? Who are you dressed up as?" He hazarded a guess, "The Masked Avenger?"

"Something like that," I answered vaguely. "Now, what was it you were going to show me?"

"Aw, yes," he said, raising a brow and sounding suddenly theatrical. "Price the Great, Master of Prestidigitation and the Mystical Arts. Come..." he patted the surface of the bale next to him. "Sit and marvel at my magic!"

As I took my place, he removed a pack of regular playing cards from his tuxedo pocket, slid them from their cardboard box, placed the empty container into his pocket, and then fanned out the cards in front of me.

"Pick a card," he commanded. "Anyone from the deck, but don't let me see it."

He was holding the fanned-out cards with their face values toward me; his head turned as I made my selection. I chose the Queen of Hearts.

"See it and remember it," he continued. "Now place it back in the pack." I did and watched him shuffle it.

He next made a show of holding the deck up to his head, as if trying to discern through some mental mumbo-jumbo the card I selected. Then flipping a card off the top of the pack with a flourish he produced my Queen of Hearts while exclaiming, "I believe this is your card! Am I correct?"

"Yes, it is. How did you do that?" I noticed some greasy thumb marks on several of the cards, so quickly added, "Marked cards?"

"No, nothing like that, my friend. Sleight of hand, just like the old girl in the tent. Anticipating her moves, I watched for it, and sure enough, there they were, allowing her to draw the cards she wanted to produce."

"Interesting, then that means that reading was of her making, and…" I couldn't finish my thought due to the sudden appearance of Coons. He was dressed as a werewolf, although holding the frightening head-piece under one arm.

"Some show in there," he exclaimed exuberantly. "Made a damn bloody fool out of Layton, which suits me fine. Damn old sod deserved it!" A Cockney by birth, Coons had climbed the social ladder. However occasionally, especially during interviews when becoming excited, his old roots showed through, as they did now.

Charlie Coons was a small, agile man. Attractive, but not in the usual way. His head was too large for his body, and not helped by the bush of curly brown hair which was combed back from his forehead. His round, coal-black eyes reminded me of a doe, and his ears stuck out like jug handles. Obviously, Coon's notorious appeal to the ladies had more to do with personality than appearance. He was gentle, smart, and funny; always willing to help others with a broad, warm smile. It was this, and nothing more, that earned him the title 'ladies man.' His opinion of Layton, however, seemed to counter this description. Coons was fired up for some reason about the man, and I had to ask why?

"You've heard 'Love Thy Neighbor,'" was his response. "Well, he loves thyself. Not that we don't all do it to some extent, but that bloke lives exclusively for his own pleasure and doesn't give a hoot who he hurts along the way. He's brutal to his mates, to strangers – even his own wife."

"He was married to Norma Daniels, wasn't he?" I interjected.

"Yes. Couldn't see why. The man's wonky."

"Do you think he murdered her?"

I might have dropped a bomb; and an uneasy silence followed. When he did decide to answer his voice was hesitant, "I really wouldn't know, Squire."

"It's what some are suggesting?" I pried further.

"There was an alibi," he countered.

"Yes. A fellow named Gregg. But do you believe him?"

"Who exactly are you, Squire?" he asked, suspicion in his voice.

Price answered for me, "He's a detective, Charlie, working for CW."

It shouldn't have surprised me, but it did; how word seemed to get around.

"Investigating, what?" Coons responded.

This time I replied, "Layton, of course."

"Oh," he said, still inexplicably on edge. "In answer to your question, I'm not sure what to believe about the bloody fool."

I wasn't going to let it go. "Your description of him earlier certainly sounded like you might believe him capable of murder."

"It was only my opinion, Squire."

"Did Layton ever do anything personally to you?"

"No," he replied shortly, but I wasn't convinced.

Another awkward silence followed, eventually broken by Price, who decided to change the subject.

"I was just demonstrating to the detective, Charlie, how that old lady put one over on Layton."

"Doing your card tricks again, Damien?" Coons replied, sounding more at ease.

"Proving the magician's adage: 'Keep the audience watching your one hand while the other does the dirty work.'"

"I'll be assisting in the séance tonight," Coons remarked. "Anthony Wells was at the earlier show and said these Gypsy blokes really deliver."

"Very convincing," Price concurred. "Smoke and mirrors – they go the whole route. I was also at the first seating, even spent time there when they were setting up – my professional curiosity being piqued. They pulled off a few tricks even I wasn't aware of." Price turned toward me, "You going to check it out, Detective?"

"I plan to tonight," I responded shortly and then making an excuse that my wife was waiting, left them.

Rita and I caught up with the Rollins inside. Jim was excited about his encounter with one of the guests, but before he could tell me, a photographer stuck his head in and asked if we wanted a picture taken. I said no and sent him packing.

"Tom," Rollins began breathlessly. "See that guy who looks like an undertaker?"

"Dressed like one, or actually looks that way?"

"Both. That's Anthony Wells, Randolph's former lawyer."

"Who's the floozy next to him?"

"Carol Keen. Get that costume, or what little there is of it. I think she's supposed to be a vamp."

"Tramp would be more like it," Liz cut in. "She looks like a real man-eater."

Ignoring Liz's last comment, Jim continued, "I think you may want to talk to him. He has some interesting thoughts on Layton."

"I'll head over there now."

"Not without me you don't," Rita admonished, placing her arm in mine. "Liz is right, that floozy is a man-trap, and I'm coming to make sure you don't take the bait!"

"Still don't trust me, doll?"

"It's not you I'm worried about. It's that honey-trap over there."

"OK," I laughed. "You can come along, but let me do the talking."

❧

Our conversation with Wells began with small talk, but before long drifted over to the subject of Layton – with my guidance, of course. And once it did, the lid came off the pot, and everything started spilling out.

"Don't mention that bastard to me," Wells snarled between his teeth. "That son-of-a-bitch is the cause of all my problems, and pretty much everyone else's who ever came in contact with him. He's a blackmailer you know, but not for money. He gets his jollies causing others to grovel at his feet. He's a sadist in that way. Gathering nasty bits of information and using them to manipulate people. It makes him feel powerful, wielding that knowledge like a sword, slashing and cutting his victims to ribbons."

"Really," I replied, feigning amazement. "I guess I don't know him that well."

"And you don't want to," he snapped back. "That man plays with fire, and I bet you someday someone will put a bullet in him, slit his throat, or pierce him with an arrow."

"Wow," I responded, continuing my act. "He's that bad. He must've done something pretty nasty to you."

"I lost CW as a client, and almost my license to practice law thanks to him."

"If I may, Honey?" Keen interrupted, addressing me.

She was a big and shapely girl in every respect, especially where it counts. Her black button-eyes, round, apple-cheeked face, and jet-black hair complete with spit-curls made her a dead ringer for Betty Boop, not to mention lips that were painted ruby red and heart-shaped. Jim was right about the vamp outfit. It left little for the imagination. If she were out in public, she probably would've been arrested.

"Sure, Miss Keen," I said. "Go ahead."

"I know exactly what Anthony's talking about. Layton tried to ruin my career in Hollywood as well. He didn't quite succeed, but did blackball me at a few studios. My chances of ever becoming a leading actress were ruined by that… by that…. Well, I'm too much of a lady to call him what I would like to."

"Could've fooled me," Rita mumbled under her breath. Fortunately, Keen didn't hear her.

"It's not that I'm cheap or anything," Keen continued. I gave Rita a slight nudge with my elbow. "But that palooka was putting the make on me, and him being married and all. Now, don't get me wrong, I don't mind men putting their hands on me, but only if it's me that tells them it's OK." A devilish smile crossed her lips. "Actually you got some nice hands, Honey."

I cleared my throat and tossed a sideways glance at Rita. She was fuming, but to her credit, stayed quiet. I commented, "Layton made a play for you, and I assume you rejected him?"

"Sure thing. Like Anthony said, Layton gets a kick out of hurting people, but not only mentally, but physically as well. He's what you called him?" She looked at Wells. "A sadder."

"Sadist," he replied dryly.

"Yea, that's it. He likes knocking little girls around."

"Did he ever knock his wife around?" I asked.

"Norma? Sure. Many times."

"Miss Daniels tell you that herself?"

"Sure. She, and others. It was common knowledge."

"Did he ever knock you around?"

"I never gave him a chance, but if he did, I wouldn't think twice about laying him out."

"Would you go so far as Mr. Wells' suggested?"

"Put a bullet in him?"

"Yes."

She thought a moment and then answered, "Sure. The way I look at it, I'd be doing the world a service."

I turned to Wells.

"What about you, Mr. Wells? Would you consider killing Layton as doing the world a service?"

"I would." A familiar voice behind me chimed in. It was Cookie Clark. All dressed up as a black cat. "Forgive me for eavesdropping, but I couldn't help but overhear. Count me in on the 'I Hate Layton Club.' CW and I were close. I was his star gossip reporter. Then Layton came along. I don't want to go into details, but that hit piece on Rogers, and my mention of her affair with Charlie, was all Layton's doing. He blackmailed me into writing it."

"For what reason?" I asked.

"God only knows. But, if I didn't do it, he would've of exposed me to more grief than I could bear."

"Even at the expense of all that's transpired since – the losing of Randolph's friendship, your newspaper job, and everything," I stated, taken aback.

"I'm afraid so."

"It's the way he operates," Wells offered. "I never would've done what I did, if it wasn't for a threat from Layton. He examines your life with a fine-toothed comb, searching for weaknesses, like long-forgotten scandals or something of that order, and when the time is right, springs it on you for his own satisfaction. Sometimes it's for his betterment, other times out of jealousy, but mainly because it gives him power over others. He's pure evil through and through. So, you ask if I could do all those nasty things to him I mentioned earlier. You bet I could, and in spades!"

The 'I Hate Layton Club' seemed to be growing by leaps and bounds. Still, all these insights, as interesting as they were, were not getting me any closer to the truth of his wife's murder – or Gregg's. It still came down to Rogers' plan, and whether it would provide the proof I needed.

22

THE EVENING SÉANCE

*"The ghosts of things that never happened
are worse than the ghosts of things that did."*

—*L.M. Montgomery*

The séance was staged indoors, in a large room occupying almost an entire wing of the castle. It was a combination library, smoking room, and trophy exhibit area – a real man's space with Randolph written all over it. Mounted animal heads adorned the walls above the many bookshelves lined with first-edition, leather-bound texts. The parquet wood floors were covered with animal skins, mostly zebra, and the walls with ancient weapons of war that hung from hooks, or were exhibited in glass cases. Full sets of knight armor were propped up in the room's corners. The furniture was antique, sturdy, and comfortable with cushions of cracked leather. Silver ashtrays were in abundance, and although emptied and wiped cleaned, a strong odor of cigar still hung heavily in the air.

Space was cleared at the far end of the room, and a large cabinet placed up against the outer wall. A round table with chairs was set a few feet in front of that, and much farther behind this, four rows of folding chairs were arranged for the audience.

For such a grand room, I was surprised to find a single entrance, two large oak double doors, and very few windows, all of which were presently covered by thick curtains. The only light provided in this vast space was a couple of reading lamps placed near the audience and the dim glow of a crystal ball set in the center of the round table.

Set the mood, and set up the audience, I thought cynically, as I navigated my way through the crowd. There was a clipboard hanging by the door. On it were, names, times, and assigned seating for the two séance performances. The first, before dinner, had already passed, and the final – this one at nine forty-five, was about to begin.

Cookie Clark, Charlie Coons, Al Bellini, Jeff Layton, and I were the lucky recipients of a random drawing that selected five guests to assist in the séance. Although, 'random' wouldn't have been a term I would've chosen to describe the process. Rogers had made the arrangements for this soiree, so it was evident that I was sitting exactly where she wanted me – at the table next to Layton.

Moving counter-clockwise, starting with the Medium, who sat with her back toward the cabinet, the seating arrangement went as follows: Coons, Bellini, Clark, myself, and Layton.

Once everyone settled, and a general hush fell over the audience, the Gypsy Medium directed the staff to extinguish the floor lamps near the spectators, leaving the room pitch-dark except for a soft circle of light around our table, cast by the crystal ball.

"I am Madame Ioana," she announced. Her voice was melodious and hypnotic. "I will be your guide this evening into the spirit world." She spoke with a Romanian accent that added charm and credence to the presentation.

Madame Ioana, I would guess, was in her early thirties, an attractive woman with a long, angular face, dark almond eyes, and shoulder-length, chestnut colored hair. Her nose was slightly larger in comparison to her other features, but not unattractive; and when she smiled, she displayed a set of pearly-white teeth that contrasted greatly with her flawless, coffee-hued complexion.

Her dress was traditional: a black dirndl skirt, heavily embroidered on the hem, with a white blouse and black velvet vest also embellished with embroidery. A colorful silk scarf was wrapped around the top of her head, and she wore an abundance of gold coins as jewelry.

"Before we begin," she continued, "I ask two things of you. First, you must remain quiet. The spirits are sensitive, and any noise can cause them to vanish. And second, I ask that whatever happens, you remain in your seats. Agreed?" She looked at us first. We all nodded, and she then looked toward the audience, who voiced their agreement as well. "Good," she responded, satisfied, and then returned her gaze to us. "I will be asking you momentarily to join hands, and once I do, I ask that you at no point break the chain. If we are lucky and make contact, it is essential that we remain joining hands; otherwise, our link to the spirit world will be broken, and any manifestation that has arisen will disappear. Do you understand?" Again we nodded our consent.

She arose and walked over to the cabinet.

"This is a spirit cabinet," she explained, gesturing toward the massive box. The coins on her bracelet jingling as she did so, breaking the otherwise dead silence of burgeoning anticipation that had everyone mesmerized. "Earlier this evening, during my first attempt to contact the spiritual realm, I was tied hand and foot with ropes to this chair..." Here she opened the center of three hinged doors on the cabinet exposing the space within. It was empty except for a chair and four musical instruments set on its floor: a small child's tin horn, a tambourine, a little drum, and a wooden flute. "But tonight will be different."

"Could I have a volunteer?" she asked. When no one responded, she indicated me. "Sir, could you please step this way?" Shrugging, I joined her. "Would you please inspect the cabinet?" And on cue, a staff member appeared with a lantern to assist me.

The spiritual cabinet was a wooden closet, approximately seven feet in height, six feet in length, and two feet in width. The entire unit was supported on three sturdy sawhorses eighteen inches off the ground to prevent any contact with the floor. The three doors made up a significant part of the cabinet's exterior. I examined inside each of these doors and found all three empty except for the center one with the contents I'd already described. I was next asked to inspect beneath the cabinet, and getting down on my knees, confirmed that there were no trapdoors or other ways of access or egress visible. There were no other openings that I could see upon the entire cabinet, except for a six-inch hole cut into the middle door, supposedly for air. Satisfied that I had completed my task, the Medium requested that I return to my chair, but not before having me confirm to the audience that I hadn't seen anything outside the norm during my inspection.

After I had sat down, she continued, "Tonight I'm going to attempt something unique. Unlike this afternoon, I plan to call forth a manifestation from here," she spread her arms toward the table. "While sitting amongst my assistants as part of their circle." She was really pouring on the theatrics now.

She returned to the table and asked that we all join hands. Layton's grip felt cold and clammy. I don't think he was keen about participating, but like us all, was following the dictates of our host.

Silence once again fell over the proceedings. You could've heard a kitten in slippers tap dance. It lasted a full minute or two, and then came some sounds of stirring, followed by a sorrowful moaning that emanated from the direction of the Medium.

"Who is there?" she asked. "Is it Lucy? Have you come to lead us through the spiritual veil?" I learned later that Lucy was Madame Ioana's spiritual guide.

A flute started playing from the cabinet, and although I knew this was all a fraud, the dirge floating on air still had the effect of sending shivers up my spine. When the tune finished, Madame Ioana repeated her earlier question:

"Is it you, Lucy?" A hush followed. "If it's you, Lucy, make a sound." Again, complete quiet. "Then if it is not Lucy, give us a sign." The rattling of a tambourine followed. "Good. Then if you are not Lucy, who are you?"

In response to her own inquiry, the Medium started moaning again, twisting her head from side to side as if in extreme pain. It was pretty effective, but not nearly as convincing as what came next. After releasing a heart-stopping scream that seemed to burst forth from deep within her chest, she suddenly started speaking in a voice that wasn't her own. It was high-pitched and mournful.

"My name is Norma," the voice uttered. I felt Layton's grip momentarily tighten.

So this was Rogers' plan. Whether it would work or not was anybody's guess. My cynical mind said that it wouldn't. Layton was smarter than that. But, who knows? At the least, this was going to prove interesting.

"Why are you here, Norma?" the Medium asked in her own voice.

"I have a question for the living," returned the falsetto voice.

"This is ridiculous," Layton exclaimed, starting to rise.

"Be quiet," Ioana admonished harshly, causing him to drop back into his seat. "We don't want to destroy the spiritual bridge."

"Spiritual bridge my..." he started to say, but the appearance of a delicate hand extending from the hole in the cabinet caught his attention, as it did ours as well. It was glowing green, and undulating hypnotically back and forth like a Swami's cobra.

"Norma," Ioana called and then repeated the name. "I sense you're longing to materialize fully. Use the cabinet's energy as a mechanism to complete the transformation and step from your world to this. Now feel the ectoplasm enter your spiritual body and take form."

"I feel it!" screamed the ghostly voice.

Tendrils of vapor started flowing from under the right-hand door of the cabinet. As it grew thicker, all the instruments: flute, drum, tambourine, and horn began making a confusion of sound that grew louder by the minute. When it reached its crescendo, the door flew open as if on its own, and the figure of a woman floated out.

For once I was thoroughly stunned. Not due to the spectacle of the manifestation. One could see how that can be faked, but by the identity of the ghost itself. In every respect: appearance, height, weight – even down to the platinum colored hair, she resembled the woman I'd discovered dying in the canyon. And even if I was asked to do so, I couldn't deny it. Here stood Norma Daniels. But how? That, I couldn't begin to explain. Norma Daniels was dead. I know that; the world knows that; yet there she stood in front of us plain as day.

This apparition, for I know not what else to call her at this point, had already floated down from the cabinet's exit to the floor and was presently advancing toward the table. Her entire body, including her hands, was shrouded in a radiating green glow, which outlined her shapely and seemingly-nude body. The features of her pale face were remarkably like Daniels, and when she finally glided to a stop just beyond our reach and spoke, I could clearly see that it wasn't a mask or some other means of deception.

"Why did you kill me, Jeffrey?" she moaned, slowly extending her left arm and pointing an accusing finger toward Layton.

A series of events occurred next which prevented me from witnessing his response to her question. It began with a scream, followed by Layton's squeeze of my hand with a grip so tight that I feared my circulation would be cut off. Then, as I was wrestling my hand loose, Layton suddenly collapsed, dropping head first onto the table, an arrow shaft protruding from his back.

At this same instant, I sensed frantic movement from behind. A darkly dressed figure rushed past. Instinctively, I shot my leg out and caught the figure mid-stride. The person tripped and fell helplessly to the ground. I was upon the intruder in a flash, drawing my Colt, and shouting for someone to turn up the lights.

The intruder was strong and struggled frantically at first, but once I warned that I was armed, calmed down and stayed motionless under my weight. I didn't cease pinning this person to the ground until the lights came fully up. His identity was a no-brainer. It tallied perfectly with the description given to me by numerous witnesses at the Grand Canyon.

"Mr. See," I announced leaning close to his ear and shoving my automatic harder against his ribs. "We finally meet."

"No wait," a woman's voice shouted. "You're making a mistake."

It was Norma Daniels' ghost, except she looked less otherworldly in the bright light. Not to say that she still wasn't a dead ringer for Daniels, but her apparel was all hoax – a flowing, sheer gauze frock over a bodysuit, covered with some sort of phosphorescent dye or paint. Her face and hands were made up too: white makeup to pale the skin, and a blue shade for lips and around the eyes. Effective under low illumination, but absurd in harsh light.

"Norma!" a weak voice suddenly cried out.

Due to the excitement, everyone's attention had been focused on the struggle, and Layton, unfortunately, cast aside. But as he lifted his head in a concerted effort and began addressing the image of his wife, all eyes turned to him.

"Norma!" he repeated again. His eyes were red-rimmed and tearing as he focused on the woman standing before him.

"What is it, Jeffrey?" she responded softly, quickly taking the cue.

"Norma, I'm sorry," he responded. "I didn't mean to kill you – it was the baby – too much to bear." He started coughing as red foam began forming at the corners of his lips. He tried to say more, but couldn't.

I called for medical assistance but suspected that it was too late. Within seconds he was gone.

"Who are you?" I asked the woman.

Without warning, Alice Rogers approached us from the corner of the room.

"I thought you could figure that out, Mr. Logan," Rogers answered. "She's Norma's sister, Anna. Her identical twin."

Inwardly I chastised myself. What is it about the most straightforward solutions that sometimes alludes us?

"And this man is innocent," Rogers continued indicating Mr. See. "Please release him."

He was still pinned down on the floor, my knee lodged into the small of his back. I rose slowly and told him to do the same, with hands clasped behind his head.

"You're making a big mistake, mister," he protested after facing me.

"Not from my perspective." I pointed to an ancient crossbow that was laying just inches from his feet.

"Honestly, it wasn't me," he pleaded. "I didn't do it."

"He didn't, Detective," added Anna. "Rudolf wouldn't harm a fly."

"Let's work this out later," I responded briskly and turning, addressed those around the table. "Nobody's to leave this room." I surveyed the audience. "And that goes for all you too." To my surprise, I caught a glimpse of Rita, Jim, and Liz. They must've joined the crowd after I'd entered.

"Jim," I shouted. "Could you come over and give me a hand?"

He did and helped me cuff my prisoner.

"I didn't expect to see you and the ladies in the audience," I commented to Jim as we stepped away.

"Seems lucky we did," he replied. "However you'll have to thank your wife. She convinced us to come along."

"I should've figured. Rita isn't one to let an opportunity pass. I bet she said I was selfish for not letting the rest of you in on the kill."

"Well, not quite like that," he responded diplomatically.

"Knowing, Rita," I replied with a smile, "*It was exactly like that.* But how did she know?"

"Perhaps you're not the only detective in the family," he suggested.

"Perhaps you're right, Jim." I threw a thumb toward Layton's body. "Did you see anything of the murder?"

"Not really. First, there was the appearance of the ghost and then someone shouting from the audience. I'm afraid my attention was divided between the two. I didn't see anything else."

"What about the girls?"

"I can't say, you'll have to ask them. My guess, we were all distracted by other things."

"You're probably right. Who shouted?"

"I can't say. It was too dark, but it came from nearby."

"Was it just a shout, or was something said?"

"Said," he answered firmly. "Look out, or something to that effect."

"It's what I thought I heard as well," I replied. "Just wanted to be sure."

I stepped away and faced the audience.

"Who shouted out during the séance?"

"I did." It was my architect friend again, Mr. Butcher.

His costume was all leather belts and black tights, and he was holding a rubber ax.

"Let me guess," I commented, approaching him. "Executioner?"

"Yes," he answered meekly. "Although I don't believe I could ever chop off a head or anything. I'm a bit squeamish. Architecture and design is my first love."

"Sure," I replied before he could launch into another dissertation about the antiquities of the castle. "I was curious," I pressed on. "What was the idea of you calling out as you did?"

"I thought that would be obvious," he replied. "I saw that man you arrested pull a crossbow off that wall and aim it at Mr. Layton."

I looked to where he was pointing, and sure enough, there was a blank space amongst some swords and other hanging weapons.

"Are you sure it was that man?" I asked. "It was dark, and there were a lot of distractions."

"Well, I'm pretty sure," he returned, a bit hesitant. "I'm ashamed to say, but when that spirit stuff started, I got somewhat nervous and was looking away. That's when I saw that fellow grab the crossbow."

"But could you swear to it?" I pressed further.

"Who else could it have been?"

Butcher got me there. Within seconds of the murder, there stood Rudolf, the crossbow, and nobody else. It had to be him.

I thanked Butcher and returned to Rollins and Rudolf. Rogers and Anna were there as well in support of the prisoner.

"If you just listen to our explanation, Mr. Logan," Rogers implored, "you will see how wrong you are about Rudolf."

"I plan to," I replied shortly. "But not here. Is there somewhere close by where I can question him in private?"

"There's the Radio Room," she suggested.

"Good. Just give me a second."

I pulled Jim aside.

"I don't know how you can manage it, but I need names, contact information, and written statements from everyone in the room." I counted a dozen in the audience, five at the table, and another half dozen or so Gypsies and castle staff – twenty-three, maybe twenty-five tops. Not impossible to manage, but an effort nonetheless. I suggested he seek the assistance of the ushers and if necessary, our wives.

"What about the body?" Rollins asked. "Shouldn't we at least cover it?"

"By all means, but let's not move it – not just yet."

At that moment I glanced toward Layton's body and spotted Coons bending over it. Hurrying over, I addressed him sharply, "What are you doing?"

"I thought I saw him take a breath," he responded quickly. "But I believe I was mistaken."

I checked. There was no pulse. However, I wasn't buying it. Charlie Coons may be a great comedian and a master of pantomime, but when it comes to acting, he had a lot to learn. There was guilt written all over his face and lies aplenty.

"What do you have there?" I asked. He was trying to conceal something.

"Where?" His demeanor was childish and clumsy.

"Behind your back."

Discovered, and with no place to go, he surrendered the item to me. A crumpled envelope which I noted was addressed to him.

"It's nothing," he objected. "It's mine."

"I'll determine that later," I responded, shoving it into my pocket. I was eager to question Mr. See, who was beginning to get anxious. "We'll talk then," I added as I started over to my prisoner.

23

MR. SEE EXPLAINS IT ALL

"A friend is one who walks in when others walk out."

—*Walter Winchell*

The Radio Room was small, comfortable, and less formal than the other quarters, just two sofas, a couple of easy chairs, and a large Philco radio console occupying its space. Immediately upon entering, Miss Rogers stated that she wanted to be present during Mr. See's questioning.

"I'd prefer interrogating him alone," I answered.

"Like Hell," she returned. "He's in this spot because of me, and if anyone needs to do any explaining, it should be me!"

"Do as you like," I conceded. I wasn't in the mood for a fight. "If you think you can help?"

"I do."

"Then let's all take a seat."

We did. Mr. See in a chair, Miss Rogers and myself on the sofa.

"First things, first," I began, addressing him. "Is See your assumed, or legal name?"

"It's not real," he responded. "It was Nadya's little joke to register at the hotel. It was her favorite operetta and mine, 'Gypsy Love.'"

Chalk one up for Jim. It's what he had figured.

"My true name," he continued, "is Rudolfo Granenski, but you can call me Rudolf."

I removed my ever-present notebook and jotted it down.

"And when you say Nadya, you are referring to Nadya Jeneko, otherwise known as Norma Daniels, correct?"

"Yes, that's so."

"I'll want to go over what happened at the canyon later," I explained, "but for now, please give me your account of this evening. Why were you at the séance, and how did you end up near the victim and at arm's length from the murder weapon?"

"The weapon I cannot explain," he said. "It could've been dropped or thrown there by the killer. How I came to be at the séance however..."

"He was there because of me," Rogers interrupted. "It was part of a plan to get Layton to confess."

"Thank you, Miss Rogers," I responded firmly. "I'll get to you in a moment, but for now I'd like to hear Rudolf's version of the events."

She huffed and pertly nodded.

Turning back to Rudolf, "Where were you prior to the murder?"

"In the Spirit Cabinet. I was assisting Anna and the others."

"This Anna you're speaking of is Miss Daniels' sister, correct?"

"Yes, her twin. It's hard at times to tell them apart. However, their personalities are very different."

"Yes, I've heard that's often true. Who are these others you've just mentioned?"

"Adrian and Marius. They're Nadya's – Norma Daniels' brothers, and the Medium, Ioana – her cousin."

"So these entertainers – these Gypsies – are made up of Miss Daniels' family?"

"Yes, that is correct. The Fortuneteller who's doing the Tarot readings outside in the tent is Nadya's mother."

So the old Gypsy woman was Daniels' mom; that explained her animosity toward Layton during his reading.

I told Rudolf to continue.

"Our jobs – Adrian, Marius, and myself are to create the illusions. Before the séance starts, and the audience arrives, we conceal ourselves behind a panel. The cabinet is double walled and put together in a way that it appears empty when observed from the outside. It's all illusion. The space between these walls is very narrow, and only two can stand shoulder to shoulder at any one time. Anna and I were in the right cubical panel as you face the cabinet and Adrian and Marius behind the left.

"After a person selected from the audience examines the cabinet and confirms that it's empty, we slide out from our concealment and go to work. There's plenty of room then for the four of us, since the middle cubical partitions are hinged, and can be swung away. These doors also give access to the musical instruments and other props we left there. Adrian's and Marius's jobs during the séance are to play those instruments and shine hooded lamps upon Anna's costume when she appears as the ghost. Mine is to manipulate a wire apparatus that gives her ghost an appearance of floating. Dry ice and warm water supply the vapor, and the rest – like Nadya's ghost, as you probably saw for yourself, is nothing more than gauze, makeup, and luminous paint."

"That's all very interesting," I interrupted. "But I'm more concerned with your movements before the murder."

"I'm getting to that. You see, just after Anna left the cabinet, and I was pulling in her wires, something on the left caught my attention. Either Adrian's or Marius's lantern had drifted away from Anna's costume, its beam, momentarily lighting the bookcase. I saw a portion of the bookcase move apart and the glint of something shiny sticking out."

"Is there a hidden passage there?" I quickly addressed Rogers.

"Yes. I believe so."

"I'd like to examine it later." Next turning toward Rudolf: "Could this object you'd seen have been an arrow?"

"Yes, although I wouldn't have been so sure at the time. It seemed strange, and while I was wondering about it someone shouted, 'look out,' and I sensed Layton could be in danger. I ran toward him, but was too late – that's when you tripped me, and you know the rest."

"Are you saying," I responded, "that you wanted to save the man who'd killed …"

"Yes," he interrupted. "That's exactly what I was trying to do, but not for the noble reason you may think. I needed him alive to admit to his crime. His confession would clear me of Nadya's murder. And besides, death was too merciful for that man. I wanted to see him spend the rest of his life behind bars tortured by the memory of what he'd done."

"Even though he'd killed your baby in the process?" I stressed.

"Baby?" he replied. "What baby?"

He seemed caught unaware.

"Didn't you know that Miss Daniels was three months pregnant?"

"I had no idea."

I looked at Rogers, and she shook her head.

"She never said a word to me either," she explained. "Three months you said?" I nodded. "It might've been longer than that since I spoke to her last. How terrible."

"You have to believe me," Rudolf spoke again. "What I'm telling you is the truth."

"I can vouch for that," Rogers added. "I was watching from the back of the room; Layton was shot moments before Rudolf even got close to him."

"And the others will swear that I was still in the cabinet at the time," Rudolf offered. "Ask them – Anna, Adrian, Marius, and Ioana."

"What's to say that they wouldn't lie for you," I countered.

"You calling me a liar?" interjected Rogers.

"No. No," I conceded with a sigh. "But the cops might think so. They have no imagination whatever, and when faced with choices, they'll always choose the one of least resistance. In this case, Rudolf here. There's a room full of witnesses who will say they saw otherwise. And when it comes to Rudolf's friends or some less prejudiced eyewitnesses from the audience, guess who'll hold the most weight with the local cops? And then there's the matter of motive. Rudolf has a great big one, especially since Layton publically confessed to the killing of Daniels. Daniels was Rudolf's lover and carrying his child – open and shut, the cops would say."

"Then you'll have to find Layton's killer before the law arrives," Rogers said. "I can get CW to delay contacting them."

"No, definitely not!" I said. "We held off calling them in on Gregg's murder as it is; and many witnesses observed Layton's murder. The cops have to be alerted. I can't afford to get into trouble. Mr. Randolph may escape the long arm of the law, but my license – my whole career – would be in jeopardy."

"CW can fix that," she offered.

"So he said concerning Gregg, but I can't chance it."

"Please. Rudolf didn't kill Layton. You'll be condemning an innocent man!"

"The law is the law. There's a certain protocol that has to be followed. They must be notified," I persisted.

"Please, Mr. Logan," she repeated. "I promise CW will cover for you. You know his influence can do it; and I would be eternally in your debt – not to mention the Jeneko family, and of course, Rudolf."

I took a deep breath and let the air out slowly. Rogers' doe eyes were getting to me.

"OK, we can delay calling them," I finally conceded.

She emitted a squeal of joy and placed her hands in gratitude atop mine. I slid them gently away, adding, "But no later than noon tomorrow. That's my final offer. After that, we hand the matter over to the police."

"Will that give you enough time?"

"I guess it'll have to," I replied, and returned my gaze to Rudolf. "In the meantime, tell me what happened at the Grand Canyon. You were there at Miss Daniels' invitation, correct?"

"Yes. Nadya and I grew up together. We have always been close. She and my family believed that someday we would be married. So did I, but she was always restless, and then this Hollywood nonsense occurred."

"I wouldn't exactly call it nonsense," I commented. "She did succeed and became famous, something others only dream of."

"It changed her," he countered. "She became wild – lost her innocence. But, mostly, I resented it because it took her away from me."

"How did you find each other again?"

"It was ten long years that we were apart, some of which she was married to that cad, Layton. Then recently, out of the blue, she contacted me…"

"How recently?" I interrupted.

"About four months." "Interesting," I commented, but let it ride. "Go on."

"We picked up again as if we'd never been apart, only more so. As I said, those ten years had changed her – she was more passionate, and our love, once innocent, had developed into something very different, almost wicked and very wild." He paused, suddenly realizing that Rogers was in the room, and flashed her an apologetic smile.

"Don't be embarrassed, Rudolf," she assured him. "I'm no angel myself. You can talk freely. God knows, there's very little that shocks me these days."

He nodded, and at my urging continued, "Nadya suggested the rendezvous at the canyon – indicated that she needed to get away and all the better if I shared it with her. 'Our days would be filled with adventure and our nights with romance' – that's how she described it. However, due to fear of her husband, not to mention bad publicity, we decided to be discreet. I registered at the hotel earlier, using an assumed name, and she later, with a disguise and phony ID. Naturally, we'd booked separate rooms, and assumed a casual acquaintance when moving in public about the hotel. We thought we were safe…"

"But somehow Layton found out," I interrupted.

"Exactly. Don't ask me how, but he did. Nadya said he was always suspicious of her, and although technically separated, kept tabs on her movements through detectives and other means. In any case, around 2 AM the morning of the murder she'd crept into my room, and we spent the rest of the time as lovers do, waking later than we should have. It was shortly before 10 AM, and we needed to get her out of my room unobserved, which might prove to be a problem since many guests were already up and about. I started dressing and urged her to do the same, but she was acting carelessly that morning – even said that she didn't care what people would think and that maybe she would just like spending the rest of the day here making love. Naturally, I didn't argue.

"Still there was the question of breakfast. I was hungry, and I knew once becoming fully awake, Nadya would be too. I continued dressing with the idea of going downstairs and scrounging up some food. However, as soon as I put on my jacket, there was a knock on the door.

I waved to Nadya and indicated the closet. Her clothes were on the floor. She kicked them under the bed and ran nude toward the closet. Once she'd hidden herself, and I'd run a quick eye over the room, I asked who it was. A voice answered, 'Management,' so I opened the door partway. Immediately I recognized the visitor as Layton – she'd shown me his picture often enough – and in a panic, tried to slam the door in his face."

"Did he yell?"

"No. But I believe I did. I can't remember exactly, but whatever it was I said it in my native tongue. Expressed surprise or something."

That jives with what the Jeffersons had told me they had heard from the room next door.

"How was he dressed?" I interrupted.

"Watch cap, turtleneck, and pea-coat. All navy colored," he replied without taking a breath.

"Good." That also tallied with Miss Iverson's description. I instructed that he continue.

"Unfortunately he was too strong for me, and he forced his way in, slamming the door behind him. Silently he grabbed me by my scarf and began to strangle me. Luckily it wasn't tied too tight, and during the struggle, the knot slipped, freeing me from his grip. To my shame, however, the moment it did, I bolted for the door, opened it, and ran, not stopping until I reached outside.

During my escape, I thought he had been chasing me, only realizing once I came to a stop that it was my imagination. Nevertheless, I waited some moments before concluding he might have remained in the room and discovered Nadya. Afraid that her life was in danger, and also ashamed that my rash actions could've left her in that predicament, I quickly returned to the room but found it empty.

"Frantic, I began searching for them, first in the hall, then in her room, and finally out on the grounds. Outside I again saw Layton arguing with another man near the cliff's edge. A series of shocks followed. First, that the other man was wearing my clothes, and it wasn't a man at all, but Nadya. It didn't make sense. It still doesn't."

"I believe I can explain," I said. "Or at least give a probable explanation based on what I found examining your room. After you fled, Layton did remain in the room and had it out with Daniels. The Jeffersons next door said they heard heated words between the two of them. He then must've decided to go after you, but not before ensuring that Nadya wouldn't leave until he could return. He threw her clothes out the window expecting that would hold her there, not counting on her ingenuity and her desperation to warn you. Your suit hanging in the closet was both her ticket to freedom and a means to her end."

"Warn me?" he asked.

"Yes. She knew how brutal her husband was, and that he was dead set on taking his anger out on you. He probably even said as much. So, she had to reach you. Her last words to me are proof of that. At the time I thought she had said, 'The Gypsies,' but knowing what I know now, I could've been mistaken, and she was thinking of you when she said, 'the Gypsy' – perhaps wanting to say, 'Save the Gypsy.'"

"That only makes me feel worse," he responded. Shaking his head remorsefully. "But, it did happen so quickly. Before I could act, he'd pushed her over the cliff, and ran. I should've stopped to check on her. Maybe I could've saved her. But once again, due to my panic, I was making all the wrong decisions and chased after him instead."

"If it's any consolation, I was there soon after, and there wasn't anything anyone could've done."

"Nonetheless, I deserved all the trouble that followed."

Rather roughly I urged him to cease playing the blame game, and move on. He took my advice.

"I didn't catch up to Layton," he continued. "Somehow he escaped me. I searched for some time, but he'd simply disappeared."

"Afterwards," I interjected. "Why didn't you report what happened?"

"To who? And whom could I trust? I was confused, frightened. First off, Nadya and I were there under false pretenses, her husband had tried to kill me, he murdered her, and I was the only witness..."

"Not true," I corrected. "There was another."

"I didn't know that," he returned. "And to make matters worse, Nadya was wearing my suit, and he had my handkerchief, which I'd remembered, he'd tossed away at the scene of the crime. I'd tried to recover it later, but it was gone. What do you think crossed my mind? What would others surmise given that evidence? Surely that I was guilty. Who would believe me, a Gypsy? And in the end, I was correct, as the newspapers confirmed. At that moment I knew I had to get away and find a safe place to think."

"Still, you hung around for a time?" I offered.

"I had to. I kept watch from a distance and saw all that happened next – the recovery of her body, her movement to the icehouse..."

"You say, you had to?" I interrupted.

"Money. I needed money. Every dollar I had ever earned was sewn into the lining of that suit."

"So that's why you took the risk and broke into the icehouse."

"I had no choice."

"And the message you left on her body?"

"Once I saw her placed in the icehouse, I slipped back into my room and gathered the items I left. I had already planned to return to where they had stored her to remove my suit, and on an impulse wrote that note as a warning to Layton – that he wasn't going to get away without paying for his crime. I was positive that the newspaper reports would mention it, and he would be sure to see it. Again, it might have been stupid on my part, but I was angry, and anger makes people do stupid things."

"The note said, 'Revenge is sure,' I believe?"

"It did, and this séance was supposed to be my revenge. Not his murder," he quickly corrected, "but tricking him into a confession. Which worked," he concluded sadly, "but as things stand, it looks like he'll have the last laugh after all."

"Not if I discover who the true murderer is," I declared.

"So you do believe me?"

"Yes. What you've told me about Layton's murder and the incident at the canyon rings true. But that doesn't mean you're out of the woods. I believe you, but I don't think just my word will convince the cops."

I took out my key and unlocked his handcuffs.

"You won't need these," I continued. "I trust you'll not try to run away. Technically you're still under arrest, but only as a person of interest in a murder and not for the murder itself. Got that?" He nodded. "Good." I looked at Rogers. "He's your responsibility. I'm releasing him into your custody. Understand?"

"Yes. Rudolf will not cause you any trouble. I promise he'll stay put."

"OK," I concluded. "Then I believe we're finished. However, before you go, I have a couple of questions for you, Miss Rogers."

"Sure. Go ahead."

"How did you get involved in all this?"

"That's simple. Rudolf came to me and asked for help."

"Why you?"

"Miss Rogers was the only person I knew whom I could trust," Rudolf interjected. "She had been close friends with Nadya – I knew this – and I also believed she would trust me. I also reasoned that Mr. Randolph was very powerful and thought he could help me as well."

"Which wasn't the case, as I recall, Miss Rogers?"

"No," she replied. "CW wanted nothing to do with it."

"Yet you went ahead and became involved anyway, even shielding Rudolf's existence from me and the law, knowing that it could get you in hot water by protecting a suspected felon. Why?"

"It was for Nadya and Rudolf. CW himself will tell you I'm strong-minded and not easily swayed."

"I've seen that myself," I commented with a smile.

"Well, I'm also an idealist, who believes in love, charity, and the power of lasting friendships. Sometimes, Mr. Logan, there are situations that are worth taking risks for."

"Very noble indeed," I replied, "But still foolish. Tell me, how did this whole séance thing come about?"

"After CW made it clear he wanted nothing to do with Nadya's – Norma's – murder," Rogers replied. "Rudolf helped me locate her family in Los Angeles. We worked this out together – her family and I, and the rest came easy. CW loved parties, and with Halloween coming up, the perfect scenario presented itself. As always he left me with the arrangements – guest lists, entertainment, and the party's theme. And the rest, as you say, is history."

"But Mr. Randolph still knows none of this, I gather?"

"No CW is still in the dark."

"For the sake of this investigation, Miss Rogers, I suggest you tell him everything. I'll need his full cooperation, and I can't be tip-toeing on thin ice around him. My focus needs to be on Layton's murderer and not on you and your little secrets."

"I'll tell him," she answered shortly.

"Very well," I concluded. "You're both excused."

Once alone in the room, I remembered the rumpled envelope I'd taken from Coons. Removing it from my pocket, I made a quick examination. It was addressed to Coons and included his post box number. It had Daniels' return address on the flap, but no stamp, so it was never mailed. The notepaper inside was crème-colored, expensive, and scented. Opening it, I read its concise message; written in what appeared to be a feminine hand: *Charlie Dear, we have a problem. I'm in a family way, and it's yours. Need your help. Love, Norma.*

24

THE SCENE OF THE CRIME

*"The truth must be quite plain if one could
just clear away the litter."*

—*Agatha Christie*

"I only pinched the letter," Coons admitted. "You're blinking looney if you think I killed him. How could I, I was sitting at the table with you."

"You might've had a confederate," I countered. "I know you weren't particularly fond of Layton."

After dismissing Alice Rogers and Rudolf Granenski, I wasted little time in locating Charlie Coons and escorting him back to the Radio Room where I was questioning him now. He wasn't hard to find, draped atop a stool at the bar trying to convince the bartender to give him a second drink.

"Look, Squire," continued Coons. "I didn't like the bugger, but I wouldn't dream of killing him, nor ask someone else to do it either."

"So, how is it that you knew about the letter, Charlie?"

"Layton approached me earlier in the evening and said that he'd discovered a letter that might interest me. He didn't tell me what it said, only that he'd found it recently among his wife's personal belongings, and that it was addressed to me. He said he had it on him, and I could see it directly after the séance."

"What was his attitude when he told you?" I queried.

"His attitude? That's a strange question." I didn't respond, so he answered, "Business-like I guess. Perhaps a bit severe."

"Business-like?" I shot back. "Like blackmail business?"

"What makes you say that?" he returned, somewhat guarded.

"Sort of fits from what I've heard about him, and might explain why you shut up like a clam when I asked your opinion on whether he was capable of murdering his wife."

"I don't follow?"

"Nothing to follow, Charlie," I scolded. "Let's quit the bullshit, and get to the truth. You were afraid of Layton because he had something on you. That's why you clammed up as you did. You felt like you told me too much, and when pressed, decided to stay mum, just in case it got back to Layton. Am I correct?"

"Could be true," he admitted somewhat reluctantly. "But doesn't mean that I would kill him."

"I don't know, Charlie. Blackmail is as good a motive as any to stiff a guy."

"But I didn't know for certain that it was blackmail," he protested.

"Still it could've been."

"Perhaps."

"Did he say what the letter was about?"

"I've already told you, no. But I would've, had you not taken the letter away before I could read it."

"I did – didn't I," I said, removing the envelope from my pocket. Coons watched my actions closely. "Care to read it now?"

I presented the letter, and he reached for it. But before he could fully grasp it, I teasingly pulled it back. "No," I said. "Perhaps I should read it to you instead."

He licked his lips anxiously, surprised, but also with anticipation on his face.

"Dear Charlie," I read. "I want to warn you that my husband is on to you and Alice. He has proof of your affair…"

"That's tosh," Coons exclaimed. "Alice and I are only mates. I've been tutoring her in the art of comedy and pantomime, nothing more. How dare he make more out of our relationship than that. It's all a lie!"

"*It is a lie, Charlie,*" I stated to his surprise. "It isn't what the letter says at all."

"I don't get it?"

"It was a test, Charlie, and you passed it." He looked puzzled, so I explained, "I was checking to see if you were telling the truth. That you really didn't know what was in the letter. I'm convinced now. Here," I handed it to him. "Read it for yourself."

I watched his eyes move back and forth across the face of the letter. Not once, but twice. Then followed a long moment, when he appeared to be staring right through it. I broke the silence:

"Is it true? Could it have been yours?"

"Maybe," he answered slowly. "But then again, maybe not."

"Explain."

"I hate to speak ill of the dead," he began. "But Norma had the morals of an alley cat. She couldn't get enough, if you get my meaning. In my country, she would've been referred to as a tart. Men were like candy to her, and she partook often, and in great numbers. Quite frankly, Squire, this isn't the first time she had a bun in the oven; and like the times before, she probably wasn't sure who the dad was either.

"Having an ankle biter was out of the question for her, there was her career, you see. And besides, pushing a pram would cramp her style. So, whenever she found herself knocked up, she visits this GP bloke, who has a side business – illegal, if you get my drift. His services aid desperate girls finding themselves in a family way and fixes them up all neat and pretty. But it comes at a price.

"Now, Norma, as you can imagine, enjoyed the music, but hated paying the piper. She had figured a way to solve this. Being the clever girl that she was, she starts contacting male acquaintances she'd been lately intimate with and puts the squeeze on them – more than one of the dupes usually – collecting moola for the GP, with some extra pleasure dough for herself. A pretty good deal wouldn't you say?"

"In a twisted way. But you were wise to her, and maybe so too the others? It couldn't work forever."

"Oh, sure it could. As long as there's a question of paternity and a bloke with a conscience, the bloke will always fall for the bait."

"What about you?"

"I have no conscience, Squire. I would either ignore it or fight it in court. My reputation's so blemished that one more scandal wouldn't make a bloody difference anyway. She probably figured that out, which is why she never posted the letter."

"Then there's a chance others might've received a similar letter?"

"Not a chance, Squire – a surety. And not all are as wise as ole Charlie here – deadly serious they may take it."

I ran into Randolph at the door as I was escorting Coons out. He was in the process of knocking and seemed startled at our sudden appearance. After Coons had passed beyond hearing, Randolph directed me back inside.

"What's this I hear about Layton?" he asked, closing the door discretely behind us. "Someone put an arrow in him?"

"Shot from a crossbow that had been hanging in your Trophy Room."

"Is he dead?"

"Last I checked."

"This is no time to be flippant, Mr. Logan," he scolded. "My castle is becoming a morgue. And here I am a newspaperman and the last to know."

I decided to change the subject. "Did Miss Rogers have a heart to heart with you?"

"She did, and that's another thing. I can't trust those around me anymore. That little girl has me twisted around her little finger so tightly my eyes are starting to bulge."

"That's what love will do to you."

He softened. "I guess you're right." And after a pause, "So, how can I help?"

"I was told there was a hidden passageway leading into the Trophy Room?"

"There is. It begins in the hallway just beyond the Billiard Room."

"Could you show it to me?"

"Sure. Any particular reason why?"

"There's a chance the murderer may have used it to gain access to the séance and Layton."

"Then you better hear what I have to say. It could be important."

"I'm all ears."

"Earlier tonight I discovered the hidden door leading into that passageway, open."

"What time was that?"

"Around ten forty-five."

"That would be about thirty minutes after the murder. Are you sure?"

"Fairly sure. It could've been a few minutes before or after. I remember glancing at the clock in the hallway."

"OK, continue."

"The entrance is designed to look like a wall cabinet, and as I happened by tonight, noticed it was slightly ajar. Curious, I stepped inside. It was dark, so I turned on the lights. I couldn't see anything out of the ordinary, nor hear any sound. Nevertheless, I waited a full minute before calling out. I shouted twice, asking if anyone was in there. Then still not getting a response, I walked its entire length to be sure. I didn't see a soul, so I returned the way I came."

"Do any of the guests or staff know about this passageway?"

"I don't believe so. It's very rarely if ever, used." He quickly corrected himself. "I take that back. There is one guest who may know about it; Todd Butcher, an architect who had a hand in the design of the castle. Have you met him?"

"I have," I replied with a smile. "A walking history lesson. I'll need to talk to him later."

Randolph led me through the castle to a short hall after the Billiard Room. Pressing a hidden lever to the side of a shelf, he released the lock, and with a click, swung a portion of the cabinet out. Inside to the right was a switch, which he snapped on. Dust and spider webs attested to the fact that this passageway hadn't been used in some time, and the air smelled of mildew.

"It's unfortunate, your being in here earlier," I commented indicating the thick dust on the floor. "Footprints are coming and going, but who can say now if they were yours or the killer's. The person these belong to had large feet, but so do you."

We continued for some yards and then halted by a seemingly solid wall. I heard the murmur of voices coming from beyond it.

"The Trophy Room is on the other side?" I asked.

"Yes. That latch," he pointed to it, "will release the lock on the door."

I started to reach for it but stopped midway as an odd impression on the floor caught my attention. I indicated it. "Yours?" I asked.

"I don't believe so," he responded. "I didn't get that close to the wall."

I knelt and examined it. There were two distinct points over a foot apart where the dust was disturbed. They seemed relatively fresh and remarkable considering that they were situated just in front of the door's opening. Having completed my observations, I released the latch, causing the door to slide open, and then being careful not to disturb the print, we stepped into the Trophy Room.

Jim was still in charge, and everything was as I had left it an hour and a half earlier. Our appearance through the bookcase, however, did cause some alarm from the occupants, who were at first surprised, and then buzzing with excitement at our sudden appearance.

"I was wondering when you were coming back," Rollins said approaching us. "These people are getting antsy, and asking when they can leave."

"Have you got all their statements?" I asked.

"In blood."

"Good. They can all go, except that fellow over there," I indicated Butcher. "Tell him to remain. I have a question for him."

"Right-o."

"And tell the girls," I shouted after him, "they might as well go back to the party, and for that matter, you too. I'm probably going to be up late, so let Rita know that when she gets tired, head to the room and not wait up."

"Sure thing."

I stepped back to the bookcase and surveyed the scene. Layton's body was still in the chair although now draped with a blanket. I walked over and lifted the cover so I could observe the arrow and its angle of entry. Having filed that in my mind, I returned to the bookcase and mimicked the killer aiming his crossbow. I simulated it a couple of different ways and then turned my attention to the actual weapon lying where I last saw it. After scrutinizing it, and running my fingers along its working parts, then making a minute examination again inside the bookcase, I concluded my investigation and returned to Randolph, who had been watching me with some amusement.

"All you need is a magnifying lens," he commented at my approach. "For a moment there I thought you were Holmes and I was Dr. Watson."

"You may laugh," I responded. "But I did discover some things."

"What's that?"

"For one thing, the killer was on his or her knees when firing the bow, and he or she had the weapon hidden inside the passageway for some hours before the murder – which, incidentally, contradicts an eyewitness account."

"There's an eyewitness?" Randolph asked in surprise.

"Yes, Mr. Butcher over there. He told me the killer removed the crossbow from the wall seconds before the murder. I now know that's highly unlikely."

"What makes you say so?" he asked.

"Follow me over to the bookcase." Randolph did. I pointed to a dark blotch inside the opening, near the right-hand frame of the doorway. "The crossbow you had displayed on the wall is an antique. Its workings are stiff and rusted. For it to function reliably, it had to be oiled, and this one was. I determined this by examining its parts. So, therefore, the weapon had to be prepared ahead of time – removed from its home on the wall and oiled in secret.

"And what better place to do that than here in the secret passageway? Now, you'll probably ask, how did I know that the crossbow wasn't oiled ahead of time and then placed back on the wall? For two reasons, one having to do with convenience and speed of execution, which was proven by how smoothly the murder was committed. And the second, this stain on the floor, which tells me that after the killer had oiled the weapon, it was not returned to the display, but leaned up against the inside wall of the passage where it sat for some hours with excess oil running and puddling beneath it. This pattern confirms it.

"And," I added. "The murderer was also right-handed."

"How could you possibly work that out?"

"The killer left the crossbow to the right of the opening, convenient to his or her reach at the time of the murder," I said. "This was no spur-of-the-moment murder, but one that was premeditated. Everything points to it."

"OK, Mr. Logan. But what about the murderer being on his or hers knees when they shot Layton?"

"Those two marks inside were made by a person kneeling and firing. The angle of the arrow on the victim confirms it. It penetrated his back straight in at ninety degrees. If it were fired from a standing position, there would have been a downward angle of at least forty-five degrees or more. Only a large sized person firing from a kneeling position would produce these results."

"Why large sized?"

"The footprints. Even though confused by your own, I didn't see any that were smaller. Therefore the killer had to be of your height, which is considerable."

"But, for the sake of argument, let's say the killer was a small person?" he persisted.

"Again, I saw no prints to indicate that, but if so, it would have to be a child or a midget to drive an arrow into the body at the angle it did. Lacking suspects with those dimensions, I believe it's still safe to assume that the murderer was tall and on his or her knees."

"So, where do we go from here?"

"I'd like to set up a place where I could work – perhaps throughout the night – read over the witness statements and such – the Radio Room for instance?"

"I think you would be more comfortable in my Gothic Study. It's on the third floor, very quiet and will offer you more privacy. Do you want me to show you up now?"

"No. I'll need to talk to Todd Butcher first. However, there's no need for you to wait. Just give me directions, and I'll find it on my own."

"Better yet, I'll instruct a servant to take you there when you're ready," he replied. "I'll go on ahead and see that it's prepared for you."

Todd Butcher resembled a child ready to be scolded by the school principal. He sat slumped in a folding chair, head bowed, with hands folded neatly in his lap.

"Hello, Mr. Butcher." My voice startled him. "Sorry to hold you up, but I have a question or two."

"Yes, of course, Mr. Logan. If there's any way that I can be of help…" his voice trailed off.

"Were you aware of the hidden passageway into this room?"

"No, well, yes, I mean it's been here a long time."

"Have you told anyone about it?"

"Do you mean ever, or recently?"

"Let's say recently, but any time will work too."

"No, no I don't think so – no, I'm sure that I didn't. Not now, or ever."

"You're positive?"

"Yes, yes, I'm positive."

"Good. Now about what you witnessed tonight. I'm going to ask you again; are you sure that you saw the

Gypsy – the man I arrested, pull a crossbow off that wall and fire it at Mr. Layton?"

"Perhaps I was wrong about the Gypsy," he replied. "But a man did fire a crossbow at Mr. Layton."

"Did you see the man's face?"

"No. It was dark. I couldn't see any details."

"Then can you be sure that it was even a man?"

"No, I guess not."

"But you saw someone take the crossbow off the wall?"

"Honestly, Mr. Logan, I'm not sure what I saw anymore. It's my nerves you see."

As a witness, Todd Butcher was a washout, but at least a return to the scene of the crime was constructive. The passageway yielded some interesting clues, as did Layton's body, and the examination of the weapon. The murderer was a big person, like Randolph, right-handed, like Randolph, and was aware of the secret passageway, again, like Randolph. So, could it be Randolph? It wouldn't be the first time I was hired by the killer, but truthfully, at this stage in the game, I wasn't rushing to any conclusions.

25

DOUBTS AND CERTAINTIES

"Our doubts are traitors, and make us lose the good we oft might win, by fearing to attempt."

—*William Shakespeare*

Charles Randolph and Alice Rogers were waiting for me in the Gothic Study. Standing in it, was like going back in time. It was an impressive room for a grander than life man. Here, Randolph ran his business amongst the trappings of a 15th- century Spanish world. Arched beams towering overhead, painted with scenes of European life, grilled upper and lower Florentine bookcases filled with rare editions, Persian carpets, and a large oil painting of Randolph in his youth at the start of what would eventually become his news empire, were some of the features of this impressive study.

The servant who had shown me upstairs dropped the pile of papers he was carrying for me onto the long Mahogany table in the center of the room and immediately exited.

"Looks like you got your work cut out for you," Randolph commented dryly. He was seated at his desk, an over-sized, antique, mahogany relic, situated at the far end of the room.

"Yep," I agreed. "Witness statements – long on words, but not on substance. I've eyeballed several of these downstairs, and none seem to add any more to what we know already."

"Was Todd Butcher any help?"

"Just the opposite. The more questions I put to him, the less sure he was of the ones he'd already answered."

"So what have you learned?" Rogers asked.

I glanced at her standing by the world globe, which stood alongside the desk. Like it, the orb was grandiose, and a not too subtle symbol of Randolph's empire.

"I've learned a lot, and I've learned little. If my investigation were limited to those present in the Trophy Room, it would still be a challenge. But that passageway opens up a whole new can of worms, making my work nearly impossible."

"How so?" she responded.

"There were twenty-five people at that séance. That number alone would take some time to investigate –

difficult, but not impossible. But due to that passage-way, anyone else from the outside – the other guests or even staff, could be our murderer. How could I possibly deal with those numbers, and uncover the killer by noon tomorrow?"

"You set the limits," she commented dryly.

"Yes. And by necessity we'll stick to it," I retorted.

"Then," she returned, "I'd just focus on those on CW's list."

Her suggestion seemed a curious one until I took a minute to consider it.

"Did you help put together that list of enemies Mr. Randolph gave me?"

"I didn't just help him. I threw it together myself." She placed a hand on Randolph's shoulder. "Didn't I, CW?"

"Yes, she did, Mr. Logan," he confirmed. "But of course, I didn't have a clue…"

"That while I was providing a list of CW's enemies," she interrupted, completing Randolph's thought, "I was secretly providing you with a list of Layton's detractors."

"Figuring that in investigating them, I might learn something useful about Layton. Correct?"

"You get an 'A,' Mr. Logan," she said with a smile that quickly faded. "However, at the time I never thought that anyone would murder him. I knew they all disliked Layton, but for one of them to kill him…"

"So who would you guess could do it?" I asked slyly. "You've been running the show. You must have some ideas."

"You tell me, Mr. Logan," she responded. "You're the detective. But I'd start by looking at those on my list who were not present in the Trophy Room at the time of the murder."

"Fair enough," I replied. "That would be Anthony Wells, Damien Price, and Carol Keen. I would probably eliminate Keen..."

"Why?" she asked. "Because she's a woman. Did she work her charms on you or something?"

"I'm immune," I retorted, shortly. "No, because of the footprints left in the passageway..."

"CW told me about those footprints," she interrupted again. "Large, weren't they?" I nodded. "Then you weren't looking closely at her costume, or only focusing on that ample cleavage of hers. She's a tall girl with big feet, and those shoes she was wearing were gunboats and styled after a man's."

"Still..."

"Don't let that dumb, child-like persona fool you, Mr. Logan, Carol Keen is as smart and devious as they come. I wouldn't eliminate her."

"Then," I relented, "I'll make a point of talking to her. Actually all three of them – Price, Wells, and Keen. And the sooner, the better."

"I can arrange that," Randolph offered, rising. "Separately or together?"

"Separately, of course."

"Good, I'll get my staff on it. Have someone assist you. Send the suspects up one at a time when you request it."

"Thanks."

Randolph was almost at the door when another request crossed my mind.

"And Mr. Randolph!" I called. "I noticed a photographer taking pictures downstairs."

"Yes," he replied. "I hired two of them. One was on duty the first part of the evening and the other relieved him later."

"They're both still here, I presume?"

"Of course."

"Is there a possibility I could get a copy of their photographs?"

"Not by tonight."

"Could I get them in the morning?"

"That's rushing it some," he said doubtfully. "But I do have a darkroom on the premises, and if they work through the night..."

"It would be helpful," I suggested.

"I'll see what they can do."

He left, and I turned my attention to the statements on the table. Taking a seat, I started poring over them. After a minute or two I felt Miss Roger's eyes upon me, and looked up.

"Something the matter?" I asked.

"If you discovered," she began slowly, "that CW might have something to do with Layton's death would you turn in him in?"

"Why?" I asked, surprised. "Do you suspect him?"

"No," she answered, avoiding my eyes. "I was just curious."

Before I could follow up with more questions, she was out of there like a flash, leaving me alone with more doubts than certainties.

Anthony Wells was the first to be escorted by a servant into the Gothic Study. I could tell that he wasn't pleased to be summoned from the festivities. His initial comment confirmed it.

"I hope this is important."

"It's about Layton's murder."

"Then it wasn't that important," he replied flippantly.

"I know there was no love lost between you…"

"I despised the man," he interjected. "He was a menace to society."

"So, you won't be attending his funeral."

"Attend it? Hah! I'll be holding a celebration of his passing."

"Did you do it?"

If I thought the abruptness of my question might shock him into confession, I was sadly mistaken.

"Wish I did, old man," he responded dryly. "They'd give me a medal."

"Where were you at the time of the murder?"

"What time was that?"

"About a quarter after ten."

"That's easy. I was having my photograph taken with a group of Randolph's guests."

"How can you be so sure of the time?"

"Because that ghastly clock in the Assembly Room chimed the quarter hour just as we were posing."

"I'll be taking a look at those photographs tomorrow."

"Good," he replied. "Let me know how my photograph turns out."

My second interviewee was Damien Price. Unlike Wells, he'd seemed to relish being called in.

"So we meet again, Detective," he greeted with a mock salute of two fingers to the brow. "Interested in some more of my card tricks, or is this about Layton? I can't say that I'll miss him, but that was certainly a nasty way to die."

"How do you know the way he died?" I asked.

"Word of mouth, Detective," he replied.

"He had a lot more enemies than friends," I commented.

"He did. The old boy wasn't too popular, but then he'd only himself to blame."

"What about you? Was he friend, or foe?" "Neither. I didn't make the same mistake as the others – I never got too close to him."

"Miss Rogers thought you might have a grudge against him."

This comment caught him by surprise.

"Really. What did she say?"

"Nothing in particular. Just that you and a few other folks might have some ill feelings toward Layton."

"She could be talking about CW's and my disagreement," he mused. "About that screenplay I wrote and was planning to shoot at RKO. It was rumored that Layton might've stirred CW up about it, but I didn't pay too much attention to it. Heaven's knows, my stubbornness was more likely to blame than Layton's interference. Still, Alice would be informed – being on the inside and all. Perhaps I should've taken the rumor more seriously."

"And if you had?"

"Go ahead and ask it, Detective. Where were you during the time of the murder? Isn't that what this interview is all about?"

"OK, Mr. Price. Consider it asked."

"I was dancing the evening away with the lovely Miss Keen."

"All night?"

"Yes. I never left her side from dinner until I was whisked up to this room."

"Never?"

"Would you leave such a delicious creature alone, Mr. Logan? I was hoping if I played my cards right, the lady might consent later to a drink in my room." He winked. "If you get my drift?"

"Yes," I replied, and then asked after clearing my throat: "She will verify this…"

"About the drinks, Detective?" he laughed. "I'm sure she suspected…"

"No," I responded, ignoring his frivolity. "About your being in her company the entire night?"

"Oh, yes," he replied emphatically. "Ask her yourself."

"I plan to. She's next on my list."

"Thanks, honey," Miss Keen said, crossing her long legs while settling into the chair. She also gave a tug at the hem of her dress, which didn't budge much. "I never thought I'd get away from Damien. He's been drooling over my cleavage all night." She ran a finger down the center of it to illustrate her point. My eyes strayed for a moment and darted back. Her devilish smile seemed to say, "I got you to look!"

"Did he at any time during the evening leave your side?" I asked, reclaiming my composure.

"Unfortunately not, sweetie. He talked. God, he talked, during most of the evening, about his career, his new movie – but mostly about himself. Then we danced. He pawed me the entire time – and what a grip. He doesn't know his own strength!" She lifted the bottom of her dress and exposed her upper thigh. "I think he might have given me a bruise?"

It was getting harder to concentrate, but I pressed on:

"Are you sure? He didn't disappear for a few minutes to go to the gents or anything?"

Here she thought for some moments, before answering with conviction that he hadn't.

"He also had his hands elsewhere," she continued. "Would you like to see where?"

"No, that's quite alright."

"Look, honey," she stated with a glint in her eye. It doesn't matter to me if you're married."

"Does to me, Miss Keen," I responded, flashing a nervous smile.

"Wonderful," she mumbled. "A good looking guy with scruples. Just my luck."

"If we could get back to the questions," I insisted.

"Sure," she answered forlornly. I guess she couldn't handle rejection.

"Was there anything out of the ordinary that you noticed this evening?"

"No."

"Are you sure?"

"Yes, I'm sure," she retorted, coming back to life. "Look, I've told you everything I know. I've spent the entire evening with the very unpleasant, egotistical, Damien Price and from the get-go, he's never left my side. Really, the only good thing that came out of this is that he'd promised me a part in his next picture." She added, "Of course you know how that goes."

After she left, and I found a washroom to splash a little cold water on my face, I returned to the study to pore over the stack of witness statements Jim had collected. They were, as I predicted, just as informative as the three suspects on whom I wasted a good hour questioning. To say that I was disappointed would be putting it mildly. According to my latest tally, everyone on that list had an alibi. Cookie Clark, Al Bellini, and Charlie Coons were at the séance table in my full view, and Damien Price, Anthony Wells, and Carol Keen were at the party with alibis to prove it – or so it seemed. Even those I spoken to, not mentioned on that list were definitely in the audience during the time of the murder – Todd Butcher, Alice Rogers, and Rudolf Granenski. So, who could have killed Layton from the concealment of the passageway? Charles Randolph? He's the only one without an alibi. But, if not him, who? Was it someone I missed? Or had I been a victim of a lie? Only time would tell, and unfortunately, I had damn little left of it.

I stayed up until 2 AM spinning my wheels. I read through every statement twice, checked and double-checked the entries in my notebook, and mentally played back every discussion, incident, and nuance leading up to the murder, but to no avail. I finally reached my limit, and decided to call it a day. Nothing gets accomplished with a tired mind, so I closed up and returned to our room.

Neither Rita nor Buddy stirred when I entered. I was careful not to disturb them. The moment my head hit the pillow I conked out and didn't wake until early the next morning. Hopefully, a good night's sleep and the opportunities of a brand new day might produce some promising developments. Ready or not, I was about to find out.

26

A BREAK IN THE CASE

*"The world is full of obvious things which
nobody by any chance ever observes."*

—*Arthur Conan Doyle*

I returned to the Gothic Study after a quick breakfast. Randolph and Rogers were already there.
Randolph was reading through the numerous
competitor's newspapers and doing some editing on
his own afternoon paper with a stub of a blue pencil.
Rogers, on the other hand, played solitaire at the other
end of the room.

"Morning, Mr. Logan. Any progress?" Randolph
asked soon after I closed the door.

"Afraid not. I keep running into blank walls."

I returned to my spot at the table from the previous
night.

"Perhaps we could help," Rogers offered.

"I can't see how. I explored every avenue last night, twisted it every which way…"

"What about Price, Wells, and Keen?" Randolph asked. "Did you learn anything from them?"

"Price and Keen alibied each other…"

"They could be acting together," Rogers suggested.

"That thought crossed my mind this morning. Questioning some of the other party guests might clear that up. And Wells claimed that he was having his photograph taken at the time of the murder. A group shot."

"Aside from candid photographs, I ask my cameramen to do group shots as well," Randolph confirmed. "I give them as parting gifts to my guests – mementos of the party. Which reminds me." He slid a large folder over to me. "Here are the copies you'd requested. I placed a sheet of paper between the two sets. The set at the top was shot earlier in the evening, and those at the bottom beginning at nine p.m."

I flipped through each of the 8 x 10s carefully, eventually locating the group photographs. Everyone present in the Assembly Room was lined up in front of the fireplace, and fortuitously, a clock. It could be seen in the background on the mantelpiece.

"Do you have a magnifying glass, Mr. Randolph?" I asked.

He asked Rogers to retrieve one from his desk, and she brought it over to me. I directed it toward the picture and scrutinized the image of the clock face. It showed ten fifteen p.m.

"She really thinks she's the bee's knees," Rogers commented behind me. I hadn't noticed, but she was leaning over my chair trying to catch a glimpse of what I was inspecting.

"Who's that?" I responded absentmindedly.

"That Carol Keen. Look at her mugging for the camera."

I was about to respond when the telephone rang. Rogers ran over to the desk and answered it. After a short exchange, she announced that it was for me.

"There's an Inspector Clancy from Los Angeles Homicide on the phone for you, Mr. Logan."

I walked over and took the receiver from her. As I did so, I saw concern in her eyes. Before answering, I whispered an assurance that I wasn't going back on my word, and this hadn't anything directly to do with Rudolf.

"Hello, Red," I said, after removing my hand from shielding the mouthpiece.

"Hello, Thomas," greeted Red over the line. It was a treat to hear my old friend's Irish brogue again. "How's life amongst da rich and famous?"

"Murder, Red," I replied. "Simply, murder. I'll fill you in later. What did you find out about those names I sent you?"

"They all tie in together. Dr. Jean Boucher was a doctor at a clinic in Tijuana, Mexico. A GP by trade wit a little business on da side – he performed abortions."

"You said, *he was* a doctor at the clinic, has he taken a powder?"

"Da ultimate one. Committed suicide a week ago."

"Do you know the reason?"

"I'll be getting to dat in a moment, Thomas. Let's not get ahead of ourselves."

Red went on to explain that Shirley Lake had come to Boucher's clinic about a month and a half ago seeking an abortion. It was all arranged, but then, Dick Pratt suddenly appeared on the scene and talked her out of it."

"Any descriptions of Lake or Pratt?"

"Yes, provided by da clinic's nurse. She didn't speak good English, and my officer's Spanish wasn't much better, but what we did get fits the description of Norma Daniels."

"That figures," I added. "She's gone this route before."

"Ya don't say?"

"An acquaintance of hers confided that it was almost a common occurrence. Didn't the nurse recognize Daniels on sight?"

"Apparently not, and dat was asked of her. She said she wasn't interested in American films or their stars."

"One of the few from across the border," I commented. "What about Pratt?"

"She wasn't much help there. Just caught a glimpse of him as she was leaving da clinic on an errand."

"What did she give you?"

"That she saw a tall man in overcoat and hat."

"That's it?"

"Afraid so. She said she wasn't paying attention."

It's funny that it hadn't struck me before, but at that moment, speaking with Red, something coincidental caught my attention.

"This doctor. How much of his background did you uncover?"

"Give me a break, Thomas. I think we've dug up quite a bit in such short order as it is."

"You did, Red, and I'm amazed. But I'm asking for another miracle. Get me what you can on him as soon as possible."

"How soon?"

"Yesterday if possible. But no later than noon today."

"And would ya be asking for me to be parting da Red Sea as well?"

"No," I responded, laughing. I'm a good swimmer, just get me that information. I'd appreciate it."

"Ya'll owe me, I'm thinking – and not dat cheap stuff."

"Sure thing, Red. Only the best Kentucky bourbon. Now, what about that suicide?"

"Here, Thomas, we hit pay dirt. It seems dat da doctor was recently contacted by someone claiming to be da husband of Mrs. Lake, and threatening him with exposure. Initially, da doctor thought it was blackmail, and said he would pay, but da accuser seemed more interested in information regarding da baby's father than money. But the doc hadn't any answers to give him. Desperate, da doctor killed himself before his crime became public."

"Another good fit, Red," I said. "Daniels' husband, Layton, was a scoundrel of the first order. I got that from more than one source, and this would fit his MO."

"So this is all coming together far ya, me boy?"

"Like links in a chain, Red," I responded enthusiastically. "Norma Daniels gets pregnant and heads south of the border for her usual fix. She's done this before. However, unlike the other times, the implicated father talks her out of it. Maybe it was his conscience, or simply a refusal to pay. In any case, she's stuck, but perhaps not for long, because she had another sucker on her list…"

"Sucker? List?" Red questioned.

"According to one in the know, Pratt may not have been the true father. Daniels was pretty wild, and a number of men could be responsible for her condition. She just went down the list. If one didn't pay, Daniels would start on another. She was probably in the process of that when her husband, Layton, somehow discovered her infidelities. He traced Daniels to the canyon, killed her in a rage, and then later followed up with threats to the doctor, who eventually killed himself rather than be exposed by him."

"Layton killed Daniels?" Red interjected with surprise. "Didn't dis Joe See – da man she was with at da canyon, do it? Wouldn't it make more sense dat See, having found out about being used by Daniels, killed her?"

"Sorry, Red," I said. "I forgot you couldn't possibly know. Layton confessed last night to killing Daniels. But, please, keep it under your belt. It'll all hit the fan soon."

"Well, I'll be kin to Saint Bridget's – dat is news!"

"That's only the half of it, Red. But it will have to wait until later. Did you get anything of interest back on Gregg's prints?"

"There too, we made progress."

Red told me that Gregg's fingerprints opened a Pandora's Box of information regarding his background – all of it shady. Petty crime as a youth, followed by juvenile detention, and later arrests for being drunk and disorderly, shoplifting, and breaking and entering. But, in spite of these illegal activities, he did find time to learn bookkeeping. For a while it seemed he'd gone straight, now running his own East Coast auditing business. However, later that ran afoul of the law, with him being accused of embezzlement by one of his clients. The charge was mysteriously dismissed, and soon after, he was hired by Layton for bookkeeping at the San Francisco newspaper office.

I reflected on this. Why would Layton hire a man with a background like that? Perhaps because he could manipulate him, I concluded.

"Is there anything more I can do far ya, Thomas?" Red's said, breaking into my thoughts.

"No, Red, thanks. Just get me that information on Boucher."

He rang off, and I returned to my investigation of the photographs. I started flipping through them again with another purpose in mind. I had gotten halfway through the top set – those taken earlier in the evening – when I spotted what I was looking for.

"I'll be damned," I muttered to no-one in particular, but got Randolph's and Roger's attention nonetheless.

"What?" they asked, almost in one voice.

"These photographs, they've revealed something interesting."

"What?" Randolph asked.

"It's hard to explain, but in one case something is missing and in another, there's something there that shouldn't be."

"Now you're talking in riddles, Mr. Logan," admonished Rogers. "Tell us simply. Do you know who killed Layton, or not?"

"I believe I do."

"Who?" Rogers asked.

"Yes. Tell us," urged Randolph.

"Please bear with me," I requested. "I don't want to say just yet. Not until I'm sure of all my facts."

"And when would that be?" queried Randolph.

"How long will it take to get the law here?"

"An hour and a half by car – sooner if I fly them in."

"Let's wait until noon, as agreed, then contact them. Let them find their own way here, which by car and calculating in delays, would bring us safely to 2 PM. I should have everything I need by then. In the meantime, please make sure that no one leaves, and…" I jotted some names on a page from my notebook and tore it out. "Here," I said, offering it to Randolph. "Notify these individuals that their presence is required. Emphasize that they're to report here, in the Gothic Study, no later than two, and that no excuses will be accepted."

"Couldn't you even give us a hint, Mr. Logan, whom you suspect? Rogers pleaded,

"Let me say that four things led me to the killer. First, you playing solitaire; second, a casual remark you made; third, the 'something missing and something that shouldn't be there,' which I observed in those photographs; and finally, the phone call from Los Angeles."

"More riddles," Rogers sighed in exasperation. "I guess we'll have to wait like the rest of our guests until you're ready to tell us."

"Isn't it the way they do it in those detective movies?" Randolph asked Rogers.

"Yes," Rogers replied dryly. "And I think Mr. Logan may have seen one too many of them!"

27

CARDS ON THE TABLE

*"For every minute spent organizing, an hour
is earned."*

—*Benjamin Franklin*

The rest of the morning went by quickly. I jotted down a few notes to make sure that my ducks were in a row, and hunted down Cookie Clark for information I knew only she could provide. I also put a question or two to the photographers. At eleven, Red called, and reliable as ever, supplied the final piece to prove that my hypothesis was correct.

Detective Avery of the San Luis Obispo Police Department arrived at one forty-five with two uniformed officers. Randolph introduced me and explained the situation to Avery. To Randolph's credit, he took all the heat, and to Avery's, he seemed willing to work with us.

Inspector Avery was a small, plump man, some-where in his late 40s, with black curly hair and a bull-dog face. He was wearing an overcoat that looked as if it had been slept in, and a fedora hat that had seen better days.

"The coroner and his boys will be joining us later," Avery said, gnawing on his cigar. He indicated Layton's body. "Thank you for not moving it until we arrived. You say he was shot by an arrow from this crossbow?"

"Yes," I replied, in reference to the weapon at our feet. "From a passageway hidden behind that bookcase."

"Anyone touch the crossbow?"

"No. It's exactly where we found it."

"How did it get there?"

"Thrown. Look, Inspector," I said, anxiously look-ing at my wristwatch. "I'll explain everything upstairs. I've asked those involved to gather in the study. I believe I know who killed him."

"It isn't the butler, is it?" he asked.

"What?" I replied, oblivious to his sarcasm.

"Never mind, just my little joke."

The study was filled to capacity. It was warm, stuffy, and buzzing with excitement. As a precaution, Avery left an officer outside in the hall. There was a small divan located to the left of the door, referred to as,

'The Hot Seat.' It was nicknamed so, because of the many employees who had sat there, cooling their heels, waiting to be chewed out by the boss. Avery's officer decided to make this his post. Slouched back into its cushions with arms folded, he kept guard over the study's only exit.

"Could we have some quiet?" I announced, and faces tense with expectation turned in my direction.

I looked along the table and then toward those who had chosen to remain standing against the wall. Everyone whom I requested was present, including Jim, Liz, Rita, and a few of the Gypsies. Wild horses couldn't have dragged them away,

"Now that I have everyone's attention," I began, "Nadya Jeneko, otherwise known as the film star, Norma Daniels was killed earlier this month at the Grand Canyon. Since then, a Mr. See, her clandestine lover, has been sought by the police in connection with her death. It now seems, however, that the police were looking for the wrong man because Miss Daniels' husband, Jeff Layton has confessed to the crime. He did so last night, moments before his death. Some in this room, including myself, heard him."

I waited for the gasps of surprise from those not present at the séance to die down before I continued:

"Apparently Mr. Layton, upon discovering his wife's infidelity, had followed her to the canyon with thoughts of confronting her. To add fuel to an already raging fire, he traced her to Mr. See's room. How

Layton knew she would be there is anybody's guess, but he did, and in a rage, Layton tried strangling him. Mr. See escaped, but Layton remained, drawing out his wife from her hiding place in the room's only closet. An argument ensued, where I assume, she'd tried to pacify him. Two witnesses next door heard a woman and a man fighting, and one of these neighbors tried to intervene, knocking on the door and asking if she was OK? Miss Daniels replied, 'yes,' indicating to me that she was attempting to take matters into her own hands. Her attempt, however, was futile, and after tossing Miss Daniels' clothes out a window to prevent her from leaving until he returned, Layton set out after her lover. I should mention at this point that the name See was an alias. He was an acquaintance from Miss Daniels' past.

"Fearing what her husband might do to her lover, Miss Daniels quickly dressed in Mr. See's suit, which she'd seen in the closet, and hastened from the room. She was desperately trying to reach her husband before he overtook Mr. See, driven chiefly by her knowledge of Layton's temper, and his propensity for violence.

"Miss Daniels was successful in this endeavor, stumbling upon her husband on a trail near the canyon's rim. Here an even more vicious disagreement arose between them, ending with Layton shoving his wife to her death over the cliff edge. Realizing what he had done, Layton fled, and Mr. See, instead of coming forward as he should have, went into hiding instead."

Inspector Avery interrupted. "Why would Mr. See do that?"

"Because he was a Gypsy, and afraid," I answered. "But ask him for yourself, Inspector, he's in the room."

I noticed Rudolf flinch, but after I gave a nod of encouragement, he came forward.

"I knew Mr. Layton was well placed and more apt to be believed than me. However, I shouldn't have run. I only made things worse. When I learned that the police were searching for me, I really became scared and went into hiding."

I could tell that Inspector Avery wanted to ask more, but I didn't allow him to as I was determined to stay on track.

"Mr. See," I continued. "Or I believe we can now use his proper name, Rudolf Granenski, may be guilty of fleeing the scene of a crime, Inspector, but not of the crime itself. We can safely leave him for the moment, and return to Layton, who was preparing his own alibi by this time.

"There was a bookkeeper at the San Francisco newspaper office which Layton managed, a Steve Gregg by name, who Layton coerced into lying for him. He convinced Gregg to say that he and Layton were going over the books in San Francisco at the time of the murder..."

"Do you know all this for certain?" Avery interrupted again.

"Layton's confession to his wife's murder is a certainty, Inspector. But if you want more, then there's also Gregg's shady past and the pinning of the account irregularities on Bellini…"

"Irregularities?" Avery interjected. "And who's Bellini?"

"Mr. Al Bellini. He's here in the room. Raise your hand, Al." He did. "He works at the same newspaper office as Layton and Gregg. They tried to accuse Bellini of playing loose with the company's funds, but for reasons I don't need to go into, I believe it was all a setup to make him their patsy. However, this is getting us off track. Now where was I?"

"The reason you know for certain that Layton is guilty," Rita reminded me.

"Thank you, Sweetheart." I turned back toward the Inspector. "Inspector Avery, my wife; Sweetheart, Inspector Avery."

"Pleased to make your acquaintance," Avery mumbled. "So," he continued, returning his gaze to me. "Finish your statement about Layton's guilt."

"There was also Gregg's murder."

"What?" Avery exclaimed, pulling at his face. "There was a second murder? And nobody reported it."

"Yes, Inspector," Randolph cut in. "We can discuss the particulars of that later. Just let Mr. Logan continue."

"Geeze, I feel like I've walked into the middle of a B picture."

I ignored the Inspector's comment and pressed on: "I believe Layton killed Gregg because he was afraid

Gregg was about to spill the beans to me about the false alibi. Gregg discovered that I was having a clandestine meeting with Miss Rogers at the indoor pool, and got there ahead of us, only to be murdered by Layton who followed him in."

This time Randolph interrupted, "What meeting was that?"

"Yes, I'd like to know about that myself," Rita chimed in.

"I'll explain to you both later," I laughed.

"I'm sorry if I sound a bit mystified," Avery responded sharply. "But what the blazes does this have to do with Layton's murder?"

"I was getting to that, Inspector."

"I wish you would," he grumbled. "But just tell me. Is there another body lying around here somewhere?"

"No," Randolph replied for me. "He was already shipped to your morgue – listed as a 'John Doe.'"

Avery threw up his hands.

"OK. Don't mind me. Just continue, Mr. Logan."

"When we pulled Gregg out of the pool, I immediately searched his pockets and discovered a list of three names. Incidentally, these persons will play a large part in revealing those involved in Layton's murder. I believe that Gregg brought the list along that night to back up his claims that Layton was a cad and the murderer of Miss Daniels.

"Dr. Jean Boucher, Shirley Lake, and Dick Pratt were the three names on that list. Lake, I determined, was Miss Daniels, but who was this Dick Pratt? That too is a crucial question. But before I tackle it, I'd like to go back to the events of Layton's murder.

"Soon after my arrival, and during the hours leading up to the murder I directed my attention to another list, one given to me by Mr. Randolph, but compiled by Miss Rogers. It named certain individuals who might have a gripe against Layton. Many of these individuals were present at the séance, and in clear view of myself and the audience, so I safely eliminated each of them as Layton's murderer.

"Mr. Rudolf Granenski, on the other hand, had decided to make his reappearance right at the time of Layton's murder, inadvertently catapulting himself again into the position of prime suspect. He had the motive, but the opportunity and means were not there. Several people could swear that he was in the Spirit Cabinet when the arrow was fired, and the angle of entry into the body would exclude any speculation that it could've been fired from there. Furthermore, his explanation of how and why he ended up near Layton's body when the lights came on led me to discover a secret passageway, and the realization of how the murderer gained access.

"Further investigation of this passageway also revealed some useful facts. I was looking for a tall person, right-handed, who had fired the crossbow from a kneeling position. Premeditation of the crime was undeniable because the weapon had been removed from the Trophy Room's wall earlier, oiled, and left at the ready inside the passageway hours before Layton's murder.

"Now, where does that leave us? Three persons on my original list were the only ones not present in the room during Layton's murder: Anthony Wells, Carol Keen, and Damien Price. All are tall, right-handed, and had motives. Wells, for losing his law license, Keen, for being blackballed in Hollywood, and Price's lawsuit by Randolph, all could be blamed on Layton's interference. And two of them openly admitted they hated him, and felt the world would be better off without him.

"All three seemed like good candidates until I questioned them. Wells, Keen, and Price had alibis. They claimed to be in the Assembly Room at the time of the murder. This I had to accept until proven otherwise by further investigation – which I did the following morning.

"I was given photographic prints of the party and upon examination, learned two things: first, two of the three suspects were not lying, but a third one was. And second, that someone who wasn't on my suspect list should now be considered.

"After these revelations, several other epiphanies followed in quick succession: Miss Rogers playing solitaire, her reference to 'the bee's knees,' and a telephone call from my source in the Los Angeles Police Department, who was checking the names Gregg had written on his list."

"Come on, Mr. Logan," Avery interrupted. "I think you've dragged this on long enough."

"Yeah, Logan," Wells added. "Who is it?"

"You're even driving me crazy, Tom," Rita voiced with the others. *"Who is Layton's murderer?"*

I gave Rita a double take, then flashed her my 'traitor' look. She scrunched up her nose in reply.

"If you were all paying attention earlier, you would have noticed that I said *those involved* in Layton's murder. There were two people. One fired the arrow, and the other made it possible to do so." I turned to the architect. "Isn't that correct, Mr. Butcher?"

"What... I mean... how?" he began to stutter.

"It took me a while, but it suddenly struck me that Boucher was French for Butcher. Dr. Jean Boucher was your son, and Layton drove him to suicide."

"No," Butcher began to deny the charge. I cut him short.

"Once I caught on to that, I had my source go back and check on the doctor. He had indeed changed his name from John Butcher to Jean Boucher, figuring no one would be anxious to go to a doctor named Butcher. Despite the name change, his practice didn't flourish in the States, so he moved it to Mexico. He didn't fare much better there until he added abortions on demand to his services. Wealthy clients who needed his safe, and more importantly discrete, assistance made the trip to Tijuana where he helped them out of their problem – Daniels being chief among them.

It wasn't cheap, but to those who had the cash it was worth it."

"But..." Butcher began again. However, I was unrelenting.

"There's no denying it, Dr. Jean Boucher was your son, and I have all the goods to prove it."

Alice Rogers spoke out: "But Todd Butcher was in the audience, Mr. Logan. *How could he be the murderer?*"

"He isn't. He was the 'means' to the murder. He showed the murderer the passageway and provided the distraction at a key moment during the séance. Without him, the killer would've had to find another way. Isn't that true, Mr. Price?"

28

THE MASTER MAGICIAN

*"Who knows himself a braggart, let him fear
this, for it will come to pass that every braggart shall be found an ass."*

—*William Shakespeare*

Damien Price looked neither shocked nor surprised at my inference. His manner, bordered
on the smug and mockingly amused.

"I don't know what you're talking about, Detective,"
he said.

"Didn't you say you were the Master Magician –
'Price the Magnificent,' or something like that?" I
retorted. "That was your first mistake, showing me
that card trick. Seeing Miss Rogers playing solitaire
this morning triggered a memory. When you sat down
to perform the trick, you dusted something from your
trouser knees. I believe that something could've of

been dust from the passageway, which you'd picked up earlier during the murder's dress rehearsal."

"That's reaching. I hope you have something better to entertain us?" he remarked.

"Oh, much more." He wasn't putting me off with this condescending act. Actually, it was encouraging. It meant I was touching a nerve. "Those playing cards you were using," I continued. "Remember that I commented that they were 'marked?' I thought initially they were made by greasy fingers, but oil could also be responsible – like the substance used to lubricate a crossbow."

"You have an imagination, Detective," Price replied. "If you ever want to change professions, I could use a good story man for my film productions."

"I don't believe filmmaking's in your future, Price. Prisons don't go in much for the arts – laundry, but not the arts. However, considering your background, they might allow you to put on a play. Shakespeare's 'Tempest,' perhaps? That might be appropriate."

"You do like hearing your own voice," he said starting to rise.

Avery motioned to the uniformed officer in the room, who responded by placing a restraining hand on Price's shoulder and commanding him to remain in his seat. Price obeyed, but not without making a fuss.

"I don't see why I have to sit here and listen to this nonsense." He turned his head in the direction of Randolph. "CW, you're the host. Tell them they can't do this."

"Hear him out, Damien," Randolph replied firmly. "He's making some good points."

"So you're on his side too," he complained bitterly. "Suppositions and far out accusations are all he's presented. At best circumstantial, and not proof of my guilt."

"Then let me finish, Price," I said. "And let others judge."

"You go ahead, Mr. Logan," Avery interceded. "I'm interested in what you're saying, and Murphy here," he nodded toward the uniformed officer, "will make sure Mr. Price doesn't interrupt again."

"Thank you, Inspector. Now, where was I?"

"The dust and the oil," Avery prompted.

"Right. Now, when I questioned Miss Keen, she told me that she spent the entire evening in the company of Price. Suspecting him now, I specifically asked if he were at any time out of her sight. She said, no, but that's not true is it, Miss Keen?"

"Well," she began, sounding unsure.

"Remember," I cautioned, "this man is under suspicion of murder. If it's proven, charges can be brought against you as well."

"He was absent," she responded firmly, "for only a short time. He said he was feeling sick and needed to find a bathroom."

"What time was that?"

"I can't say."

"You can't, or you won't?"

"I don't remember."

"Was it before or after ten?" I persisted.

"It was late in the evening. It could've been after ten p.m."

"Let me help you. Do you recall taking a group photo?"

"Yes."

I turned toward Randolph and Rogers.

"Remember this morning, my commenting about something missing in one of the photographs?" They both nodded. "It was Price that I was remarking upon. The group shot included everyone in the room. I verified that with the photographer this morning. Anthony Wells was in it, as he'd said he would be, and so was Miss Keen – you made the 'bee's knees' comment, Miss Rogers, when you'd noticed her, but said nothing about Damien Price because he wasn't there. And as you recall, I had the exceptional luck of the mantle clock being captured in the photograph, which set the hour precisely at ten fifteen p.m. – the time of the murder."

"But you also said," Rogers interjected, "there was something in the photo that shouldn't have been?"

"That I discovered in a second photograph – a group shot taken earlier in the day. It's what put me onto Todd Butcher. He was dressed as an executioner, and when I talked to him in the Trophy Room after the murder, he was missing a key component of his costume – a black hood. His outfit was tight, with no pockets nor any other compartments for concealment, yet the only object he carried was a rubber hatchet.

"However, in the group photograph taken earlier in the evening, Mr. Butcher had his hood. Some other candid shots showed him wearing it, and in that group shot, it was clearly in his hand. So, where did the hood disappear to? What I think happened to it, I'll admit, is part conjecture, but I believe it will match the facts.

"Damien Price told me that the Dr. Jekyll outfit was the only costume they had in his size. The suit was black and had a full cape, but the mask was of rubber and uncomfortable. According to him, that's why he wasn't wearing it. But of more significance, however, I believe the real reason he wasn't wearing it was that the mask was unsuitable for its true purpose – concealment during the murder of Layton. This mask was highly recognizable – a grotesque monster face designed after the likeness of Fredrick March's Mr. Hyde – and not dark enough to make him invisible within the recesses of the passageway.

"An executioner's hood, on the other hand, would be perfect, and the reason he found it necessary to borrow Butcher's. I'll even go so far as to venture that Price probably used the medical bag that came with his costume to carry the hood in secret until it could be used later.

"Getting back to Miss Keen." I looked intently at her. "Why did you lie to me?"

"I didn't mean to..."

"Let me be direct," I interjected. "Did Price ask you to lie for him?" She squirmed a bit but didn't answer. I repeated my question, and added, "Did he promise you anything if you did? Remember, if you don't come clean now, you could be considered an accessory to murder."

"OK," she cried. "You already know he did. I mentioned that to you earlier. He'd promised me a part in his next film. But believe me, I didn't suspect Price was guilty of murder. I wouldn't have lied for him if I did."

"*You didn't even suspect that?* Even after the details of Layton's murder became public?" Or did you not wish to? You'd hinted the offer was made as a prelude to something more sexual he'd had in mind?"

"I guess I was turning a blind eye to it," she admitted. "I didn't want to believe Damien was a murderer. Still, I was telling you the truth about how he was pawing me all evening, and trying to put the make on me. I'll swear to that."

"I don't disbelieve you, Miss Keen. Actually, what you say makes sense. Let me offer some more supposition. If a man is planning to commit a murder, I doubt that a sexual conquest that same evening is very high on his list. That is, unless there's something perverted about him, which I don't think is true of Price. He was planning to use you, take you up to his room, get you drunk, or dope you, or whatever, so you would unwittingly act as his alibi. However, as you expressed to me, you resisted him. So, not succeeding with this plan, he had only one other choice; to take a chance, and boldly ask you to lie for him, using the promise of a role in his picture as an incentive. Sound plausible?"

"Sure. I wasn't as dumb or easy as he thought," she admitted proudly.

"Still, you thought it was OK to accept his offer?"

"Again, I didn't think I was lying to protect him from murder. A role in his dumb picture wouldn't have mattered if that was the case."

"Then why precisely were you lying for him?"

"I've told you. He said he was sick and needed to go to the boy's room."

"And you believed that?"

"Not now, but I did at the time. Damien was so convincing. He said because of his absence they would try and pin the murder on him and begged that I act as his cover. It seemed like he was gone only a few minutes, so I thought, what's the harm? The role in his picture was just as a sort of thank you – that's how he presented it."

"And it might have worked," I continued, now including my audience. "Except for the group photo. It was unexpected, and gave his game away."

"I'm sorry, Detective," Price finally spoke up. The officer made a move toward him, but I held up a hand, indicating that he should let him speak. "But this is all conjecture and unverifiable information. It still comes down to one question: Why would I want to murder

Layton? And don't bring up the lawsuit, I was sincere when I said it wasn't important to me." He made a broad, sweeping gesture with his arm. "Everyone in this room had it in for Layton. And for reasons weightier than my own. Clark, Coons, Wells, Keen, and Bellini could just as well seem as guilty as me. And what about that Gypsy creep? He had a real motive. Layton killed Norma, his sweetheart. Why aren't you accusing him?"

"I'm afraid you haven't been following me, Price. All those you mentioned may have had the motive to kill Layton, but you were the only one with the means and opportunity to pull it off."

"Motive, Detective," he taunted. "You still haven't demonstrated motive. You can't possibly say that I showed any animosity toward Layton, not like the others."

"True," I admitted. "And all the more reason why I should suspect you."

He laughed.

"Good try," he insisted. "But you need to come up with something better than that. I'm sued and threatened with lawsuits all the time. My film schedules are delayed because of them. I've learned to live with that, so killing Layton because of some mundane lawsuit seems incomprehensible."

"How about him killing your baby?" I asked, watching his reactions closely. It stopped him cold, and his eyes shifted. There was a long pause.

"I don't know what you mean?" he finally managed to mumble.

"Dick Pratt. I decided to act on a hunch and hit the jackpot. Your vanity was your undoing, Price. Dick Pratt, I learned, was a breakout character for you on stage, a minor role that got the attention of Hollywood. Miss Clark enlightened me this morning. It was stupid of you to use it as an alias at the clinic."

"Are you so sure of that?" he responded defiantly.

"Just as sure, as I am that if we pass your photograph around at the clinic, someone will identify you." That was a stretch, mainly because the nurse hadn't been too helpful in that direction, but he didn't have to know it.

"Price as Dick Pratt," I continued again to the crowd, "convinced Norma Daniels not to have the abortion – maybe he liked the idea of being a father or that another Price would soon grace this world. In either case, Price didn't understand, Norma. She had no intention of keeping this child, just as she hadn't others in the past. To those who knew her, this pattern was almost routine – accuse one of several men that she had recent relations with of being the father, and have him fork out for the operation, with a little on the side to fatten her own bank account.

"Surprised?" I asked after I saw Price flinch. "Knowing that this predicament you're in could've been avoided if you had only known the truth. The child Daniels lost during the fall at the canyon may not have been yours at all."

There followed another long pause, during which I indicated to Inspector Avery that I was finished. Instantly he took charge, cuffing Price and Butcher and reading them their rights. Todd Butcher came out of his shell and started protesting his innocence, but Price remained silent and glum. Only for a moment did he cease his brooding, to give me daggers as he was escorted toward the door.

"I'll remember this, Logan," Price growled in passing. "They won't be able to make this stick, and then I'll be paying you a visit – you, and that lovely wife of yours."

I lost it at that point and landed a haymaker squarely on his jaw. As he staggered to regain his footing, assisted by the officer in his charge, I turned toward Avery.

"You didn't see that Inspector," I stage-whispered.

"What's that, Logan?" Avery replied. "See? See what?" He made a play of looking around and then pointed the stub of his cigar toward a marble statue of a nude maiden. "I must've missed it. I was admiring the little lady, here."

I heard a few snickers from the crowd.

29

END OF THE CASE

*Without ambition one starts nothing. With-
out work, one finishes nothing. The prize
will not be sent to you. You have to win it.*

—*Ralph Waldo Emerson*

Inspector Avery, his men, and the prisoners were
long gone. So were the coroner and the meat
wagon carrying Layton's body. Most of the party
guests were in the process of leaving, as were the
Gypsies loading up their trucks. The household staff
had already removed most of the decorations and were
sweeping and discarding trash. On the surface, everything appeared to be back to normal. As normal as any
household that had just hosted two murders.

Alice Rogers was walking alone in the western garden when I happened upon her. It presented an ideal

occasion to clear up the one final mystery that was bothering me.

"Miss Rogers," I began, "the last time we spoke alone you seemed apprehensive about something."

"I did?" she responded, smiling. Her attitude seemed exceptionally cheery.

"You seemed concerned that Mr. Randolph might be Layton's killer."

"Oh, that," she exclaimed, laughing. "Just my imagination running wild."

"Based on what, if I may ask?"

"Oh, it was silly," she replied. "The morning of the murder, quite by accident, CW made a mention that he was getting fed up with Layton, and suspected that he was trouble for his business – that's all."

"That's it?" I queried.

"And the fact that he had no alibi and seemed to fit the criteria you'd mentioned for the killer. CW is a private man, a deep thinker, and quite honestly, he keeps me guessing what he's capable of, all the time. Thanks to you, my suspicions were proven unfounded."

Toward evening, Rita and I were packing in our room – or attempting to. Buddy kept jumping into my open suitcase and rolling from side to side as if it were his dog bed.

"Tom?" Rita asked suddenly. "How come you didn't mention you were meeting Miss Rogers at the pool?"

"I was wondering when you were going to get around to that." I laughed. "I didn't know it was her, to begin with. I had been left an anonymous note."

"You could've said something."

"And have you worrying. Or worse, insisting on tagging along."

"You said we were partners?"

"We are, but there are some things I still like to manage on my own. Force of habit I guess. Believe me, doll; I didn't even ask Jim for his help. Besides, the note specified that I come alone."

"All the more reason that you should've told me," she rebutted. "That's a force of habit we'll have to break!"

Before I could respond to the contrary, Liz and Jim stuck their heads in the door.

"How's the packing going?" Jim asked

"Better, if I could keep Buddy out of my suitcase," I responded. "How about yours?"

"Done."

I sensed that there was something they wanted to ask, and commented as such.

"In your explanation," Jim began, "we think we may have missed something regarding Layton's actions before and after the murder of his wife."

"What specifically?" I asked.

"With respect to his wife, and her pregnancy, what did he know, and when?"

"I'll give it a shot," I answered. "I'm not sure if Layton knew of her pregnancy before arriving at the canyon, or if she only revealed it to him there, but it was a factor in him losing his temper and pushing her to her death. He probably suspected that the father was her Gypsy lover, and when digging around with the hope of discovering his whereabouts – Layton was probably still determined to find him – stumbled upon Dr. Jean Boucher's name instead. This revelation led Layton to threaten the doctor, pressuring him to reveal whatever information he had on the father. Boucher couldn't, or wouldn't give Layton what he wanted, so now the threat of exposure reared its ugly head, driving the doctor eventually to suicide. Somewhere along the line Layton also uncovered his wife's unposted letter to Charlie Coons, which also mudded the water. In it, she claimed Charlie was the father."

"So, who was?" Liz asked.

"Damned if I know," I replied. "And from what I've heard, Daniels probably wasn't sure either."

"Are all your cases this complicated?" Jim commented with a chuckle.

"You don't know the half of it."

Liz chimed in with another question:

"You said Damien Price and Todd Butcher conspired together?"

"They did. Whether before, or once they got to the castle and saw their chance, I can't say, but whatever, Price observed everything about the séance figuring it would provide them the ideal opportunity for murder. He watched the Gypsies set it up, attended the earlier show, and then prepared things within the passage-way which Butcher had revealed. In the tradition of all great magicians, as Price claimed he was, he placed Butcher in the audience to distract from the one hand while the other – Price's hand, was performing the evil deed."

"Regarding Layton," Jim said, "I assume he killed Gregg?"

"I'm sure he did, although I hadn't any evidence to prove it. The poker still hasn't been found. Maybe if we had located it, I could've made a connection. But based solely on the events, it's my only conclusion.

"Layton had been closely watching Gregg and my dinner conversation that evening of the murder. From it, he concluded that Gregg was weak and likely to con-fess the truth about the alibi. It worried him.

"Then there was that note from Miss Rogers, which I found at the table. The one, instructing me to come to the indoor pool at midnight. It was evi-dent that someone had tampered with it. Now let's say that not only Gregg, but Layton somehow saw it, and because it was unsigned, assumed that it was Gregg's invitation. As a consequence, Layton decided that Gregg had to be silenced, so at the appointed hour, caught up with Gregg and murdered him at the pool with the poker."

"My God, you couldn't make this stuff up," Liz commented as I concluded. "And to think, we were a part of it!"

"Tom," Jim began. "We're going to miss you and Rita. This has been a blast. I can't imagine a better crash course on what it's like to be a detective. Now if I could only figure out how to use it on stage."

"If anyone can, you will, Jim," I replied with a grin. "And by the way, thank you for all your help. Here's your check from Randolph." I handed it to him. "As you can see, he has been more than generous to the both of us."

I thought Rollins' eyeballs were going to leave their sockets.

"Holy moly," he exclaimed. "Getting paid for this much fun almost seems criminal."

Liz looked at it and said, "I've never seen so many zeros after a one!"

"Isn't it, wonderful," Rita cooed. "I wish you two weren't rushing back to New York. Liz and I could've done some serious shopping."

"Then, I think it's fortunate for us both that we are," Jim said under his breath, nudging me in the process. And then adding, "With paychecks like this, I'm beginning to think I may be in the wrong profession."

"I'd stick to acting, Jim. If you make a mistake on stage, the only thing they'll be throwing at you is tomatoes. As a detective, it's usually lead, and that's guaranteed to bring down the curtain."

About two months later, Christmas Eve, in fact, I was relaxing comfortably in my easy chair. Rita was by my side in her rocker reading, and Buddy, napping with his chin resting on the stuffed camel we got him for Christmas. It had a squeaker inside, and I believe he had tuckered himself out squeezing it all evening. It was an unusually cold night for Los Angeles, so the radiator in our Bunker Hill apartment was doing double duty. The warm, colorful lights from our Christmas tree filled the room, as did the melodious holiday carols being playing over our radio by the Los Angeles Philharmonic Orchestra. Rita had prepared a hearty Christmas Eve dinner of roast beef, whole potatoes, carrots, and Yorkshire pudding. Combined with the cozy atmosphere, excellent meal, complemented by a glass or two of some fine Petri burgundy, I soon found myself dozing.

"Tom," I heard my name called from somewhere in the distance. "Tom, are you asleep?"

"I was," I mumbled, still bordering on the twilight. "What?"

"We got a Christmas card from the Rollins today."

"That nice."

"They wrote a note in it."

"Hum, hum."

"Would you like to hear what it says?"

"Tomorrow would be fine."

Rita didn't get the hint.

"Hope all is fine," she began reading. "Miss you both. Jim has been getting great reviews – his role as Inspector Perry has been the talk of the town. He says he owes it all to you. We hope to get back to Los Angeles someday. Maybe get around to that shopping outing you suggested, Rita, before we left. I know the boys will like that. Ha. Ha. If you ever come to New York, don't forget to look us up. We miss that California sunshine; the East Coast as you might have heard is frozen in. Love and kisses to you and Buddy, and a very Merry Christmas. Liz and Jim.

"Wasn't that nice, Tom?" *Silence.* "Wasn't that nice, Tom?" *More silence, plus the sounds of Buddy snoring.* "Tom!"

"Yeah."

"Have you been listening?"

"Ah, ha."

"What did I say?"

"You want to kiss the dog."

"You're insufferable," she grumbled, then after a pause: "If you're so tired why don't we go to bed. It's almost midnight anyway, and we need to go to mass in the morning."

"Let's wait for Christmas."

"Why?"

"It's a tradition to stay up until midnight," I replied, still with my eyes closed.

"Very well," she sighed. *Another moment passed.* "Tom?"

"What is it?" I sensed this was a losing battle.

"Do you think this apartment is too small?"

"Not for the three of us."

"I was thinking," she replied, pensively. "With all that money in the bank…" At which I opened one eye. "Thanks to Mr. Randolph's generosity, I thought, perhaps, we might be thinking about putting a down payment on a house."

"Soon, Sweetheart," I responded. "There's no rush." I closed my one eye again.

Another long pause followed, and then she said, "But, what if there was a need."

"A need for what?"

"A need for a bigger place," she replied, growing impatient.

"Someone moving in with us?" I asked, sarcastically.

"It's very probable."

"Oh, God, I hope it isn't your Aunt Katherine."

"Don't be silly, Tom. But if she asks, she's always welcome."

"Not if I can help it," I muttered under my breath.

"What was that?"

"Nothing, dear."

I started to doze off again when her next seven words had me wide awake and sitting straight up in my chair.

"Tom, we're going to have a baby."

"When did that happen?"

She gave me one of those, 'that was a dumb question' looks, so I re-cooped instead, "Are you sure?"

"Very sure," she answered beaming, and then added, "Some detective you are."

"What do you mean?"

"My symptoms. Morning sickness."

"I thought it was the flu."

"Strange food cravings."

"I like catsup on rice."

"Mood swings. And don't answer that."

Just then our clock struck twelve, and Rita leaned over and kissed me.

"Merry Christmas, Darling," she whispered lovingly.

"Merry Christmas," I replied, and then added with a warm smile, "Mommy."

THE END

ABOUT THE AUTHOR

Tony Piazza is a Central Coast mystery writer, film historian, lecturer, and a veteran storyteller well-known for his passion for writing and movies. He is the author of five mysteries, "Anything Short of Murder," "A Murder Amongst Angels," "Murder is Such Sweet Revenge," "Murder Will Out," "Murder in the Cards," and an action/adventure novel, "The Curse of the Crimson Dragon," all available through Amazon. His memoir from SansTree, "Bullitt Points," provides a behind-the-scenes look at the making of the classic Steve McQueen movie "Bullitt" and the involvement of the Piazza family in the production. He worked regularly in the 1970s as an extra and stand-in on multiple Hollywood movies and television productions. His inventory of stories reads like a Who's Who of Hollywood from that era: Clint Eastwood, Steve McQueen, Darren McGavin, Paul Newman, Karl Malden, Michael Douglas, Raymond Burr, Walter

Matthau, Fred Astaire, Robert Vaughn, and Leslie Nielsen. He now blogs regularly about his Hollywood experiences at **authortonypiazza.com.** He is also a contributing author to two anthologies: "The Best of the SLO NightWriters Published in Tolosa Press 2009-2013" and "Deadlines: Murder & Mayhem on the California Coast." Mr. Piazza has also done many interviews for television, radio, and the print and electronic press. He is a member of Mystery Writers of America, Sisters in Crime, and California Writers Club.

Made in the USA
Middletown, DE
20 September 2020